PITKIN COUNTY
library
inspire growth

PITKIN COUNTY LIBRARY
1 13 0003344359

D0014533

blue
rider
press

THE KNIFE

THE KNIFE

ROSS RITCHELL

Blue Rider Press
a member of Penguin Group (USA)
New York

blue
rider
press

Published by the Penguin Group
Penguin Group (USA) LLC
375 Hudson Street
New York, New York 10014

USA · Canada · UK · Ireland · Australia
New Zealand · India · South Africa · China

penguin.com
A Penguin Random House Company

Library of Congress Cataloging-in-Publication Data

Ritchell, Ross.
The knife / Ross Ritchell.
p. cm.
ISBN 978-0-399-17340-0
1. Special forces (Military science)—Fiction. 2. War stories. I. Title.
PS3618.I7556K66 2015 2014040709
813'.6—dc23

Printed in the United States of America
1 3 5 7 9 10 8 6 4 2

BOOK DESIGN BY AMANDA DEWEY

This is a work of fiction. Names, characters, places, and incidents either are the product of the author's imagination or are used fictitiously, and any resemblance to actual persons, living or dead, businesses, companies, events, or locales is entirely coincidental.

For my wife and children. Love.
And for the boys.

THE KNIFE

To those who do it, those who did, and those who will.
And for those who have loved and lost them.

1

He was Shaw to everyone in the squadron, nobody to the rest of the world. His given name was Dutch Robert Shaw and his grandmother raised him. She called him her Little Dutch, or the more formal Dutch Robert if he was in trouble, but with her gone his pre-squadron life might as well have been buried in the Minnesota soil along with her lifeless body. She was gone now and he was changing.

Special operators lived in the shadows and he was a team leader in the darkest of them. Their lives were classified and they liked it that way, for it let them do their job. The next deployment would be Shaw's tenth, the team's fifth together, and he didn't even think about it as killing after a while. Besides someone having an interesting mustache or getting whacked in their underwear, the kills weren't worth much of a second thought. Holding a weapon? Two in the chest. Strapped with a vest? Two in the head. If he'd wait a second longer it'd be him on the floor leaking into the ground, or one of his buddies. Maybe a building full of people. It was work. Living over life, way of the knife.

Summer was just giving way to fall then. They weren't slotted to head out on their next hop for another couple months, but the warmer weather brought an influx of farmers and goat-herders with pockets fattened by jihadist contracts. They'd swarm out of the mountains, deserts, and villages and attack anyone in uniform. Just like back home in the cities, the violence increased with the temperatures. So teams and squads back in the States cleaned their weapons and kept their eyes on the news. There were one hundred three coalition deaths in June. One hundred thirty-four in July. One hundred sixty-one in August. Speaking averages, the numbers usually dropped in September, but then one of their sister squadrons lost fourteen men after a Chinook and a Black Hawk went down in the mountains on the same day. The tally for the month rose to nearly two hundred. Shaw knew they'd be getting spun up early. Bets were placed with each passing day.

"Sir, a refill?"

The girl pouring coffee stood in front of him, her blond ponytail splayed over her shoulders and chest like parted curtains. Her name tag read *Stephanie* and she'd drawn a little heart to dot the *i* in her name. She wore khaki pants and a dark green sweater and a little too much eye makeup. She was cute, beautiful soon if she didn't start smoking or fall in love with any of the guys like the one seated before her. Their profession aged people.

She looked sweet and relaxed and she had her eyebrows raised, as if she wasn't yet annoyed but was thinking about getting there. Shaw looked older with a beard, so she probably didn't see him as someone liable to hit on her. He was safe, thus was she, she might have thought. But he wasn't safe in that regard, merely distracted. He'd been drumming his fingers on his empty cup, focused on the TVs nailed to the walls. The news had been broadcasting widespread suicide bombings in the Middle East for the last few days and the beeper he wore in his pocket weighed heavier than normal. He hadn't noticed her sweater-strangled breasts hovering mere inches from his face.

"Sir, a refill?" she repeated.

He turned toward the sound, quick and abrupt. He nearly nosed her breasts. The longer strands of his beard pricked the loose wool of her top. He nodded and tipped his cup toward her. Smiled. He had a good smile, deep dimples on both cheeks. "Please."

The dimples were a strong peace offering. She smiled back and poured.

"Cream?"

He nodded. "Thank you."

She held her smile longer for him than she did for most customers. She poured from a small silver creamer and stopped when he cut the air with his fingers. He thanked her again, and she had probably just started staring through his beard, recognizing the handsome face buried beneath it, when an older couple seated at another table called her over. An old woman held her white coffee cup in the air with arthritic fingers while her husband sat across from her, asleep, with his head in a book. The old woman looked like she wouldn't be able to hold the cup up much longer, so the waitress backpedaled quickly over to the old couple, running her fingers through her hair. She kept her eyes on Shaw as she moved and he watched her while he blew waves in his coffee, the tattoos on his wrists freed and visible from his sleeves. His lips hovered over the rim of the cup and he mouthed her name. Stephanie. *Stephanie.* He watched her pour for the old woman and liked the way she rested her hand gently on the old woman's brittle shoulder.

He could see her smooth hand and the fragile, delicate wrist emerging from the sweater she'd rolled up to pour the coffee. A leather bracelet emerged on her wrist and he wondered who'd given it to her. A family member or friend, maybe. Another man. She probably hadn't seen Shaw's fingernails, stained with gun oil, but she might have learned to love that about him.

The news continued blaring in the background, but he was too busy counting strands of the blond hair cinched into her ponytail to care. And she might have started noticing something in him beyond what everyone else in the shop could see: a tall blond guy with a wild beard and large back muscles shifting beneath a trim blue sweater that hugged his chest and waist.

And then the beeper in his pocket rumbled.

He took it out and black stars filled the screen with a minus-2. He let out a breath. The stars meant rush—two hours to get back to base—and it was October second, which meant he owed Hagan fifty. Hagan bet on the first week in October and Shaw the second.

He opened his wallet and fingered the fifty he now owed Hagan and the five that would cover the coffee. He'd just thought of asking the waitress for her phone number when the beeper went off. It was pointless now—he'd be leaving in hours—so he stood up and made sure to catch her eye when he did. He waited for her to turn away from the old couple's table, and when she did her blond hair caught the sunlight. For just a moment, he let himself think of what it might look like lying next to him on the grass of a farm in the summertime, a baby on the way. Maybe two or three others further down the life line. Then he smiled at her, held the fifty up in his hand, and left it on the table for her.

He'd tell Hagan to shove it. Hagan would be upset only for as long as it took him to talk about the girl he was with the night before.

Huge tits," Hagan said.

He was smiling wide and appeared to be quite in love with himself. Shaw thought he might have forgotten their bet entirely. The youngest guy in the team, Hagan had a round, doughy face but carried nothing but muscle on his frame. Dressed in cargo pants and utility shirt like everyone else, he had flecks of dip stuck in his bottom teeth and his lower lip bulged with the brown flakes of tobacco. He stood propped in the doorway leading to the pit, his hands flexed around invisible breasts he'd given himself, and was rocking back and forth on his heels. He looked like a hulking, giddy idiot. A middle-school pervert.

"Huge."

Shaw nodded because to Hagan they were always huge, and because he needed to be believed. Hagan was fragile like that. Plus, keeping his mind on tits would keep his mind off the money Shaw owed him.

"Congrats on the huge, Hog." Shaw slapped Hagan on the back and walked around the wooden pallets being filled up with all their gear. Hagan didn't ask for the money, so Shaw laughed and continued on past him. "And you've got shit in your teeth."

"Huge, man," Hagan yelled after him, running into the pit. "Did you hear me? Huge!"

The pit was dim and humid, loud. Hagan stopped in the entryway and looked to the ceiling. He yelled, "Huge! Tits!" as loud as he could, his arms spread like Christ on the cross and his chest trembling. Hagan liked tits. Hagan also juiced. Yelling about tits like that all roided out, he looked like a rabid beast and devout sex saint.

The pit was full of tall gray metal lockers and the team bays were separated by numbers and squadron colors. There were footstools housing disassembled, fully automatic weapons lying on rags or propping up half-naked operators drooling into plastic-bottle spitters and ornate metal spittoons the room over. There were lots of sharp, blind corners and dead ends and the smell of sweat and metal ruled the air. State flags and captured weapons hung from the ceiling or outside lockers, along with a few crucifixes and a single Star of David. A clock taken from a raid on one of the royal palaces hung above the pit, attached to a metal D-ring and chained to an anchor in the roof. The hands of the clock traced the face of a dead tyrant's son and his ghost slowly turned on the chain, keeping watch over the guys who killed him. The reek of gun oil and damp concrete made the men dizzy for the second it took to get used to it. Then they did and knew they were home.

The team bays were alive and frantic. Electric guitars shrieked through speakers nailed to the walls and hop bags were pulled from the tops of lockers and spread out on the floor, their owners hunched over and among them, frazzled or calm, running their fingers through ammo, banger, and frag pouches. Looking for small holes that might lead to big problems. The lockers were doubles and opened in the center like French doors. Extra fatigues and civilian clothes hung inside them, along with the occasional newbie with his mouth and hands bound with flight tape. Shaw had also seen blow-up sex dolls, kegs, and a pet dog or cat in lockers as well. He heard about an MP stashed in one to avoid a DUI charge once, too, though he never saw it.

Dalonna stood in front of his locker with his arms crossed and his eyebrows raised, the folds of his shaved head wrinkled like waves running on the tides of the ocean. He had two daughters and a wife and looked like Gandhi if the latter had lifted weights his entire life. He was expecting a son.

"You'll never guess, Donna," Hagan said, when they entered the bay.

Dalonna looked at Shaw. Shaw shook his head, removed his lock, and sat inside the locker on a stool he kept at the base.

"I'll take a shot," Dalonna said. He scratched his beard and looked at the ceiling. "She was a supermodel—no, a porn queen. A real dick diva. And they were gigantic, beautiful flesh mountains. Everests."

Hagan was nodding along aggressively. It seemed like his head might fall off or that he might make himself sick. Shaw was getting dizzy just looking at him.

"Cut that out, Hog," Shaw said. "Necks aren't supposed to move like that."

Hagan waved him off and looked at Dalonna.

"Donna. Check it."

He brought his hands in front of his chest and flexed them around the invisible breasts that'd gone from cantaloupes when he first showed Shaw to watermelons for Dalonna. Hagan was generous like that.

Dalonna laughed and shook his head. "You're a caveman. And you're not allowed near my daughters."

Someone blasted a stereo and the Rolling Stones drowned out their voices. "Gimme Shelter."

Ever, Dalonna mouthed over the music. *Stay away.*

The lockers rumbled with the rifts and guys on their first or second hop ran around hurriedly, anxious to make sure everything was in their hop bags, while Shaw and the other salts pretended to worry about their bags. They didn't want to be bothered so faked being busy. Anybody not frantically searching for extra pouches, or pretending to look for them, leafed through their wills. Everyone had to figure out who would get what and what they wanted done with their bodies when they died—wouldn't be allowed on the bird without it—so guys put pen to paper and got morbid. Bagpipes were a common request at funerals, and books, tins of dip, cases of beer, and pouches of tobacco kept pictures of kids or faithful wives company along with the bodies in the caskets. Guys signed over insurance policies to their kids or girlfriends and not their estranged wives. Shaw once knew a guy who requested the ex-wife he hated to be buried with him, though she hadn't passed yet.

There'd been a shift in Shaw that summer. He might not have fully recognized it, but the exact date, the source of it all, was inked in black on his wrist. He hadn't changed his will for years before his grandma passed that July. July the twenty-third, to be exact. His grandparents had raised him as their own when his birth parents died in a car crash when he was a toddler, and his grandma had been a mother to him his whole life. He had been home with his grandparents during the crash and couldn't remember having guardians who didn't wear Velcro Keds, hadn't fought in the Second World War, and didn't bake apple pies religiously instead of attending church every Sunday. He had a teenage phase during which he played up the tragedy of losing his real parents; it helped land a girlfriend or two, but he recognized it as disingenuous and kicked it. His grandparents were his parents. His mother looked beautiful from pictures he'd seen and his father seemed like a man worth knowing from stories, but he couldn't remember his mother's smell or touch and couldn't remember his father's strength or laugh. Instead, he remembered the smell of his grandpa's Pabst Blue Ribbon and how his grandma let him get away with anything. That free pass first fanned the dickhead in him as a youth. He'd throw drinking parties in their basement and unhook bras while they slept. Then one night they found him in his room, passed out with an empty bottle of Jack in his hand, puke all over his face and hair, and he decided to stop hurting them. His grandpa's *Now, that won't do* and his grandma's tears were enough to rearrange his stomach and outlook permanently. And they did. He went on to college, studied business, and graduated magna cum laude, and then the Twin Towers were hit. He was in his first month with an accounting firm in Chicago and quit before the end of the week. Then he went back to Minnesota and told them he was leaving.

Before she died, the details of his will read more like a grocery list, mundane and hardly worth a second thought. He didn't have a wife or serious plans for one, and no children because of it, so he figured he'd leave everything to his grandparents. When his grandpa died eight years before, on June eighteenth, he had the date inked in black on the wrist protected by the black metal KIA bracelets he wore. Then he listed his grandma as the sole beneficiary. He missed the way he and his grandpa could talk without saying a whole lot. His grandpa had been a Ranger in France, so he understood. The smell of any alcohol reminded Shaw of the stale PBR his grandpa always had in his hand. The dimpled smile and tip of the can as common as his cane. His grandpa's death hurt, sure, but he still had her. Shaw liked to think of what she would do with the government insurance, nearly half a million, if he died. She probably wouldn't do anything with it, maybe get another dog, but he hoped she would hire some help for herself. If not, maybe get a nice foot massage twice a day for the rest of her life—the old Vietnamese ladies in town charged only a couple bucks for a half hour. Or maybe she could travel to France. See Pointe du Hoc, where her husband was nearly killed so many years ago in so many different ways.

Then she died on a Saturday night in July and he got piss drunk with Hagan and Massey. He got the date of her death tattooed on the wrist covered by his watch before the hangover had time to sprout. Massey tucked him in that night, wrapped a blanket in the caves of Shaw's big body, and set a trash can by his face. When Shaw woke, the first thing he saw was Massey sitting on the floor against the wall.

"You okay?"

"No. I'm not."

Then Shaw looked at the fresh tattoo on his wrist. The ink shiny and black, the skin red and raw. He smiled. Then he cried. Then he threw up.

He needed her. He didn't know it at the time, but whenever he visited her back home in Minnesota her smile absolved him of every mistake he knew he had made or ever would. She was his mother, his grandmother, and as he was a godless man, his single savior and saint. His kills weren't murders or ending the lives of others. They were protecting the country like his grandpa had, keeping his sweet grandma from getting blown up on the bus on her way to the market. She was his anchor to the civilian world. To peace. She was the only person he was close to outside the squadron—the boys from high school and college didn't understand him anymore—and after everything he'd seen and done, that didn't seem likely to change. When he saw her he saw approval, redemption. He was her Little Dutch, no matter how big he got or how many years passed. When she saw him she still saw the little boy with grass stains on his knees and truth in his heart. And he would be okay with that if he knew. But he didn't and never would.

After her death he replaced her as beneficiary with a Labrador retriever shelter back home. He loved dogs and had a yellow one named Patch growing up. Patch had a white tuft of skin scarred under his left eye that he got dogfighting before Shaw's grandparents adopted him when Shaw was five or six. He was a good dog, loyal and smart, with the right mix of goof. Patch used to steal Shaw's grandpa's hairpiece while he napped on the couch and then leave it on his slippers for him to find when he woke. Patch lay under the casket for hours after the cancer beat Grandpa—it had taken him like a bullet, unexpected and quick. Grandma ran her hands through his fur on their deck in the summertime, and Shaw and Patch would both fall asleep in her lap. A boy and his dog. So the Labrador rescue would get all his money when he died. He requested cremation over burial, and that made figuring out the contents of a casket pretty easy.

When Shaw finished looking over his will, Hagan was still gesturing with his air breasts. He was closing his eyes, rubbing and slapping the breasts around. Really getting graphic and into it. Dalonna just stared at him. Shaw laughed.

The team. The squadron. The only family left.

A Briefing Officer came into the pits carrying a megaphone and shouted, "Briefing room in twenty, buses in ninety," and a couple guys booed him and he gave them the finger and walked out. Hagan let go of the breasts and smiled at Shaw, raised his eyebrows.

"Love me some Afghanipakiraqistan."

Shaw nodded and took his kit out of his locker.

Fitted flush and tight against chest and back, the kit was an operator's life source. Everything on it had a purpose, and operators could access anything they needed blinded or in total darkness. They were consistent, yet unique. Each man had his tailored to his person and no two were alike. Shaw ran his hands over the dusty straps, fabric, and worn patches. He could smell on his fingertips the earth of a dozen countries and the smoke from countless firefights.

He shot righty, so he kept three mag pouches next to one another, starting to the left of his belly button and continuing to the right for quick changes. His bleeder kit was on his rear left side so if he had to harness his rifle and use his pistol, knife, or hands, he wouldn't have to worry about it catching on the bleeder and getting all snagged up. Snags lose time. Lose time, lose lives. Bleeder kits were for the wearer and no one else. Nothing selfish about it, just business. If a guy got hit, whoever came to his aid would be able to locate the wounded man's bleeder and not have to use his own to patch, clog, or wrap him back up. If a responder used his own to help a buddy and then got shot himself, the next person on the scene would lose time trying to find stuff to clog him up with. Again—lose time, lose lives. Shaw made sure his bleeder was packed tight with anything and everything getting shot or blown apart might necessitate. He packed reams of gauze, stacks of wrap bandages and cotton compresses, a few tourniquets, scissors, tape, and a hollow metal cylinder with plastic wrap for sucking chest wounds. He kept a pack of Skittles or two in there as well, plus a few tampons to plug bullet holes the size of a fingertip. Above the mag pouches he had a pouch for signal tape and others for frags and bangers. Flex-cuffs and ChemLights bridged the space between his radio and bleeder, and the rear of his kit had a water reservoir and eight other pouches for bangers, frags, and other things that smoke, bang, or flash. Front and back ballistic plates weighed about seven pounds each and three-pound plates the size of index cards protected his vitals from the side. All loaded up for a house call, the men's kits weighed anywhere from twenty to forty pounds. Shaw carried 5.56 in mags, not drums, so his kit weighed in at twenty-seven pounds all topped off. Carrying rucks on longer missions or in remote areas and they're humping another thirty to one hundred pounds. The teams slept and ran in their kits, climbed ropes, shot thousands of rounds, ate, and shat in their kits. They didn't fuck in their kits, but Shaw wouldn't have been surprised if some guys had tried. Hagan was a likely suspect.

Everything was in its place, so he strapped the kit to his ruck and laid it outside his locker.

. . .

The men grabbed seats in the briefing room wherever they could. In chairs. On or under tabletops. Sprawled out on the floor. Elements of two squadrons were relieving the one that had just lost nearly half its strength after the Chinook and Black Hawk went down. Multiple terrorist cells had claimed the kills and the government was still investigating. The party that fired the RPGs wouldn't take credit for it, though. Their founder forbade it.

The BO stood at the front of the room. He opened the file folder he held in his hands and started reading. "Those of you with families won't head home to them tonight," he said. "Those with hot dates should consider them iced, and if you were trying to get out of one, you've got an excuse."

Most of the family men's hands found their pockets and their fingers started fluttering. The unmarried and childless laughed. The BO spoke slow and calm, a smile curling on the edges of his lips. He looked pleased with himself and continued the speech, telling the men they would be relief for the sister squadron that had lost the fourteen men. Instead of visiting the familiar pussy they were used to, they'd hop on a plane for twenty-three hours and land in the country that'd been on the news lately for its recent surge in suicide bombings, executions, and kidnappings. He told them Intel had noticed a splintering of leadership among multiple terrorist cells and organizations. High-value targets from al-Qaeda, al-Shabaab, the Taliban, al-Qaeda in the Islamic Maghreb, and al-Qaeda in the Arabian Peninsula were leaving their organizations and joining under a new veil called al-Ayeelaa: the Family. Al-Ayeelaa primarily stressed bombings and avoided gunfights with coalition forces, and as a result, they were staying alive longer and causing problems. They also avoided the limelight, never putting out videos or accepting interviews. No one knew who led the cell or the full structure of the network. Intel barely knew any of the major players.

"So we're going to find them and hunt them down," the BO said. He took a deep breath and paused. "If anything can roll down the damn street they'll put a bomb in it. Even if it doesn't have an engine, they'll blow it. Bikes, donkeys, dogs, fruit stands. Fuck it, they'll blow it."

He closed the file and looked around the room for a while, tapping his palm with the folder. "Bad fuckers, men." He let the room get quiet and then he pointed the folder at them. "Well, now they're fucked."

Shaw shook his head and the room laughed. The BO tried not to smile and walked out. He was slight and clean-shaven, with brown hair cropped close at his ears, temples, and neck. He walked without moving his head or neck much, a desk jockey with his time on the ground so far behind him he probably couldn't remember what dirt on his boots felt like.

Hagan leaned in to Shaw.

"When's he moving to the Pentagon?"

"You don't move there, Hog. You get assigned. And I don't know."

"He spoke well."

"Yeah."

"You think he practiced that speech?"

"Without a doubt."

"You think he's jealous of us?" Hagan asked.

"Jealous how?"

"I don't know. Not kicking in doors anymore, sitting behind a computer all day."

Shaw looked at him and raised his eyebrows. "You jealous of his job?"

"Hell no. Maybe. Yes. Kind of. I don't know. Dude drives a Lexus. He has a hot wife and doesn't have to worry about Hajji throwing a barrel in his nuts and shooting his guts out. That's not too bad."

"Then yeah," Shaw said, and laughed. "I'd guess it's probably mutual. He probably misses kicking in doors because he never will again and you think sitting behind a computer would be nice because we'll never do it. He's got his hot wife waiting for him at home and not just the Glock and bottle of Jack that's waiting for us."

"Damn, that's depressing." Hagan narrowed his eyes and bit at his fingernails and then turned up his palm. "And I don't have a Glock."

"No, you don't. But you can use mine," Shaw said.

"Thanks. And I'm gonna have a hot wife. No doubt."

"Of course," Shaw said, and the room cleared out.

The teams had an hour to get all their gear together and onto the wooden pallets assembled on the hot concrete outside the pit. Rucks, hop bags, and TVs all went in. Shaw saw a couple footballs and a recliner, too. The Commanding Officer of one of the squadrons that didn't get spun up was sitting in the recliner on top of one of the pallets. He was in his underwear, drinking a bottle of whiskey, and the top of his balding head was getting sunburned. His blond chest hairs gleamed in the light. He was whispering *Fuck you* to everyone as they put their bags in the pallets. It took only a few minutes to pack the pallets, so Shaw dropped his stuff in, received his *Fuck you*, and winked back at the CO and headed into the pit.

Back inside, some of the younger guys were beating their chests, grabbing ass, and mouthing off, but it seemed forced. Most guys just sat together in circles quietly and didn't say a whole lot while Walker, Beam, and Daniel's made their way around in handles and fifths. They had at least twenty hours of flying ahead of them, so most guys took advantage of getting their last drink in for the next couple months. Once they got in-country they couldn't even smell it. They were on a twenty-four-hour mission clock. When Shaw got back to his bay, Hagan was sitting on his footstool with his eyes wide. A bottle without a label sat at his feet. It looked like half piss and half moonshine. Copenhagen was swirling around and settling at the bottom.

"Did you see Thomkins?" Hagan asked.

Shaw nodded and shook his head.

"He was drunker than shit," Hagan said. "Than. Shit."

"Yeah. Good thing he missed church."

"Did he tell you to fuck off?"

"No," Shaw said. "He said 'Fuck you' to me. But the sentiment was probably the same."

Hagan laughed. "How old is he, like fifty or sixty?"

"I don't know, Hog. Probably not any older than forty."

"He looks old. Too old to be all pissy in his boxers because he didn't get spun up. Doesn't he have kids?"

"Yep. A wife, too."

Hagan shook his head. "Man, what a goof." He looked at his feet and rubbed his boots together. "I think I saw one of his nuts."

"Bummer, Hog. Sorry about that."

Then Dalonna came into the bay, grabbed something from his locker real quick, and left. "Shitters," he mumbled.

Hagan watched him leave.

"That sucks."

"What does?" Shaw said.

Hagan rubbed the back of his neck. "Donna was talking about taking the girls to some lake up in the mountains this weekend. He wanted to teach them how to swim. He's gonna be pissed. The girls probably don't understand it yet, though, huh? They're what, two and three?"

"Just about three and not yet two," Shaw said. "And no, they probably don't understand it. Not yet."

Hagan nodded and started chewing at some calluses on his trigger finger, and neither one of them said much for a while. "Did he have his phone?"

"Yeah, I saw him grab it," Shaw said.

"Tough, man."

Most of the men had codes set up with their families. They'd run into the bathroom stalls and call with a code word or send a text that let the wife and kids know Daddy wouldn't be home for a while. Rumor had it that the bathroom stalls deflected some of the bugging devices, so all the married guys and family men coincidentally headed for the shitters right after the briefs. It seemed like every time a squadron got spun up early a minivan would come through the gate, tires screeching toward the pit, and a wife or soon-to-be would jump out of the car, hair a mess and wearing workout clothes under a sloppily buttoned sundress. They'd hug and kiss their men, restrained for the most part—sometimes a guy would get some tongue or a slap—and the rest of the squadron would give them their moment and then joke about it later on the bus. Kids coming along was different, though. Usually they didn't know exactly what was going on, the younger ones especially, but they fed off the mood and it messed guys up, family men or not. Pissed-off teens were old enough and knew what was happening, so they would stand by their mothers with hard faces, but the tears still came. No one had gotten kicked out of the unit for breaching classified material in years, so the codes or deflecting walls must've worked.

Hagan spat some part of himself on the floor. "I bet a guy'd have to shit in the sink right now, huh?"

"Probably," Shaw said.

Hagan nodded and then looked at Shaw like he smelled something out of place. "Where the hell are Cooke and Mass?"

Cooke had his kit, ruck, and hop bag lined up immaculately in front of his locker. He still hadn't been in the bay since Hagan and Shaw arrived, but Dalonna said he saw him messing with his weapon in the arms room after he got back from the bathroom.

Cooke always seemed to be messing with his weapon. He had a dry sense of humor, was hard to understand or get to know, and unnerved people in general. He was dependable, a natural, and probably some kind of redneck genius. He didn't talk a whole lot, but when he did he had a way of being heard without ever raising his voice. The team watched *Jeopardy!* every day in their bay on a little analog TV they had wired up and Cooke always won even though he claimed to have never graduated from high school and Shaw was the one with a college degree. Cooke was from the red-rock brambles of far West Texas, beyond Odessa and Pecos and civilization in general. He could run forever and bench twice his weight despite the standing myth in the squadron that no one ever saw him in a weight room. He also had a habit of lying about his family life.

During their first few months together, Shaw and Cooke were shooting partners on the range one day and Shaw asked Cooke about his family. "My dad liked his whiskey," Cooke said, spitting on the dirt. "He liked beating us with electrical cords, too." Shaw didn't remember his response to that, conversation killer as it was, but remembered sending a mag downrange and that they didn't have a whole lot of in-depth discussions about Cooke's family after that. Later on, Shaw found out Cooke had told Hagan his father was an angel preacher who never raised a hand to anyone but the blacks. The team confronted Cooke about it and he had a good laugh and told them his real father went to Vietnam and the jungle swallowed him for good. Cooke said he was adopted by lesbian nuns from Sacramento. The men never found out about his real home life so they just stopped asking. Shaw had seen long scars on Cooke's lower back, though—thin and red and knotted like a worn-out rope—so Shaw figured he lied about his past so he didn't have to relive it. Shaw could give him that. Cooke would take over the team if anything happened to Shaw.

Hagan pulled his footstool next to Shaw and offered his tin. "They were huge, man."

He sounded sad, was looking at his feet like he had spilled something on his boots. He looked like a puppy after a shaming.

"The tits? I know, Hog."

Shaw grabbed a bite from Hagan's tin and settled it into the groove he had going at the time. Upper jaw, left side. They had to rotate their sweet spots or the gums would start to blister and thin, *Get all cancerous and shit,* an older operator had warned Shaw years ago. He worked the upper left to rest his lowers.

Chewing and dipping was an art form. No one smoked because of the cherry tip that'd get them blown away and the smoke signals that'd do the same, so their jaws were always packed to the brim. Every man had his own sweet spots and preferences. Long cut, fine cut, leafs or plugs. They dipped or chewed because they were bored and because it calmed them and sometimes just because they needed something to focus on to keep from focusing on everything else. Shaw was a long-leafer but accepted a dip whenever offered. Refusing a man's tin was almost an insult. Teams sat in circles in their bays like Hagan and Shaw the whole pit over, drooling or otherwise spitting straight streams of juice into empty bottles. It was an operator's version of a peace-pipe ritual. Guys who had given it up or never chewed or dipped to begin with even had a habit of keeping gum where the tobacco would've gone. It must have felt right to them. Hagan wasn't picky. He liked his tobacco like he liked his women. Whatever's available.

"I think I love her, Shaw."

"Really?"

"Yeah."

"What's her name?"

Hagan looked like he was giving it a thought for a second, and then smiled, shrugged. "Hell, I don't know. Claire, or Meredith. I think I called her Mere and Claire at different times last night. Man, she was hot."

"Did she get pissed when you called her the wrong name?"

"I don't remember."

"So you love Mere or Claire?"

Hagan laughed. "Probably not, I guess." Then he crossed his foot over his thigh and looked up at the ceiling, let out a slow breath. "This'll be the one, man. I'm not coming back. I know it."

Hagan was a bruiser, brawler, and womanizer but a softy underneath it all. He talked about dying all the time. He would admit to being scared with no reservations or second thoughts and then switch gears immediately and talk about something else: tits, a drum set, something that was growing on his nuts. One time he told Shaw he dreamed his own death the night before. *It was a real bloody mess,* he'd said. Then he brightened and asked if Shaw knew anything about neurons and glial cells. *Not a lot, Hog,* Shaw told him. Hagan shrugged and turned away, and Shaw looked up the definitions later.

Shaw packed the dip together with his tongue and swallowed the stray flecks.

"No, it won't, Hog."

Hagan looked at him and raised his eyebrows. Then he shook his head. "Huge, man." He whispered it over and over, quietly, until he trailed off and was silent. "Huge."

Huge.

. . .

The wind was blowing through the open doors leading outside the pit as they made their way to the arms room to get their weapons. The burnt leaves and crops added a harsh bite to the air and it smelled like football and sunny fall weekends. Sweatshirt cookouts.

The arms room was a lead-and-metal paradise. Racked full from floor to ceiling and wall to wall, black metal and camo-painted weapons from pistols and snub-nosed little babies to full-sized scopers sat in metal crates, muzzles pointed to the ground. Suppressors and ammo crates sat stacked neatly in boxes like toiletries in a drugstore. The men could shoot whatever they felt like, whenever they felt like it. They shot every day and had classes and hands-on training with different historical and present-day weapons every few weeks, even though they would see the majority of them only as display pieces in museums. Gun nuts could get hard-ons daily and everyone could master new instruments to add to their steel symphony repertoires. They'd been messing with the German MP40 for the last few weeks and were getting a kick out of it. Some of the guys even had their grandfathers stop by to shoot what the Nazis had thrown at them in France and the Fatherland, and everyone enjoyed themselves like real Greatest Generation cowboys. Shaw held the MP40 in his hands and admired its sides as if the black metal would tell him something worth remembering. When he pulled the trigger he wondered if his grandpa was ever shot at with the weapon. It was likely, but he couldn't ask him.

Operators grabbed their weapons, racked them to make sure they were cleared, and slung them over their shoulders or fit their hands around the grips and stocks. They'd massage the ribs and divots lovingly, as if checking a newborn for deformities. Each weapon was sure to be the cleanest part of its owner. A man might let his beard grow scraggly, give up toothbrushing and showering for good, but his weapon would be clean at all times. Always. Men not yet fathers, or never to be, would find their babies in the metal molds of the weapons they carried. The men knew when their cough didn't sound right and what to do to fix it. They cleaned and pampered them, never let them out of their sight, and worried about them constantly.

Shaw and Hagan found Cooke sitting rigid in a corner of the gun room with his weapon disassembled in front of him. Cooke was slim but coiled with muscle, like a steel snake. He obsessed over his weapon, cleaned it more in a single day than he ate. He also mixed his dip with a little bit of gun oil, so there was that, too. Hagan tried it once and threw up. Cooke looked up at them and smiled. His hands were stained black with gun oil and he assembled his bolt without looking down at his hands.

"Boys."

"It's clean, Cooke," Hagan said. "Always is."

Shaw grabbed his snub-nosed shorty, racked and cleared it, and looped the black sling over his shoulder and around his neck. Hagan did the same and they left the room.

"Save you a seat," Hagan said over his shoulder, and Cooke gave a nod.

The ride to the blacked-out airfield took less than ten minutes. Gravel hit the undersides of the bus and the sweet southern air flowed through the open windows and wrapped around the men's faces. As the buses wound their way through the pines and red hills, Shaw's world slowed. Voices registered and carried through the cabin but in indecipherable sentences. The tones, pitches, and meanings lost in the rumbling of the bus. His hands tingled, so he wrapped them around his weapon. The grooves, dips, and metal ridges were familiar. Comforting.

Massey leaned in to Shaw.

"I'm on pill duty. Need extra?"

He was the second son to a Guatemalan mother and a white corn farmer from southern Illinois, and people laughed when they heard his name, thinking Martinez or Valdez would be more apt. Massey looked distinctly exotic, especially with a beard, but had a white man's name and couldn't speak a lick of Spanish. He was organized, and had a sweet tooth and an admirable knack for fitting in. He started conversations with strangers in supermarkets or gas stations and didn't walk so much as glide or saunter. He had friends everywhere. Everybody liked him. Even high-value targets would seek him out on objectives, probably trying to catch a sympathetic eye from a look-alike captor.

"I'll take a few," Shaw said.

Massey gave him four packets, eight pills total. Shaw could've probably killed himself if he took them all together.

"Save me a seat by the shitter, huh?"

Shaw told him he would.

Approaching the airfield, the guys were talking either too much or not at all. The lit cabins of the four C-17s that were waiting for the operators and their gear were the only lights visible on the airfield. There was no parade or receiving line bidding them adieu or good luck, and it would be the same when they came home. Most of their families didn't even know they were leaving. They left in anonymity and returned the same way, if not in boxes. If guys had the chance to let their wives know they'd be gone, the women wouldn't be able to tell their kids where Daddy had gone to because they often didn't know themselves. He was just gone, sometimes for good. They hoped he'd come back. The buses downshifted in groans and hissed to a halt. Men grumbled awake from short sleeps, stretched and yawned to wake themselves. Shaw shook Hagan's shoulder.

"Let's go, Hog."

Sprawled over the seat across the aisle in a jumbled heap, Hagan had fallen asleep. He snored and drooled, and true to form, he woke up and wiped some spit and snot off his shoulder and onto the back of the seat to his front. He smiled and shouldered his pack, sprang to his feet, and ran off the bus. The clean air was ruined by the harsh diesel spitting from the buses and the aviation fuel splattered all over the runway. It smelled like oil changes and greasy kitchens. Shaw's beard danced in the wind on his way to the lowered ramp of one of the C-17s, and Massey took his place opposite Slausen, beside the entrance of the bird. The two medics stood across from each other, handing out Ambien to the operators as they loaded onto the plane.

Slausen was missing one of his front teeth and had a problem taking in stray cats. The men joked that Slausen's heart would take them in but his brain would forget he was gone most of the year. The cats would tear his place to shit, clawing one another to death for food. The guys made sure to come with him when he got back home from hops to see his reaction. He'd walk into his place after months of being gone and say, *Again? Goddamn,* all thick in his mountain-man accent. As if the concept of starvation and neglect shouldn't apply to his animals. He told bar girls he was a hockey player and liked to give his cats milk—when they were alive—by shooting it from the gap of his missing tooth. One night he was attached to a four-man perimeter team stationed outside the objective while two teams cleared the inside of the home. The first team breached the doorway and cleared the first floor without finding anything more than a wife and her two young children asleep on the kitchen floor. When the second team hit the stairs leading up to the second level, the perimeter team saw someone open a window above them and drop a grenade, then tumble out the window after it. The explosion blew an arm off one of their guys, so Slausen slapped on a tourniquet, but not before Slausen leveled his weapon and put two in the head of the guy who had just come tumbling out the window. One of the wounded guys said Slausen hit the guy while he was in the air, and the other claimed it was after the landing. Either way, the window jumper had an eight in his forehead. Two holes with a shared middle. Slausen finished bandaging the wounded man, then flicked away an apple slice–sized piece of shrapnel smoldering in his calf. Squadron lore was that he was smiling and brushed it off like some crumbs he'd spilled on his pants. Smiling during the ordeal or not, Slausen was still missing half the calf of his right leg. It wasn't hard to imagine him grinning without that front tooth while his flesh burned and blistered. He was an animal.

"For your zzzz's, you goofy bastard," Slausen said, tossing a bag of Ambien at Shaw's chest. He winked. "Save me a seat by the shitter?" Shaw told him he would, and then Slausen gestured behind himself with his eyes wide. Shitter seats were prime spots. Foot traffic and fumes were better than navigating over sleeping team members sprawled out on the floor. Step on some groggy or drugged-out buddy's balls, stomach, or head on the way to the john and the aggressor would have his own knocked around some.

As Shaw made his way to the ramp a shorter man emerged from the dark behind Slausen, wearing the operators' mission tops and bottoms—a mixed salad of earth-toned camouflage. He had a salt-and-pepper crew cut cropped to cliffs on his head and the skin of his face was taut to the bone, lined like dried-out riverbeds. He offered his hand to Shaw and mumbled, "Shoot straight." It sounded like he was chewing on gravel.

The man had four stars pinned to his top. His face, familiar from press conferences, took on a ghoulish pallor in the moonlight and the wrinkles cast deep shadows on his face. He looked like a corpse. Shaw realized that the man had just been appointed commander of Joint Operations and the new commander tried to strangle or otherwise break Shaw's hand. Shaw returned the death grip and the four-star clapped him on the shoulder. Shaw walked past him, and a priest standing at his side threw the sign of the cross at Shaw as his boots slapped the ridged base of the ramp. He felt the cool metal ridges under the balls of his feet.

A voice laughed out from behind him.

"No blessing, Father. I'm a Jew!"

"Then you're fucked!" someone answered from the dark.

Shaw smiled and the cabin of the bird filled with laughter.

The C-17 was a giant steel cross on wheels, more than half a football field in length, with a wingspan to match. Hundreds of men could cram into the empty cabin, but the squadron had two gun-mounted vehicles with .50-calibers on their roofs shackled down in the back of the bird and a few of the wooden pallets. The twenty men of Shaw's squadron could split up and enjoy the ample space left on the two birds as they saw fit, and the operators did so, spreading their belongings along the floor and canvas seats as if they were claiming territory in a dorm room. The other twenty men, of the other squadron, would do the same on the remaining two C-17s.

Shaw found a couple seats next to the shitter. He grabbed the seat closest to the plastic door and settled in to the canvas, Ambien in hand. He tried not to sleep a whole lot and didn't feel like tripping, so he aimed to trade. Some guys would give almost anything for the pills. Most men wanted as many pills as possible, but hounding medics would give off the impression of an aspiring doper, so they would get thrifty and trade among themselves. Hagan stood in front of Shaw right away. Hagan did not believe in caution.

"Neck pillow," he said. "Neck pillow for your poppers."

He thrust the black-padded crescent at Shaw, hadn't even sat down yet. Shaw nodded and tossed Hagan a pack and Hagan lobbed the pillow at Shaw's chest. Hagan took a seat across the aisle. He sat smiling and lusting at the packets, like they had naked women pasted on the plastic. Shaw sat on the pillow and waited for his ass to go numb as Massey moved Shaw's pack off the seat next to him and yelled over to Hagan.

"Did you trade with him, Hog?" Massey pointed his thumb at Shaw.

Hagan nodded and Massey asked for all of Shaw's packs. Shaw gave Massey the four he had left after trading and Massey held them up for Hagan to see.

"Oh, fuck you, butt buddies."

Hagan flicked them off from across the aisle and Shaw laughed.

"Give him a couple more, Mass," Shaw said.

Massey threw two packets across the aisle and shouted over the awakening engines. "Don't take more than three at once or they'll kill you."

Hagan grabbed the three packs and mocked swallowing them all together. "Better these than Hajji."

The ramp closed and guys started clearing space with their feet, calling spots on the floor and laying down their sleeping nests. Massey let himself sink into the canvas seat and drummed his fingers on his thighs. He looked at Shaw.

"I feel old, man. Tired."

"We are old," Shaw said. He put a chew in, a lighter one so he'd have less to worry about if he fell asleep, and tried to get comfortable in the canvas with the pillow under his ass. "And did you pop already?"

Massey nodded.

"Then there you go, bud. Shit'll make you drowsy before you nod off."

Shaw offered him his pouch and Massey shook his head.

The metal clicks of belts buckling spread through the cabin of the aircraft and conversations died down. Everything seemed quiet for a second and then the frame of the bird shook as the engines fired up and drowned out the remaining voices. Guys shifted in their seats and ran things through their hands: rosaries, pictures, bullets that had been shot into their bodies and dug out by doctors, and other small stuff that wouldn't make much sense to anyone who wasn't holding it for luck. Shaw saw one guy holding a small pink blanket and running his fingers over a matching beaded bracelet on his wrist. Shaw remembered hearing about the daughter that'd just made the man a father a couple weeks ago. Dalonna had his eyes closed with some pictures on his lap and Cooke ran his fingers softly over his weapon, like it was an old guitar. Everyone looked at peace, calm.

Shaw didn't have anything to run through his fingers, but he was into smells during the fall in the South. The air is sweeter that time of year to a Yankee, especially when there's still a little heat left before the winter arrives and the leaves are starting to burn. He couldn't get enough of it the last couple weeks in September, had the windows open in his room at night and rolled down in his truck all the time. It was clean air. Pure. So he inhaled hard and tried to find any fresh air through all the exhaust fumes, hydraulic oil, and personal touches filling the cabin. The closest he got to the outside air smelled like a woman's perfume and he shrugged and figured Hagan probably had some panties in his bag. Then he thought of the waitress in the coffee shop and wondered if she'd watched him leave there a few hours before.

The bird rocked free from its blocks and carried them down the tarmac, away from their homes and families and dogs and cats and to a land that didn't want them.

The men were left to their thoughts during the flight carrying them to war. Fathers, brothers, and sons turned into trigger pullers while others enjoyed the highs from their Ambien or the whiskey they'd smuggled aboard. Shaw thought of his grandma, how for the first time she wouldn't be waiting for him on the Minnesota plains when he returned. Usually he'd get on the first flight back north after landing in the States and he'd let himself skip workouts for a whole week. Fatten himself on her cooking. She pampered him and he'd find himself venting, telling her classified information while they split a couple beers on the back porch, looking out over the snowdrifts or the mowed summer grass. He'd tell her about missions and she would shake her head lightly, not in judgment or displeasure but, so it seemed to him, out of a total surprise that the world moved as it did and that men like her grandson were involved in the pushing and pulling of it.

Hagan and Dalonna came across the aisle shortly after takeoff. The three of them got a poker game going with Massey and Slausen, but it wasn't serious—mostly just to kill the time until the Ambien kicked in. They were all terrible. The lights were blacked out in the cabin, so they played under red headlamps, legs splayed and locked with those of the next guy to form a playing surface on the floor. After the Ambien had weighed down his eyelids, Hagan kept saying, "Hit me," and the rest of them stopped caring enough to tell him they weren't playing blackjack. They wouldn't hit him and he didn't seem to care. He must've just liked the way it sounded coming out of his lips while he was half asleep. Eventually he mumbled, "Bombers are fucked," and then he grinned slightly and fell asleep sitting up. Dalonna checked Hagan's cards and then threw his own on the floor of the plane.

"Hog's got a damn flush," he said. "I don't have shit."

No one had anything to beat Hagan's hand, so they decided to quit as long as the sleeping one among them had the best hand.

"I'm gonna zone, boys," Slausen said.

He put on his headphones and lay down across a couple seats above Hagan, who'd fallen asleep on the floor with his back propped up against a seat. Slausen was from Vermont, or maybe New Hampshire—somewhere in the woods of the Northeast—and seemed like he'd been a doper in a past life, or might still be. He'd pop an Ambien or any other sleep aid he had on hand, keep himself awake, and then ride out the high as long as it lasted. Then he would crash into a near coma. He'd come out of it with bloodshot eyes, snot and slobber splattered across his chin. After he put on his headphones he tore open a bag of pills, then another, and held the baggies delicately over his mouth, letting the white capsules tumble over his bearded lips. He crossed his arms behind his head and closed his eyes. A smile spread across his face.

The temperature dropped the higher they flew, so Shaw and Massey took out fleece tops from their packs and Dalonna brought a field blanket out from his. Plumes of white breath started floating in the dark cabin like the clouds had seeped into the bird. The smell of moonshined whiskey and cool laundered clothing mixed with tobacco and farts and emerging hangovers. Hagan started to drool on his shoulder, so Dalonna eased him down to the floor and wrapped a corner of the blanket around his feet. Hagan lay scrunched on the floor with his knees huddled at his chest, a big man sleeping like a fragile baby. He was a man-child. A guy who brought an engagement ring he'd bought for a stripper to the team bay to get Shaw's opinion on it. The ring, not the concept. Shaw asked for some time to think about it, and before he told Hagan what he thought about the idea, Hagan had pawned the ring and bought a drum set instead. Hagan didn't play the drums, before or after he bought the set. Hagan's wallet was loose and he was known to drive remote-controlled cars around the pit with beers and nudie mags taped to the roofs. Some guys didn't like Hagan because his chest looked better than theirs or because his tattoos fit him well, but he was an animal on the objective—wouldn't know quit if it hit him in the face with a wooden plank. Shaw loved the contrast in Hagan. He could punch three full mags into a quarter from fifty meters away yet had a habit of gravitating toward kids on the objective. Shaw had seen Hagan put down two HVTs on a target once, then sweep up a little boy with the gentle arms of a father to keep him from running into the room with the dead bodies. Shaw imagined Hagan as the little brother he might have had if his parents' car hadn't hugged that oak tree. Hagan fought a lot in the squadron gyms. After one bout, when Hagan had mashed in a guy's face rather impressively, he'd looked defeated and worn out, the other man's blood still wet on his gloves. Shaw put a towel over his shoulders and asked him if he was all right. *It's so damn personal,* Hagan had said. Shaw asked him what he meant. *Hitting guys in the face,* Hagan said. *Don't like it.* Shaw laughed and asked him how punching a guy in the face was more personal than taking his life. Hagan shrugged and offered his upturned bear-paw hands in response. *That's different,* he said. *Our job.*

"Hog's got the right idea," Dalonna said. "I'm out, too."

He brought out a black watch cap and pulled it down over his eyes. He sat with his back braced against Hagan's large feet—an arm draped protectively over his calves—and fell asleep immediately.

They were an unlikely duo, the short Filipino father of daughters and the womanizing hulk. Dalonna fought in Golden Gloves bouts growing up in Chicago and taught Hagan how to box right, with finesse and patience. Dalonna's fatherly touch must've appealed to a guy like Hagan, who appreciated anyone who didn't call him a dumbass or a meathead, and Dalonna must've seen Hagan as a big kid who needed looking after. The pair got along well despite their differences, and it was known throughout the squadron that if you wanted to fight one you had to fight both. Dalonna was paternal like that. He reminded the team of things constantly. *Don't forget water. Extra batteries. Oil the shit out of that barrel. Condoms, Hog.*

Massey looked over at Shaw and gestured to Dalonna. Dalonna's mouth hung open and his head kept falling back. As his neck strained, the tendons and veins would enlarge and pop out of the skin. Shaw could see Dalonna's pulse. Massey smiled and then his hand disappeared in his bag. He handed Shaw some papers.

"I made corrections."

Shaw had finally convinced Massey to get out of the squadron and give college a shot after years of talking about it on foreign airfields. Shaw could see Massey as a doctor, going home to a beautiful blond wife and three kids after a day in surgery, *How was the day, honey?* and all that good shit. Massey was an operator but a medic still, his job centered primarily on saving lives, not taking them. The rest of the team seemed destined to grow old kicking in doors, but Massey did not. Massey started applications at around the same time Shaw's grandma died, and he would enroll in classes next fall. Massey asked Shaw if he would think about getting out, too. They could be neighbors and get drunk and fat together while their kids threw rocks at one another, Massey had said. Be normal people. And Shaw entertained the thought for a moment, but normal to him had become having dirt under his boots at all times. Normal was being clipped into a Black Hawk or Little Bird, flying nap-of-the earth over foreign dirt on the way to raid some towel-headed motherfucker plotting to blow up the Statue of Liberty or his sweet grandma. And his normal was falling apart into something foreign and unknown, like the runoff of a glacier melting into the sea. He couldn't tell anyone who didn't do it himself what he did for a living, legal or personal reasons aside, and if he did, he knew they would look at him a little too long. As though if only they looked hard enough they might see the blood on his hands and recognize it, appreciate it as necessary but nevertheless unfortunate, before being relieved that they weren't the ones stained. There was no other world for him.

Massey handed him one of his personal essays for admission, written in pencil. The script looked like crusted blood under the headlamp. Massey wrote in harsh strokes, nearly stabbing through the pages, but he could write well. The prompt was a funny one. It made Shaw laugh. *Describe a time of difficulty and how you overcame it.*

"What? It sucks, doesn't it? It felt like bullshit on the paper."

"No, you're good," Shaw said. "The question is funny."

Massey frowned and shook his head, looked at his lap. He was writing about applying tourniquets to arterial wounds, having a guy die under his care. Shaw could imagine the graduate student or crusty academic salt tasked with reading Massey's essays. They would try to determine how well someone like him would do in a biology lab. *Tourniquet application, sure—but how would he do in an academic environment? Could he handle the pressure?*

"You need to clarify what you're trying to say here," Shaw said.

He gave Massey the essay, pointed at a paragraph that needed some clarifying. Massey took the papers and stared at the words.

"You told them about tying off guys." Shaw raised his eyebrows and tried not to laugh. "What about those experiences would enhance a classroom?"

Massey stared at the pages. "I don't know, man. Enhance? That kind of thing doesn't enhance shit. A guy died."

"Exactly. Mass, you'll get in. They'll probably beg you to come. Just try to explain how the experience affected you. Tell them about death. They want to know about leadership, problem solving, and worldly experiences. You've got more of that in what you leave behind in the shitter than the person reading your essay." Shaw looked at him and winked. "Just don't say that to them."

The fuzzy red bulbs of distant headlamps kept Shaw awake long after Massey put his essays away and went to sleep. The lights went out one by one until hours later they were all gone. Then the bird was just cold and dark. It felt like being in a tomb. Shaw imagined his grandma lying alone in the cool Minnesota earth. It made him sad and he wished he'd taken the pills. Every now and again guys passed his face on the way to the shitters and he could feel a slight brush of wind and a little warmth as they walked by. They each carried their own scent. Waxed tobacco pouches. Sun-bleached tops and bottoms. Shampooed beards.

Shaw grabbed Massey's essays from the pack and was going over them again under the red light of his headlamp when Bear walked by, grabbing his crotch on his way to the shitter. He carried his own toilet paper and patted Shaw on the shoulder with the roll. Bear was a graceful sniper, a gum chewer, and unlike an actual bear in every way except for his hair. He was thin and short, with dark features. With jet-black hair and eyes to match, he grew his hair and beard so long it was hard to tell where his beard ended and the hair on his head began. He could close his eyes and blend into the dark. He was good-looking, but it was hard to tell through the mop of hair that was his face.

Bear walked out of the shitter after a few minutes and tapped Shaw again on the shoulder with the toilet paper. Then he walked away, tossing the roll in his hand, and dropped the roll on Mike's face. Bear walked on, laughing loud after Mike failed to wake up. Mike was Slausen's team leader. He was tall, thick and veiny, and wore the Alaska state flag next to the American one on his kit. His auburn beard was overpowered by a mustache with long, wispy hairs running away from the rest on the far ends. They looked like black licorice tails in the dark cabin of the aircraft. He was older than most of the guys in the teams, had three kids out of high school already. Ohio was sleeping next to Mike on the floor. He would take over the team if Mike went down. Ohio was shorter than Mike but broader in the shoulders. He bypassed the squadron beard, opting instead for a mustache darker than oil and thicker than a candy bar. He played lacrosse in college on the East Coast, an Ivy League—Princeton or Cornell, it was said—and had a young daughter he didn't see much. His ex-wife sent him pictures of his daughter every few months and his locker in the pit was a collage of his daughter's school pictures. She was a pretty girl, with dark black hair like her father, and was almost at the age when she'd change from being cute to being beautiful and making her dad worry.

Coughs interrupted the steady drone of the bird as it made its way over the Atlantic. If Shaw could forget where he was it might've sounded like a lawn mower running in the summertime. He could almost see his grandpa coughing out flecks of tobacco that had loosed from his cigar among the rivets, screws, and tiles of the bird's cabin. In reality, there were ten operators on that bird and thirty more on another three just like it flying through the dark and the clouds. They were the knife of the military, expressly used to hunt down and eliminate terrorist networks throughout the world. And they'd all be out in the night soon enough, doing their best to kill the right people. And the right people were asleep in their beds while those who would bring them their deaths flew over the ocean. The men and women would soon be waking up next to their husbands and wives, boyfriends and girlfriends. They'd stretch and share a kiss before brushing their teeth. Or maybe they'd already been up for hours with the sun, connecting circuits to car bombs or packing lunches for their children on their way to school. Some of them were probably standing in their kitchens, in their bathrobes, holding cups of coffee and blowing steam away from their mouths. Planning explosions on the dark walls of their homes and organizing dinner the same. Some would be innocent and might wonder if the war had finally reached the apex that would necessitate a move to another country. Perhaps they could move in with family or loved ones who would provide refuge from the car bombs, assassinations, and Western raids that usually got their targets but sometimes didn't. A little boy would rise from his bed in a remote mountain pass, and one of his uncles would do the same outside a crowded city before pushing his kids on a tire swing in their front yard.

Shaw lay awake in the dark long after putting away the essay and turning off his headlamp, his arms a bed for his head. He thought of the people they'd be after during the night and wondered if they were thinking of him. Then he thought of the little girl from the poppy fields. He could see her face lit by the moon in the steel divots of the ceiling. The steel cables running along the length of the cabin seemed like silver trails of tears if he looked at them from a certain angle. He opened two packets of pills, chewed them to powder, and swallowed them dry. When his hands and thighs got heavy and his head felt thick, he hoped if there were others like that little girl out there in the dark that they'd run.

Because the men were coming.

The C-17s refueled in the air, and hours later a dip in the trajectory startled the men awake. Shaw found half a ball of chaw sitting wet against his neck, the other half still loose-leafed in his cheek. Dom was awake and sitting across the aisle from him, panting with his thick pink tongue hanging half a foot from his mouth. He dipped his long brown snout to the floor and nosed a tennis ball toward Shaw. Stephens, the Belgian Malinois's handler, smiled through his red beard and stroked the smooth crown of buff fur between Dom's ears.

"Might want to roll that back," Stephens said. "He's grumpy after a nap."

Dom's eyes widened as Shaw reached toward the ball; then Dom lowered onto his haunches, his forepaws resting in a dignified stance of patience. His long white teeth glistened eerily in the light of the red headlamps turning on here and there as men awoke and prepared to land. Shaw rolled the ball back and Dom snatched it in his jaws. He moved into a sitting position and nosed the ball back at Shaw.

"Steph," Shaw said. "I'm exhausted. Call the Dominator off. He's just going to get mad at me for underperforming and bite my ass for insulting him."

Stephens laughed and patted the dog on the side. "Down, Dom."

Dom dropped to his stomach, forepaws stretched out toward Shaw as before, and rested his snout on the floor. He watched the ball with dark, alert eyes, and when Shaw nudged it back with his boot he snatched the ball in his jaws, dropped it by his paws, and rested his snout on it.

The small white lights lining the floor of the cabin illuminated guys getting to their feet, waking others, and settling into seats. Metal clips snapped and echoed throughout the bird and everyone buckled in the same as they had some twenty hours before. The landing gear descended and a lawless smell filled the bird. A mix of tire fires, sunbaked animal shit, and burnt trash bit at their noses. Some guys smiled as the stench settled in and others coughed. Voices welcomed it in the dark.

There it is, boys.

Shitty stench for a shittier country.

Freedom isn't free, a voice giggled through the Ambien runoff.

Then it's not worth it, another answered.

It was a smell of warning. As long as the men smelled it they could never fully relax. Men had gotten blown up in chow halls and checkpoints and shot while instructing locals in counterinsurgency tactics. CIA agents had gotten blown up by their own sources. In this part of the earth, the world was on fire.

"Every time," Massey said, shaking his head. "It's been the same damn smell for almost a decade. How do people live in this shit?"

"Birth shit," Hagan yelled across the aisle. He was all excited, the whites of his eyes gleaming and glassed after the Ambien.

"Bird shit?"

"No. You deaf? I said it smells like birth shit."

The entire cabin looked at Hagan. The air itself seemed to switch from a smell of warning to one of confusion.

"Haven't you ever been in the delivery room and seen the women crap while giving birth?" Hagan asked.

None of the men said anything for a long time. Eyes widened and lips strained against rows of teeth waiting to unleash deep laughs from tired throats. Hagan raised his eyebrows and spread his palms.

"Jesus, Hog," Massey whispered.

Shaw looked at Dalonna, thinking that having had two kids with a third on the way, he might be able to lend an opinion on the matter. Dalonna stared at Hagan, his mouth open a little. He shook his head real slow. It appeared any personal opinion or experience he was keeping as such.

"Donna, you know what I'm talking about." Hagan looked at him with his hands open. "Tell 'em about it. They poop when they push, right?"

Shaw put his head in his hands, ran his fingers through his hair. The way Hagan said *poop* made him sound like a middle-school kid explaining his potty mouth to one of his teachers. Dalonna stared at Hagan and ran the tip of his tongue over his bottom lip. He took his time, wet his lips. Then he put his hands on his knees.

"Hog. Do not. Sit next. To me. On. The. Bird. Back. You degenerate."

The bird seemed to shake with all the laughter as it approached the runway. Cooke had his eyes closed, a wide smile on his face, and Slausen grinned through whatever he'd popped that'd taken him away from everyone, undoubtedly harder than the Ambien did for everyone else. Slausen's eyes were half shut and he drawled slowly through the drugs, giggling quietly to himself. "A mess of a man," he said. "That's you, Hog. Big ole messy Hog."

"I saw it on TV," Hagan said, his arms spread wide, preaching or begging. "No shit." His voice had started loud but seemed to lower with each word. "Swear to God."

The wheels touched down and the screeching breaks drowned out all the laughter. Hagan's face was red, his features shrunken and strained. It looked like he'd bitten an especially tart lemon. The sudden bump of rubber meeting earth after dancing weightless on the clouds for so long made the bird groan and shudder. The engines hissed and whined and everything got loud. It seemed like the plane might explode.

"I know you've seen it, Donna," Hagan said, slow and quiet, almost to himself. "I know it."

The bird rolled to a stop near an empty hangar and the ramp lowered, the men's laughter draining out into the humid morning air. It was just before 0400 hours and the heat had already found its way into the cabin. Daylight wouldn't break for another hour or two, but sweat already pooled at the base of Shaw's neck. Forklifts unloaded the pallets first and the men followed. Shaw picked up the neck pillow, wrapped it around his neck, and walked down the ramp and grabbed his hop bag from the pallets sitting outside the bird. The hot wind stung and the air was thick. Hagan walked down the runway, rubbing his crotch over and over again. He couldn't seem to find a comfortable place for his balls to rest in the heat. His voice followed the men to the hangar. He hadn't given up, rarely did.

"It was on a nature . . . science channel, or some crap. A documentary, maybe. PBS?"

Shaw walked ahead of the others. He couldn't hear a rebuttal, but he imagined heads shaking and guys spitting. Dust leapt from their boots and clouded at their knees, laughter the only thing more prevalent in the air than the heat.

Dim ceiling lights lit the hangar, making the land and dark airfield surrounding it disappear. It looked religious. Like God, if there was one, might be lighting their way and theirs alone. The engines of fast-movers heading out for nighttime bomb runs screeched above the hangar in the dark and Shaw watched the blue-and-orange rings of their engines leaving the ground and burning the sky. It looked like the Devil, if there was one, had come to earth and left his eyes behind. The fast-movers could be a relief, the screeches comforting to those surrounded on a hillside, outmatched and outgunned. They could blanket bombs for miles and split the world in half. The men started gathering in the hangar and set their bags on the concrete slabs. They craned their necks to the fading stars and watched the trails of jet fuel burn up in the sky, listening to the aircrafts shrieking like wraiths.

"So I'm disgusting for watching that?" Hagan followed Massey into the light. "It's education." Hagan kept his bag shouldered. He ran his thumbs across the nylon straps. "Every dad sees it. Donna's full of shit. The nurses clean it up."

"It's educational, you mean," Massey said, dropping his bag on the concrete. "And regardless, you're sick, that's sick, and you're making me sick."

Hagan slammed his bag on the floor. Dust fanned out and clung to his pants.

"Educational? What the hell's that? Whatever. It's the miracle of life, Espresso. Everyone knows that."

Shaw laughed. He pointed at Hagan.

"There. Espresso was good. End on that." Massey had dark skin, so the men got clever with him. Hagan, especially, liked it. He probably wrote down good ones that came to him while he was alone in his room. Coffee and bean relations were common. Burrito. Beaner. Java. Jo. Java-Jo. Tobacco-Jo. Cocoa-Jo. Cocoa Puff. Fudge. Brownie. Fudge brownie. "The birth shit's a stretch. This place doesn't smell like birth shit, which is probably no different than my shit or your shit, or anyone else's shit. PBS or not, giving birth or not. It just smells like shit. No one wants to think of birth shit, you animal. Especially not Donna."

"Why not? He's the only one that's seen it. Live show, at least."

"Hog. Think about it. He just left his daughters and wife. His ladies. He's got a son in the oven. You think he wants to think of that now? More than that. You think he wants you, or any of us, talking about Mirna like that? Thinking about Mirna like that?"

Hagan nodded and looked at the ground. He lifted his face, bounced his eyebrows, and smiled. "Espresso was good, wasn't it?"

He looked relieved after defending himself for so long. Proud.

"I thought of that a while back." He pointed behind himself with his thumb. "During poker."

"You fell asleep during poker, you big idiot," Dalonna said. He and Cooke dropped their bags next to the rest and Hagan shook his head at Dalonna. He mouthed, *I know you've seen it,* and kicked Dalonna's bag. "And why the hell didn't we carry our rucks instead of the hop bags? I think I've got one of Hog's dead prostitutes in mine."

"You bitching already, Donna?" Hagan asked.

Dalonna spit at Hagan's boots and Hagan looked at Cooke and brightened. Cooke was smiling. He had his head tilted back and took in a deep breath of air.

The men were briefed about the air quality after each hop. Government reps would welcome them from the bird, tell them they were glad they made it home safe, and then shake their hands and let them know they'd receive compensation in the future if the air they just left carried carcinogens and they got sick. They meant if the men got cancer and died.

Hagan smiled. "Nowhere else you'd rather be, huh?"

Cooke shook his head.

He looked comfortable, relieved. Happy.

Home.

. . .

The squadron they were relieving lined the outside walls of the hangar. There were twelve men. Beards trimmed, shaved, or styled. Skin tanned. Their gear formed a protective perimeter around themselves and most of them sat with their backs propped against the wall, sleeping or staring at the ceiling. They looked deflated in their wrinkled fatigues and they sprawled limp across the floor like they were shrinking or trying to hide in their clothes. A few guys stood in tight circles with their arms crossed, toeing the floor with their boots. They'd leave in a few hours, after their bird gassed up and passed its checks. None of the men from the exiting or entering squadrons spoke to the other teams as the forklifts dropped off the rucks for the entering squadron.

Red taillights crept up to the hangar in the dark and four black short buses wheeled onto the concrete floor. The squadrons just off the bird threw their hop bags and rucks into the trunks and Shaw sat in a middle seat with Massey, in front of Cooke, Dalonna, and Hagan. The seats were rough with dirt and hard spots. Mud or melted hard candy was worked into the fabric. The buses left the hangars, the smooth concrete giving way to rough rock, and Shaw looked back through the dark windows. None of the men in the hangar watched the buses leave.

"Man," Hagan said a little while later. "That smell."

"I'd already forgotten about it," Cooke said. He winked at Hagan.

"At least we're not building a FOB out of a damn hillside with Hajji pissing down on us," Hagan said. "Remember that, Donna?"

Dalonna didn't answer, so Massey and Hagan looked back.

Dalonna had his head on the window glass, and his snores and the sound of rocks hitting the underside of the bus filled the cabin. He might have been faking it but was more likely already asleep. Cooke stared out the window and, though he'd dug the forward operating base out of the hillside with Hagan and Dalonna years ago, said nothing. Massey and Shaw had been with another team then, another country. Hagan shrugged and closed his eyes.

Their FOB was one of the largest in the country. Not yet a full-blown base with Burger Kings and McDonald's, it was nestled in a low valley separating Shiite and Sunni communities where a formerly private airport had been turned into a public engine of war for the Americans. The original dirt airfield had been paved, expanded, and maintained for the cargo planes that unloaded endless troops and mountains of munitions daily. Numerous helipads had been erected on both sides of the runway, where gentle mounds of earth and air-traffic shacks once stood, and rows of dust-colored clapboard buildings erected from cheap siding and tin roofing housed expensive air conditioners and even more expensive computer systems. The rows of clapboard buildings expanded from the airfield in all directions like the ripples sent out from a rock thrown into a pond. The ripples spread throughout the low valley until the land had been turned into a blanket of concrete slabs, watchtowers, concertina wire, and temporary architecture linking the two Islamic communities that were often at war with each other. Most of the structures lining the perimeter of the FOB housed supplies and troops who would patrol the nearby Sunni and Shiite communities. Smaller communities that flanked the main airfield were separated from the larger FOB by twelve-foot-high concrete blast walls on all sides. Special operators lived in the small communities and built their own private helipads off the main airfield. They maintained their own aircraft for the missions that would take them hundreds of miles away from the FOB in all directions. The maze of concrete checkpoints leading from the main airstrip to the Special Operations communities took the longest to navigate even though they were closer to the airstrip than the conventional unit communities—in some cases by five miles or more.

The buses maneuvered through the endless concrete barriers and checkpoints in the moonlight while small flashes of light burst through tiny holes and cracks in the concrete. If Shaw had strained his neck he could have seen stars and clouds floating above the barriers, but he was asleep. They all were. The buses wheeled past two large concrete slabs joined by a large metal gate with concertina wire coiled from the ground to the top, and then took a nauseating set of sharp turns to pass through a quarter-mile of stone switchbacks, erected to prevent suicide bombers. Then the brakes hit and the buses stopped. The men woke up, got out of the buses, and grabbed their bags and rucks from the trunks. They stacked their bags against a section of wall so the GMVs could pass through and then the buses backed out, navigated the switchbacks in reverse, and sped off.

"Walk it out," their CO called out. "Briefing room's got a green ChemLight, war room blue, phones and computers yellow. Tents are red. Anything without a light is a shitter. I'll check on the chow. Briefing room at 0530."

Their CO was tall and dark-haired. He had a sharp face with angles that could cut a hand. His mind was tireless and quick, and he didn't sleep much. He couldn't stand still or grow a beard the way he wanted, so he grew the hair on his head to his shoulders and kept his face shaved close. Never one to comb his hair, he embraced the mad-scientist look but was handsome enough to be in a boy band. He never doubted his men's decisions or let anyone else take the fall for a fuckup. The men loved him and would do anything he asked.

It was 0500 hours when the buses had offloaded the men, and their bags and the sun had already begun softening the dark. The men didn't need headlamps since they could see by the sun preparing to jump from beneath the horizon. Shaw grabbed his hop bag and ruck and followed Hagan and Massey down a wooden walkway to the last tent with a red ChemLight taped to the door handle. Four tin shacks without lights sat opposite the four tents with red ChemLights. A bathroom opposite each tent—four ribs on either side of the wooden walkway sternum. Cooke got to the door of the tent first. He opened the handle and stepped into a fridge. The tents were air-conditioned and running full blast. Years ago they'd land somewhere and have to carve out living quarters in rock or dirt and sleep in the holes they'd dug. Their beds were mounds of dirt and sweat-stained rock. Now they had climate-controlled tents. They were certainly winning the war of comfort.

Hagan danced the length of the tent with his hop bag cradled around his shoulder like a girl he'd decided to fireman-carry. He moved his feet gracefully over the wood floors and each step kicked up a small cloud of dust that vanished in the dark of the tent. He threw his bag on the top bunk of a set in the right corner and Massey took the bed next to Shaw, and Dalonna and Cooke spread out along the opposite wall. The men put their hop bags on the top bunks and unrolled sleeping bags and blankets on the bottoms.

"Let's find some bottles," Hagan shouted.

Pissing outside when the temperatures would stay above the century mark for another few weeks was frowned upon. The sun would bake the tin-shack shitters into ovens, so the men used empty bottles. Empty Gatorade ones were a favorite for the large mouth. Bowel movements demanded tolerance for the shit ovens or well-timed breaks during the dark hours.

"That's fine," Dalonna said. "But take that shit outside every morning. Last hop I grabbed for some water and drank someone else's dip spit or piss. I don't want to know which it was." The guys laughed and Dalonna turned around to a whiteboard nailed to the door of the tent. It had black lines taped in a grid pattern. "I'm serious. It was sick."

Dalonna wrote their names in the empty column on the left with a marker tied to the board with a white string. They'd mark an *x* under the column where they were at all times. Shitters. War room. Briefing room. Gym. Chow hall. Phones. The range.

Shaw grabbed his baseball glove from his hop bag and threw it on his bed. It was ashy black and beautiful, the gloss faded from a decade of sun and dirt and being broken in under the tires of Humvees. It fit like a surgical glove. The ball practically hit his bare palm. Massey threw his on his bed, too. It was a ratty brown, dried-up nightmare. Shaw's fingers nearly bled just looking at the sharp edges and frayed straps around the mitt.

"Did your dad bring that from Cuba?" Hagan asked.

"Guatemala," Massey said. "And no. And fuck you."

Hagan laughed. "Guys," he said, and put his big arms around Shaw and Massey. "I forgot mine."

Hagan never had a glove. Hagan was a mooch. Shaw grabbed a catcher's mitt from his bag and threw it at him.

"It's stiff," Shaw said.

"That's okay, Shaw. I love stiffies."

Hagan smiled and hugged Shaw from behind. Shaw knocked on his ribs with his elbow until Hagan let him go and Cooke smiled and brought a foot-long metal pole out of his bag and some horseshoes.

"Yeah, you do," Cooke said. "But stiffy lover or not, we're gonna knock down these shoes." He had a huge wad of fine-cut in his lower lip and raised his eyebrows. Then he left the tent.

Dalonna said he was going to the war room and grabbed his rifle and ruck and left the tent. Shaw and Massey followed him while Hagan helped Cooke put the horseshoe stake in the ground outside their tent.

The three found the blue ChemLight leading down a set of stairs not far from their tent. The room was built into the ground, the roof raised a few feet above the earth. Wooden lockers spanned the room from floor to ceiling and end to end. Everything smelled of metal, Velcro, gun oil, and dust. Other teams had already claimed spots, set their helmets on top of the lockers, with their rucks, kits, and weapons placed neatly in the lockers. Cases of batteries and full mags lined footlockers with the tips of their rounds winking bright in the light. Someone had taped up a picture of a woman spreading her legs and pointing a pistol through her panties with *Local pussy kills* written underneath her in black ink. Hagan kissed his fingers and tapped the woman's crotch when he passed, and Shaw found a spread of open lockers spanning two walls and a corner and grabbed five. He put up a couple pictures of his grandparents and Hagan saw them and nodded.

"How do, Gramms." He said it slow, with respect.

Shaw smiled and looked at his grandma. His favorite picture had her billowing white hair tied up in a handkerchief while she held tomatoes from her garden in her hands. She smiled wide and the tomatoes looked huge in her small hands, her pint-sized body. His grandpa's hand was reaching toward the vegetables at the edge of the shot he'd taken himself. She had a smooth face until the day she died and she wore an agate necklace in the picture. It was deep blue, with smoky white lines running around the circumference. His grandpa said he'd found it on a beach, which was a known and loved lie. Shaw held the necklace in his pocket. He'd had it with him ever since she passed. Dalonna took out a picture of his family and taped it at eye level, flush on the wood that would house his helmet and NODs. His daughters held a shared hand over his wife's belly. One of the girls was prettier than the other, but they were both cute. They were dressed in purple and pink ballet leotards and smiling wide, both missing a whole mess of teeth. One of the girls had orange painted across her lips and must've gotten into a bag of Cheetos before the shot. Dalonna never tired of saying his son was high-fiving his girls in the picture. He smiled while he taped the pictures to his locker. Besides the pictures of his girls, he taped up a photo of an ultrasound that made his son look like a wrinkled old man, a picture of his wife on their wedding day, and one of himself with his grandfather during a visit to the Philippines years before.

Hagan stood at Dalonna's locker and propped his hand on the wood and leaned in to the pictures.

"Donna, did you get married in the eighties?"

"No, dickhead. We got married in the Philippines. It's hot as shit there and Mirna's hair was all frizzy."

"No shit. All her hair?"

Dalonna looked like he was trying to remember something he'd forgotten. Then he looked at Hagan and shook his head.

"Dammit, Hog. No. Not cool. Not all of her hair."

Hagan laughed and wandered over to Massey, who was putting up a picture of his niece, Penelope.

"She's five, Hog," Massey said. "Don't perv out."

Cooke laughed, Dalonna shook his head, and Hagan held up his hands like he'd dropped something on the floor and broken it. Penelope was cuter than Dalonna's girls, but they all had that careless, invincible shine to their faces. Shaw looked at the pictures of Penelope and Dalonna's girls. They all looked like the girl from the poppy fields.

At 0530 hours the operators of the two squadrons, wearing baseball hats and sunglasses pushed up on the crowns of their heads, sat around white tables facing a large whiteboard.

The exiting CO was a thick colonel with a Civil War mustache. Not fast-food thick but hypodermic-needles-before-the-gym thick. Veins were visible through the sleeves of his shirt and the mustache was likely an effort as long as the hop. He could've waxed it at the tips, it was so full, but he must've used up all his wax or never had any to begin with, because the ends flapped ragged. Like a half-inch rope cut with a knife. He was tapping his foot, held a metal pointer against his forearm, and kept his eyes on his watch. He began right at 0530.

"We've got a nice football field–sized community of nylon tents snug between two-foot-thick, twelve-foot-high concrete walls."

He sounded hoarse, like instead of using scissors, he'd chewed the ends of his mustache off and was having a hard time swallowing the hair. He spoke in declarative fragments.

"Airfields are here."

He paused to spit in a foam cup on the table behind him. Then he stabbed a large area southwest of their tents with the pointer.

"About a two-minute drive."

He hit the pointer on a bare spot beyond the phones and computers.

"GMVs and other vehicles here."

He pulled at his mustache, nodded, and held out his hand.

"About a minute walk from the war room and the TOC."

He traced a large perimeter to the west of the tents.

"Range is here. It was ours. Now it's yours. We run it and use it. You see anyone outside your unit on it, they probably shouldn't be there."

He didn't tell the men what they should do in that situation. Just looked at them, shrugged, and continued with his brief. He told them that out of more than a hundred house calls, they took fire from all but three. He cracked his neck, closed his eyes, and shook his head.

"We lost fourteen men to these fuckers."

He spit in his cup.

"They can't shoot for shit, but they can blow shit up. Al-Ayeelaa is everywhere. Every house we hit led to more of them. They're in the damn air you breathe."

He hit his pointer on a black-and-white photo of an overweight man with glasses.

"Intel's been looking for Tango1 for the last couple weeks. This is him. He's likely been involved with recent bombings in the area, but after our two birds went down we weren't in any shape to look for him."

He opened his hands and shook his head. Then he hooked his thumbs in the loops of his pants and toed the ground for a little while. Shaw thought of the fourteen men going down in the birds in the mountains. He wondered if they'd felt anything.

"That's why you're here. With any luck he'll pop hot for you guys and you can get the shithead."

He nodded to himself, spat again into his cup, and walked out the door. Everyone watched him leave the room.

"Great 'stache," Hagan said.

The two squadrons spoke briefly after the outbound CO's talk and then went their separate ways. They would operate as individual squadrons throughout the hop, hitting their own targets in different lands, unless a particularly enticing target required their collaboration. Shaw's CO told the squadron they wouldn't get the green light for missions for another couple days, so they made final preparations to their kits, zeroed weapons, watched the news, and straightened out all their shit in general. The muezzin's *salat*s echoed throughout the FOB from mosque speakers in the surrounding neighborhoods, and the prayers were already merging into the soundtrack of the war. Soon the men would hardly notice the noise at all.

It was hot out even in the early hours after the brief. They shot in T-shirts, without body armor or helmets, and finished their day-zero after a couple minutes, to ensure their rounds would hit where they wanted them to. Then the teams threw rounds downrange for a couple hours to stay warm and give their trigger fingers the work-outs they'd become accustomed to. Just before noon Shaw's trigger finger was pulsing and cramping. He hollered that he was done, and most of the others agreed and decided to call it a day before the night-zero.

"Clips to end it?" Cooke asked.

"Only if the loser really gets nailed," Hagan said.

"You'll lose, you idiot," Dalonna said.

Everyone laughed and Hagan adjusted his sunglasses. He held his weapon in one hand and pumped it to the sky. "I'm a fucking hollow-point god! Invincible and with a foot-long cock! I can take anyone here."

"I got you," Cooke said. "When I win you go ahead and take that nice foot-long and sit bare-assed on a GMV that's been sun-ning for the day."

Hagan looked at Cooke for a while, his face set and eyes nar-rowed. "Cooke, you're a genuine grass-fed Texas pussy." He threw a leg forward theatrically and bowed. "Challenge accepted. What do I get if I win?"

"Whatever you want, sweetheart."

"Good. I've been considering this for a while. Years, maybe." He looked around the range, beyond the concrete blast walls lead-ing to the tops of the mosques and neighborhood homes to the drab specks of mountains in the distance. He spread his arms wide, holding his weapon by the grip. "Gentlemen, we're in goat country now. Cooke, if I win, you need to take your longhorn-humping ass and go find a goat on an op and stick your small Texas thistle weed in its crusty goat ass."

Cooke laughed and spit at the targets downrange. "Goat sex. Sure. Sounds like something you'd consider for a while. You got it, bud."

Hagan looked confused. "What?"

Cooke smiled and shook his head. "Nothing. Don't hurt yourself. We got a deal."

Massey, Shaw, and Dalonna brought out some used ammo clips while guys from other teams stood in a line with their arms crossed, weapons slung, and teeth blackened by dip and chaw. Shaw set the clips in a triangle on the wooden base of the target stands. Each clip was no wider than the fingernail of a pinkie and a couple inches in length.

"Three rounds," Cooke said. "One in each clip, no more than two seconds."

Hagan stared at him. "Your dick. One goat's ass."

"Call the time, Mass," Cooke said.

The teams stood shoulder to shoulder behind the shooters, their arms crossed and muscled shoulders blotting out the sun and laying a solid block of shade at their feet. The teams stood far enough behind Cooke and Hagan so none of them would catch any brass, but close enough to see the rounds' impact. Massey told them to get ready and aim, then fire. He clocked the two seconds on his watch and both of the pops from their rifles coughed *pop, pop, pop* in time.

The teams and shooters walked toward the targets and Cooke let out a rebel yell. He'd hit all three clips square in the middle. There was a neat, clean hole through the center of each. Hagan had holed two and nicked the third.

"I hate my life," Hagan said.

Cooke whistled.

"Don't worry, Hog. I'll pick out a nice one for you."

It had to be close to one hundred twenty degrees in the sun. The walk from the range to the GMVs really got their swamp-ass running—Shaw's armpits and crotch seeped through his top and bottoms, and Dalonna was so wet it looked like he'd pissed himself. Hagan's back tattoos were visible through his soaked white T-shirt and the men had their bottoms rolled up to their knees.

"That one right there," Cooke said. He pointed to the GMV at the far end of the column. Heat waves shimmered off its armored sides. It was last in line and had taken the sun since it rose hours before.

"You're still a pussy," Hagan said, unbuckling his pants and walking to the vehicle. "Big grass-fed pussy from Texas."

"Ass on, you bum," Cooke said. "Clock it, Mass."

Massey looked around. "When did I become the time bitch?"

Laughter trickled around the dry shooting range but no one offered his watch instead. Breaths of wind kicked up small puffs of dirt.

"Fine. Ass on, Hog," Massey said.

Hagan's ass was large and meaty. Hairy. The blond hairs twinkled in the sunlight and the operators winced as he eased onto the hood of the GMV, cupping his distended, hairy balls with his hand.

"Foot-long, huh?" Cooke shouted. "Hope you're as generous with the charities back home, Hog. Lots of puppies and little kiddies could use your help."

Hagan flicked everyone off and sat on the vehicle with a quick jerk of his knees. He cried out immediately and the men were bent at the waist so fast and laughing so hard they hardly noticed his screams had died off and he wasn't on the hood anymore. Hagan was howling and shrieking and he'd made his way about halfway to the line of men with his pants at his ankles before most even noticed he was off the hood, standing bare-assed in front of them. He pointed at the hood and said the GMV had grated his ass. Everyone walked over to the GMV and Shaw peered close. He saw little flecks of skin curling toward the sky in the paint of the hood and Cooke whistled again.

"Damn, Hog," Cooke said. He picked up a small scrap of Hagan's skin between his fingers. "Just like shredded cheese." He offered the skin to Hagan. "I'll give you fifty bucks to eat this."

Hagan winced and slapped at his behind with the back of his hand. He craned his neck over his shoulder, looking toward his backside. "I'm not eating any part of my own ass, Cooke. I have principles."

"Principles, maybe. But you can't shoot for shit."

"Cooke, fuck yourself. Mass, do we have any ass cream?"

Massey looked at Hagan and raised his eyebrows. "What the hell is ass cream? That's not a real thing. So no, I don't have any ass cream."

"Dammit, Mass. Ointment." Hagan cupped his ass in his hand and came away with small flakes of skin on the palm. He held the skin up for the others to see. "Balm. Ointment. I need some damn ointment for my shredded arse."

"Of course I have ointment," Massey said. "And did you say *arse*? You trying out for SAS or something?"

"I don't know what I said. And maybe. I hate all of you. My ass is on fire."

"Well, thank God it's your ass and not your arse," Massey said. "I'm out of British ointment."

"Mass, seriously. I'm burning. Where's it at?"

Massey turned toward the tents and pointed. "The tent, you bloke."

Hagan turned around and walked off to the tents, his pants at his ankles and dirt clouds kicking up at his feet.

"Learn to shoot and you won't be so ass-hurt!" Cooke yelled after him.

"I bet he would've eaten it for a hundred," Dalonna said. "Hog doesn't even know how to spell principles."

With hours left to waste before the night shoot, Massey and Shaw went to the gym while Dalonna called his girls back home and Hagan rubbed ointment on his backside. The fear and anticipation kept them awake, so most walked with rucks for hours in the hot sun or shot at the range. The gym was private and beautiful and packed with guys who had witnessed Hagan burn himself on the GMV hours before. Muscles were tightening and tested under strained barbells, and white teeth gleamed bright through ragged beards. Heavy metal screamed through speakers one moment and then switched to classic rock, country, or rap the next, and no one seemed to notice or care. The gym was packed with kettlebells, bench presses, pull-up and dip bars, and rows of dumbbells and treadmills. There were even big box fans in the corners of the room to keep the place a little cooler and to keep all the stink out. In the first couple months and years of the war, poles and water cans full of sand or water sufficed for weights and exercise equipment. Sometimes men would just find large rocks and boulders and haul them around for hours.

Squadron and team rules were set in place for working out on hops. They might have seemed restrictive to the true meatheads of the unit, but they made perfect sense to those who didn't juice. No maxing out on weights, and cardio sessions were maxed out at eight miles or an hour. Whichever came first. There weren't specific checks in place, but since it affected operational capacities, most operators followed the rules. *Screw personal records if they would get anyone shot or blown up.* It was a squadron mantra on hops.

Same as with the gym, the chow hall was a noticeable improvement over their food sources in the past. The men were used to eating MREs in birds, GMVs, or in the hamlets, homes, and villages they visited, but the chow hall had wooden tables and chairs and clean metal utensils. There were big steel vats of hot food and it was available at any minute of the day. There were a couple TVs on the walls and local staff had been hired as servers. They stood behind the vats and smiled at the men, saluting them with steel tongs.

Shaw looked at Massey's tray as they walked over to a table.

Massey had four chocolate milks in a line along with a straw set on top of a napkin and a single piece of rye bread.

"What the hell are you eating?"

"I'm on a liquid diet," Massey said. "You know that."

"I remember," Shaw said. "Liquids and peanut butter cups, sure. What the hell's that?" He pointed at the bread.

"That's rye bread that's about to be eaten. I'm expanding my horizons. Let me eat my rye bread in peace."

Shaw sat down and poked a hole in the rye bread with his finger. "Fair. Eat."

"You've tainted it now."

"So that's why you won't like it? Okay. Enjoy."

Massey shrugged and turned to the TVs. He ate like a child. He ate turkey with ice cream on top; bacon and pickles and Hershey's Kisses; peanut butter cups and whole milk. Four chocolate milks and rye bread. It wouldn't be fair to say he was on a particular diet, because he rarely ate anything at all, yet even the most proven gym rats were in awe of his physique. He was a scientific anomaly, a man ripped from marble after fueling himself with shit. More than one operator had joked that Massey simply wasn't human, had to be spit from the sack of Zeus. Trips to the cornfields of southern Illinois had been planned to test the water and corn.

Massey finished two of the milks and started pecking at his rye bread with his fingers like a bird on the street. He and Shaw were alone in the chow hall, watching the TVs and eating in silence. Reporters were commenting on the increasing violence and bombings in the country, and a male reporter with dark features and nervous eyes stood outside a mosque that had been blown apart. He held up the wheel of a shopping cart, said the bomb might have been wheeled outside the mosque and detonated after prayers let out. The headline stated that at least twenty-three were dead.

"That'll rise. The reporters always get there too fast."

Shaw watched the video feeds intently, hadn't heard what Massey had said. Blood was spread over the streets like paint and Shaw was staring at a leg strewn among the rubble that the editing team forgot, or didn't care to blur out. Massey pointed at the screen, and Shaw broke his gaze from the TVs.

"What?"

"Did you see that?" Massey said. "The Mexican cartels are cutting off heads and just burying them. Leaving the bodies out on the street so no one knows who got killed."

Shaw hadn't even noticed the stories had changed. He looked back at the TV and pictures of a Mexican field of red rock and police tape filled the screen. He still saw the streets outside the mosque covered in car parts and blood. The leg the camera had failed to blur out.

Massey picked up his bread and gestured around the room with it. The bread flopped loosely in his hand like a rag. Seeds fell on the table. "You think we'll get sent to Mexico soon—take a shot at all the cartels?"

"Probably not, Mass. The cartels don't come after us and I think we're busy enough here."

"Man. Mexico. Colombia. Everywhere. World keeps churning, no matter how many guys get wasted."

"This is the world, Mass." Shaw stuck another finger in Massey's rye bread. "You know that."

"Yeah. You're right. You know what else I know?"

"What's that?"

"I don't like rye bread."

They laughed and got up, cleared their trays, and then walked out of the chow hall. Massey grabbed a couple brownies and put them in his cargo pockets on the way out. Outside, the moon made their shadows dance on the walls of the tents.

Night shoots were a colorful affair, a favorite among the men. The heat was kept at bay when the stars were out, and with the NODs down and lasers all fired up, the shooting was more like something out of *Star Wars* than zeroing and throwing rounds downrange. Green lasers swept the range, and orange and yellow fire bursts cracked the dark air. The *pop, pop, pop* of their weapons quickened and slowed like a rainstorm that couldn't make up its mind. Gunpowder, dirt, and lead ruled the air. It smelled good. Familiar and right. If townspeople had looked over the concrete barriers from the town surrounding the FOB, they wouldn't see a thing except for maybe a small glint of the rounds reflected in the moonlight from afar. They would hear only the slight puffs of air from the suppressors and the *thwack, thwack, thwack* of the rounds finding their targets and punching into the dirt mounds set behind them. It probably sounded like a whole army of housemaids had come outside in the middle of the night to beat their carpets clean at once. Among the spent casings and bottles of water stacked behind them, the CO walked slowly behind the teams, his hands clasped together at the small of his back.

"We're green in twenty-four," he said. "Try to get some sleep."

Nobody cheered or grabbed ass. They welcomed the news by

finishing off the rounds they'd loaded up and then by stacking all their gear neatly in the war room and surgically cleaning their weapons.

Shaw didn't sleep much. He watched baseball with Massey because the latter was a diehard Cardinals fan and then he got up around 0600 hours after having gotten to bed a little after 0300. The tent was completely blacked out and the air was blasting when he woke. Massey and Hagan were both still sleeping in their bunks, snoring loud, legs kicked out of their blankets. Dalonna was on the phones talking with his wife, and Cooke had marked down that he was at the range. Shaw took a marker and checked off *War Room* next to his name.

He opened the door and light flooded inside the tent. Hagan and Massey started groaning, but Shaw shut the door before they could start swearing at him. It was warm out already, but bearable. He crossed the sternum wooden walkway from the tents to the shitters and let out a strong stream of piss. The bathroom smelled like stale, flat beer. He scratched his beard and mopped away the sweat already forming at the roots. Then he walked to the chow hall and ate a breakfast burrito and watched the TVs again. There were highlights of the Cardinals game he and Massey had watched just hours before and then updated coverage of the earlier mosque bombing. The death toll had risen to nearly forty. Shaw saw a little girl being carried through rubble-strewn, trash-littered streets by grown men shouting and pulling at their dark hair and yelling into the video cameras. The camera zoomed in on the girl's pale face and she looked a lot like Dalonna's girls, only instead of orange

Cheetos powder on her lips she had blood streaking her face. His stomach knotted and tightened, so he got up and racked his tray and left the chow hall. The servers stood with their hands behind their backs, smiling at him. One of the servers tipped his white paper hat, said, "Thank you."

Shaw walked outside and found a shaded section of wall by the war room and pulled up one of the empty ammo cans. He placed the can on the brown dirt that coated his boots and sat down. Then he took out his earphones and tobacco and set a chaw in his cheek. He turned on Pearl Jam and closed his eyes. A light breeze offset the heat nicely and the sun felt good. He enjoyed the smell of the dirt baking in the new day's sun and thought about baseballs hitting leather palms and how the blades of grass had shined so bright they looked wet under the lights of Busch Stadium the night before. He thought of playing baseball as a kid, the way the dirt felt like soft buttered clay or hard schoolyard blacktop, depending on the neighborhood they were in, and remembered getting raspberries on his thighs from rough slides. The bedsheet would stick to the open sores and he'd have to cut the sheet around the scabs in the morning to keep the sores from ripping open.

It was nice.

He tried not to think of dead little girls getting carried through the streets or live ones crying for their mothers. He felt at peace.

Getting to your happy place, huh?"

Cooke nudged Shaw awake with his boot. Cooke's black beard shined in the sunlight. His gloves were streaked and dyed with gun oil and he had six empty mags in his kit.

Shaw nodded and raised his hand to shield the sun. "How was the shoot?"

"Good. I could clip with Hog again, that's for sure."

Cooke's trigger finger was tracing along the trigger guard of his weapon. He looked down at his weapon and then around the FOB, over the concrete walls toward the neighborhood mosque's minaret.

"He's probably going to be rubbing crap on his ass for a while before he clips again with you," Shaw said.

"Poor Hog."

Cooke spat in the dirt and looked at Shaw. He nodded toward him.

"You okay? You look anxious."

"Yeah," Shaw said. "I'm good. Hate sitting around."

"That's for sure. Need to get our hit list and start burning through it." Cooke checked his watch. "Well, we're greened tonight. That's good."

"Yeah, Cooke." Shaw laughed. "It is."

Cooke nodded and walked away.

Shaw watched him go. He moved light and airy, like a little kid.

The beeper lit up with their first 4 of the hop an hour after Cooke walked off. The beeper was crammed down deep in Shaw's pocket, so the vibration had woken him. The 4 meant that the teams could expect to be on the birds in four hours, so were expected in the briefing room within forty minutes. When Shaw got to the briefing room it was nearly full. Everyone sat at the tables closest to the whiteboard, their knees bouncing up and down.

Taped to the board were printouts of an overhead view of the target house they'd visit in a couple hours.

Shaw looked at Hagan when he entered. He and Cooke were sitting next to each other, their faces turned inward, elbows on the table. Cooke was trying to teach Hagan how to get a dip the size of a golf ball into his lip to match the one he sported himself. It was a fruitless effort. Hagan's fingers were black from all the runoff and he had dip all over his pants. He saw Shaw and smiled, dip falling from his mouth.

"Listening to your suicide music?" Hagan asked.

"Suicide music?"

"Yeah, what were you listening to?"

"Pearl Jam," Shaw said. "What's suicidal about that?"

"The lead singer killed himself. Right after they hit it big. He used a shotgun."

Massey rolled his eyes and let out a deep breath. "Hog, that was Nirvana. Pearl Jam's still together."

Hagan narrowed his eyebrows and let his fingertips rest on his thighs. "Nah, that's not right."

"Yes, it is," Massey said.

"All alive?" Hagan asked.

Shaw smiled. "All alive, Hog."

"That's one of their songs," Massey said.

Hagan looked at Massey. "We're all alive?"

"No," Massey said. "'Alive.'"

"Just 'Alive'?"

"'Alive.' That's it. One word."

Hagan nodded, the dip still trickling out of his mouth. He stared at the ceiling, like he'd seen something small on one of the roofing tiles. "Whatever. You should be listening to Metallica or Pantera. Billy Joel."

"Billy Joel?" Massey asked.

"Hell, yeah," Hagan said. "Dude is badass. 'It's the End of the World'? That's the shit."

"That's also not Billy Joel," Massey said.

"What?"

"That's R.E.M. Billy Joel is 'Piano Man.'"

Hagan rolled his eyes. "Fine. Then R.E.M. is badass."

Shaw sat down and patted Hagan on the back.

"Hog, you look like shit," Dalonna said.

Hagan had dip spread all over his pants. It looked like he'd spilled a filter full of used coffee on his lap. He frowned and stuck his chin out. "Donna, I'm aware. Thank you." He pointed at Cooke. "No one can get a dip the size of a golf ball into their lip. It's not possible. Cooke's a mutant."

Cooke smiled.

"I bet Billy Joel could do it," Massey said.

"Or R.E.M." Dalonna laughed.

Their CO walked in and Hagan mumbled, "Thank God," under his breath. The CO held up a copy of the printout hanging on the back of each seat in the room, and the guys stopped joking and quieted down. Small enough to fit once folded in a pocket, the printouts had a headshot of the HVT they were going after, along with personal information. Habits and likely movements. Known family members and acquaintances. Bodyguards liable to be with or around him. Aliases and possible cover stories. Intel's search during the previous squadron's hop had paid off. He was overweight and bearded, with glasses. He was also a bomb maker and reputedly had his nose broken at some point in his life by his own mother.

"He looks like Ron Jeremy," Hagan whispered.

The CO told them the name of Tango1 and began the brief.

"Tango1's from Yemen. As you know, the outbound squadron had been tracking him. He's been operating with al-Ayeelaa for the past year. He left AQAP after his father got hit in an airstrike along with his uncles and some other AQAP HVTs. He didn't like the new leadership, so he left."

The CO nodded to himself and winced, ran a hand through his long hair. The room got real quiet.

"Tango1 has targeted unusual members for his bombing ranks. Apparently he breaks into homes and buildings known to house mentally handicapped folks. Then he sends them out into markets and crowded public places. He blows them up if they try to take off the vests or get back in the car, or, of course, once they've found a large group of people. Sources on the ground have verified the last three bombings in the area—two in bazaars and one at a police station—are his, implemented with these individuals. A guardian of a teenager identified the head of a recent suicide bomber found at a blast sight. He had Down's."

The heads of bombers wearing suicide vests usually cleared the bodies from the pressure of the blast before the rest of the body was destroyed. Heads would pop off relatively intact, like the cork of a wine bottle. Heads could clear the roofs of neighborhood homes and fly through the air like a home run out of Fenway. Some of the men in the room had had heads roll in front of them after a bomber detonated a street or two over.

"Intel's been monitoring likely locations and phones and he's popped hot," the CO said. "We've traced him to this two-story compound." He pointed to the satellite images of the compound tacked on the whiteboard behind him. "He makes it back to the compound from town before sunset and has guards stationed outside the two entryways. They carry AKs and are allowed to sit on chairs flanking the doorways. They don't seem too interested and are probably just locals forced to protect him."

The CO pointed to the target house and the teams flipped over their sheets. The same satellite images posted on the board were shrunk and pasted on the other side of the printouts. The men bowed toward the pocket-sized sheets.

"The compound is two stories and secluded. The nearest building is roughly four hundred meters from any angle of the house. I want one team on each of the two entrances, follow-ons behind them, and the last pulling security. I don't give a shit who goes in first or in what order, so you guys can flip for it as far as I'm concerned. We'll get a 1 as soon as we confirm he's in the compound, so I'd skip the gym until daybreak. Questions?"

Cooke raised his hand. "Known and expected personnel?"

"Should be four known once we've confirmed he's there, and expected could be close to ten," the CO said. "The guards rotate inside, so we're not sure if the shifts stay in a lower level or not. Keep a lookout for potential bombers. First, they're likely innocents. Held against their will and clueless about what they're there for. Second, we don't know how they'll react. If they're strapped, they're strapped. Headshots like anyone else. But they'll probably be scared shitless with all the noise, so be on it and stay flexible. Don't take them out unless you have to."

He asked if there were any more questions and Massey raised his hand, a faint smile spreading across his lips.

"Sir, I think Tango1 works at an Italian deli back home. My mom buys pastrami from him every week. I can have her go over there and off him in like two minutes. Just give me a sat phone."

Hagan nearly swallowed his chew and the printouts trembled on the tables with all the laughter. The CO nodded and smiled until the noise died down.

"That's good, Massey. It's a kill call, so let her know she can finally make some use out of the rolling pins she's been using as fuck toys since you left."

"Yes!" Hagan yelled, and the room broke up. Guys nearly fell out of their chairs and gasped for breath. Massey smiled with his arms crossed and the CO raised his hands. Clapping and whistles filled the room.

"Good," the CO said. "Loosen up."

The laughs trickled to sniffs and giggles, and Hagan rubbed tears from his eyes. When everyone recovered, the air seemed lighter.

"Nobody else?" the CO asked.

No one raised a hand.

"All right. See you on the birds."

He left and everyone got up from the tables to figure out flow patterns for the assault.

Shaw and his team were taking the house.

Once the 1 got beeped through, they would have ten minutes to get to the birds, so the guys stayed close. Guys took last-minute dumps, made last-second phone calls, and gathered in the

Tactical Operations Center to watch the kill TVs. Shaw and his team gathered in the war room, making last adjustments to their kits and triple-checking the batteries in their NODs and weapon sights.

"I need batteries," Dalonna said.

Hagan grabbed a pack of triple-A's and tossed them over.

"I'll take more, too," Shaw said.

Hagan threw a pack at him.

"Me too," Cooke said.

"Sweet Jesus in Jerusalem," Hagan said. "I'm not a battery slut. Get your own shit."

They all laughed, and Massey came in with his arms full of bandages, wrappings, and compresses. He grabbed an ammo can and dropped everything inside. "Take what you want. You guys see Mike's team yet? They shaved."

Before anyone could respond, Mike and his team entered the war room. They had carved their beards into prominent mustaches, just like the Civil War colonel who had given them their entering brief. Except for one of the newer guys with red hair, the mustaches were thick and untamed.

"Excellent, guys," Cooke said.

"Terrible," Hagan said. "You guys look terrible." He pointed at the newbie. "Mrs. Rawlins. My first fuck was Mrs. Rawlins a few doors down the street. I was twelve. She had a thin line of strawberry pubes sitting on top of her happy place just like that. It was beautiful. You are not."

Slausen laughed. He wagged his finger at Hagan.

"Hog, you're just jealous because your blond ass can't handle this kind of lip dressing."

"Nope. Vaginas. Your mouths look like vaginas now," Hagan said. "Congratulations on the mouth vaginas."

Ohio stroked the ends of his mustache and raised his eyebrows. "Hog, you'd be arrested for pedophilia if you ever shaved a mustache out of that half-assed pubic mess of a beard on your face. And as the father of a daughter, I'd be the first to call the cops."

They walked outside laughing and Hagan yelled after them.

"Nice to see you again, Mrs. Rawlins!"

He looked at his team after Mike and the others left and he spoke in a soft voice.

"Guys. I could rock a 'stache, couldn't I?"

Dalonna turned to Hagan and shook his head.

"First, no way any Mrs. Rawlins let you have her when you were twelve, Hog. Second, Ohio's right. Don't chase the 'stache. Your blond ass would look like a two-bit recreational porn star from the eighties. And not the cool eighties. I'm talking like last gasp of disco, early eighties." He shook his head and looked to the floor. "You with a mustache would easily be the worst thing that could happen to any one of us. Why would you do that to us, Hog?"

He walked outside without waiting for a response, and Hagan stood in the war room, his mouth hanging open as the rest of the team passed by him, laughing.

The 1 came through just after 2330 hours and they put their business suits on. Dalonna kissed the picture of his family he had tacked on his locker, and Cooke and Hagan threw in a large chaw. Shaw looked at the picture of his grandma and traced the agate necklace in his breast pocket. The ballistic plate pushed the stone into his chest. No one slapped the top of the door frame walking out of the war room like they do in football locker rooms or beat their chest. They all fingered their kits and weapons, made final adjustments to their helmets and Peltors, checked radio frequencies, and tried to feel as limber as possible. They bent down to the ground to stretch, and operators throughout the war room jumped up and down to make sure nothing bounced or flapped, fixing anything that did.

Outside, the moon shined down bright and the stars were green under their NODs. Gravel crunched beneath their feet. They hitched onto pickups that drove them to their small airfield, and they arrived as another group was taking off. The rotors of the exiting birds pounded the air and kicked up dust from the dirt surrounding the airfield, and the teams offloading from the pickups were hit with a warm slap of air as the birds took off, blended into the night, and disappeared. Then the wind was the only sound for a moment until the birds waiting to hunt Tango1 screeched to life in high screams. There were four Little Birds and a Black Hawk. Another group of birds a few klicks out were getting spun up at the same time and would mirror their movements in case things got bad.

Shaw sat on the bench of one of the Little Birds, a small helicopter with a fuselage slightly larger than a VW Bug, and clipped the D-ring of his safety line onto an anchor bolted into the floor of the cabin. The bench was cool and he swung his boots over the tarmac. Cooke sat next to him and Dalonna and Hagan sat on the other side. Massey linked up with Slausen and grabbed a seat inside the Black Hawk.

The men plugged their comms in and waved to the pilots.

"One okay," Shaw said.

"Two okay," Cooke said.

Hagan and Dalonna sounded off *Three* and *Four*.

The pilots ran over final checks and the men waited for them to get the go.

It came and they went.

The air was clearer away from the cities, and it would be another couple weeks before the wind started biting with any force, so the draft from the bird's flight felt good. Shaw's tops and bottoms rippled on the wind and the moon lit up the ground like it was daylight under cloud cover. The birds would hug the earth and foliage to hide from view when possible, flying at a hundred knots and keeping at least two klicks away from the objective at all times to minimize the sound of their approach. As they flew on, the earth looked like the chalked bones of pale skeletons. The rotors of the Little Birds sounded like swarms of bees in distant forests. Lasers from the bird's gunners painted the ground in wide, green arcs below them. Cooke and Shaw took turns painting the ground below with their lasers, and Dalonna and Hagan did the same on the other side. There was an empty sedan in a charred field. A full sedan driving down a highway. A herd of goats grazing on harvested crops. A group of kids on top of a roof, some who waved and some who shook their fists. Slums had given way to open fields, and the fields had led to ravines and lush riverfronts. They even flew over palm trees for a few minutes.

It was nice.

After nearly an hour of flight the pilot keyed in.

"Five mikes out."

Cooke and Shaw each held a single hand up with their fingers extended and Dalonna and Hagan did the same on their side. The teams dangling their legs from the other four birds followed suit at different points in the sky. It looked like the men were waving to one another with their feet. After the five-mikes call, chatter on the comms picked up and Shaw's hands started tingling. He felt hot. His pulse rose. They received updates from the pilots and the surveillance teams monitoring the satellite footage every few seconds.

No movement outside the compound.

Two guards stationed in front of doorways.

Two mikes out.

Guard entered building.

Guard exited building.

One mike.

They flew over a small lakebed between trees flanking both shores. Then the bird decelerated and banked for its approach. Shaw unplugged his comms, keyed into the team frequency, and grabbed the D-ring anchored to the bird. He and Cooke gave each other a thumbs-up, and the bird touched down and they unclipped their D-rings, got off the benches, and ran off the bird. Shaw scanned the sector to his front and right while Cooke, Dalonna, and Hagan mirrored his movements on their own sectors. It was loud and blasts of air beat down off the rotors. Dust swarmed Shaw's face. He tasted dry earth and dead crops. Grains of dirt got stuck in his teeth. Hagan had spit out his chaw as soon as he touched the ground and got a mouthful of dirt and animal shit instead. The four took a knee and the birds lifted off and left them. Then the other birds climbed away from their loads and it was quiet and the twenty of them moved east.

Their footsteps seemed loud.

The compound sat just over two klicks to the east on the western outskirts of a relatively sparse village, and Intel had ten or twelve dwellings strewn east from the objective across another klick. The target house itself was isolated, and at a slow, deliberate pace, not even a half-hour walk away. They walked over the dried earth and over the shorn crops in the fields, their lasers lighting up the countryside. Shaw painted a depression in the ground to make sure it wasn't hiding anyone or anything that would blow. There was a small tangle of weeds but nothing else. He kicked aside large rocks and hard clumps of earth at his feet and they crumbled apart—either goat shit or baked mud—and Hagan and Cooke scanned their flanks, Dalonna the rear. Snipers were attached to each of the assault teams and Barnes, their sniper, joined them on the move south while Bear moved with Mike's team. Barnes was a redheaded woodsman from Appalachia, tall and thick. He had thighs like the base of an oak tree and he held his long-scoper at the ready, muzzle down, while the others scanned their sectors. The three-foot-long rifle looked like a crowbar in his big arms. Massey linked up with them on the movement and he and Barnes settled in the middle of the other four. After a short walk over the dirt farmland, the lead element came over the comms in a whisper. It was Mike.

"Lights ahead, six hundred meters."

Four lampposts marking the perimeter of the target house cast a hazy bulb of light against the darkness in the distance. The cloud of light seemed fuzzy and jumpy, like it was moving. A soft wind blew. If there was tall grass it would've bowed at their feet. The teams kept moving toward the compound until Mike whispered again.

"Three hundred meters from the light posts. Synch watches on me."

Shaw took a knee and fingered the buttons on his watch.

"Three. Two. One. Mark."

Shaw started his watch and nineteen others lit and beeped the same.

"Jump-off at fifteen flat," Mike said. "Radio silence until positions confirmed."

Shaw led his team south while the others broke off on their respective approaches to the objective. The halo of light surrounding the compound spread as they neared, and Shaw could make out a guard seated in a chair. Shaw brought his hand up and made a circle around his head. He took a knee and the rest of his team hugged the ground. The guard had a weapon cradled over his lap and wore a dark baseball cap turned backward on his head. A baggy white T-shirt and brown pants. He had his legs crossed and his foot was bouncing, like he was bored or anxious. Shaw couldn't quite tell if he was wearing sandals or shoes, but it looked like they were black low-tops.

Barnes crawled up beside Shaw at the head of the element. He laid a couple mags down on a towel he had grabbed from his kit and placed them in front of the trigger guard of his rifle. "Jittery fucker," he mumbled. He brought the rifle against his shoulder and checked his sights. "Go ahead and move that foot. But don't move out of that fucking seat."

The team formed a static line a few meters apart. Barnes at the head, Shaw and Cooke beside him. Massey faced the rear, directly behind Barnes, and watched their six. Dalonna and Hagan turned away from the compound to watch their flanks. Their watches hadn't hit ten minutes yet.

Barnes kept his eye to the scope, shooting hand on the grip and finger inside the trigger guard. He picked loose bits of tobacco from his teeth and rubbed his fingers on his pants. It looked like he was picking at, and eating, small shreds of dried grass from in front of him. Barnes was mumbling quietly to himself and Shaw could see waves of red hair flowing out of his helmet. Hagan wiped the dirt and earth from his tongue and Dalonna brought his sight to his eye and then relaxed. The wind had blown dried earth into the air and it looked like dust kicked up by someone running, but there wasn't anyone around. Cooke rocked back and forth on his knee and took out his chew, buried it, and put another in. He tested the seal on his suppressor and sent a stream of tobacco forward. A few stray clouds passed quickly in front of the moon and then carried on down the sky. The night was beautiful, temperate and with a light breeze. Shaw thought of Florida nights during training hops.

Shaw watched the guard bouncing his foot and wondered if he would feel the air splitting before the point of Barnes's rounds found him. Then the guard leaned forward and started picking at his feet. Shaw could almost see the bones of the guard's back shifting underneath his shirt. He was so skinny. Then he righted himself and threw something to his side.

"Yeah," Barnes whispered. "Throw that shit away. Clean space, clean life. Good boy."

Shaw checked his watch. Thirteen minutes. His head and hands throbbed and the ground seemed to pulse up and down. He tried to breathe slowly, tightening his hands on his rifle and running his tongue across his teeth. If there were any kids inside he hoped they'd locked themselves in a bathroom.

"Show's on, boys," Barnes whispered.

Shaw checked his watch. Fourteen minutes and running. He keyed the comms once and a short static went out. Three others echoed in return. Then it seemed like the wind stopped and everything got real quiet. Peaceful. His head felt heavy, like he could lie down and sleep for hours. He counted individual blades of grass and could see the circular treads in Barnes's boots.

Then the guard put both of his feet on the ground as if he were going to stand.

And he did.

The guard turned to walk inside and Barnes released a breath. Shaw felt air kick back on his face and tremors rippled through his chest and arms. The round tore through the guard's back and he crumpled behind the chair, legs splayed at impossible angles.

Shaw and his team were up and running before the shot finished its echo. They entered the light of the lampposts, running over soft dirt that crumbled at their feet, and Barnes came over the comms as their legs pumped to the doorway. "South guard down."

Then Bear. "East guard down."

Shaw ran straight to the opening, his sight fixed on the doorway just a few steps from the dead guard's feet. He put two rounds in the body lying in the dirt, *pop, pop,* and pressed against the wall to the right of the door as the team stacked behind him. Blood was splattered all over the wall and he could see there wasn't a door but an open entryway leading inside the dwelling. The hem of a shag carpet stuck out from inside in the moonlight.

"Bang it," Shaw whispered.

Hagan came to the other side of the door from the last spot in the stack, banger in hand. Then Cooke squeezed Shaw's shoulder twice. Shaw nodded at Hagan and Hagan threw the banger into the entryway.

Shaw charged through the doorway and the banger lit up the room, flashing and bursting loud. *Bam, bam, bam, bam, bam.* The smell of metal, spices, and stale sweat hit harsh and hot. Like a bag over the head. Cooke peeled off Shaw and a high scream pierced the air. Shaw hugged the wall, moving quickly along the perimeter of the room, kicking aside boxes until he felt carpet give way to concrete and a landing of stairs. The layout was open. There were two doorways and a staircase in three corners of the room. Flashes and a banger from another breach point had already popped in the room off to the left when Shaw entered the door. There'd already been shots. Hagan and Dalonna entered the room to the right and Cooke and Shaw climbed the staircase on the left. They curled right toward the only doorway on the second level.

An overweight man in a white tank top and with a black mop of hair came into the frame of the door, groggy and holding an AK-47 loosely in his hand by the wooden stock. Like it was a stage prop. He looked dizzy with his eyes half closed and ran his thick pink tongue over the ends of his mustache. Shaw sent two rounds through his chest and the rounds punched through the loose white shirt and coughed out the back. The man wheezed and snorted blood from his nose and then collapsed over a bedside table before falling to the carpet. He bobbed and trembled slightly, like a fish out of water for a moment. Then he lay still.

Cooke and Shaw stepped over him and entered the room. The blood blooming from the body had saturated the carpet and painted the ground a deep red. Shaw kicked the AK away from the body and Cooke started opening drawers, moving boxes, and leafing through papers. Shaw looked at the man. His eyes were partially open and they twitched toward Shaw and then away toward the door. Shaw ran his hands along the man's arms and legs and didn't find anything in the pockets, but the man had wet himself, so Shaw's gloves were wet. They shined as if rubbed with a gloss. The piss was warm on his hands. The dead man's skin looked sickly in the bright light of Shaw's tac light. The curly dark hairs of the dead man's belly stood out sharply on the pale flab of his stomach.

Shaw keyed the comms. "Upper level secure. One EKIA. Probable Tango1."

"Got a thumb drive," Cooke said, holding it over his shoulder. He put it in a baggie and kept shuffling through a drawer. "IDs and a checkbook. Lists, too."

Hagan came over the comms from below. "Lower level secure. We've got a live one down here."

Mike came over the comms right after Hagan. "Three additional EKIAs confirmed in North sector, lower level."

Shaw radioed in *Objective secure* and the CO came back over the comms, told them they had ten minutes for SSE. "Exfil at South ORP in twenty mikes," the CO said.

Cooke and Shaw began searching and toeing the walls of the room. They checked the paneling along the wooden floor and the sections of drywall for hidden compartments. There were more ID cards in a cigar box under the bed, along with handkerchiefs and a rifle-cleaning kit and two full mags of 7.62. Dust piles clung to the corners of the room and it looked like someone had kept the place clean but didn't plan on needing to for long. A pair of black tennis shoes sat neatly under the bed and a teal windbreaker hung on a nail in the wall. Shaw opened the drawer of the bedside table and found a copper slimline cigarette holder and a few pictures sitting in a white envelope. He smelled the holder. It had a sweet, peppery odor, and Shaw wondered when the dead man had smoked it last. He looked at the pictures before throwing them in Cooke's bag. There was a picture of the man on the floor holding a weapon. A picture of the man on the floor smiling. A picture of the man on the floor not smiling. A picture of the man on the floor looking serious with other men looking serious and cradling rifles across their shoulders like yokes. Shaw took a large black bag out of one of his cargo pockets and grabbed the shoes, windbreaker, and cleaning kit, and put them all inside the bag.

"All right," Cooke said. "I'm good. Let's go see what Hagan's got alive down there?"

Shaw nodded. They looked around the room one last time and left. A team member came up the stairs to take pictures and fingerprints of Tango1 as they walked down the stairs. Command wouldn't want them lugging six bodies back to the FOB if they didn't need to, so prints and photos were enough.

The lower level was mostly bare except for boxes full of automobile parts. Cooke and Shaw joined the follow-on teams rifling through the things scattered all over the floor of the room they had first breached. Wires were splayed randomly among dirt and oil-streaked carburetors and gearshifts on the floor. Boxes of Winston cigarettes and discarded clothes were set on the carpets, and prayer rugs were rolled neatly in the corners of the room. The northern room, the one Mike and his team had cleared, held a large table in the middle with cardboard boxes set on top. The boxes held metal ball bearings, nuts, bolts, screws, and washers, along with other small, lethal bits that would rip and tear and cut. Maim. Shaw grabbed a handful of the small metal pieces. They drained from his gloved hands like steel confetti. Large jars of industrial glue lay around the boxes, and paintbrushes were lined up in a cup. The walls and floors were white and the room reeked of machinery, bleach, and the dead men's dinner. There was a small stove with hardened rice in a saucepan and a jar of curry sitting broken on the floor.

Two slight men with dark hair and clean faces lay on the floor around the table. They looked asleep, as if pleasantly dreaming. Blood formed in small ponds around the bodies from the holes in their chests. A fatter, bearded man lay slumped over the table. His beard was graying around the jaw and neck, and his mouth was open and seemed frozen in mid-sentence. Mike and Ohio had breached the room, killed the men, and were running their hands along the dead men's arms and legs. They had two rifles and a pistol gathered into a corner of the room. The cardboard boxes on the table were wet and soggy from the runoff of the fat man. The room was spotless without the bodies and the blood. There were large Ziploc bags of white powder strewn about, and Cooke held one up.

"TATP?"

"Probably," Shaw said. He shrugged. "Or cocaine."

Cooke laughed.

"Hey," Hagan said. He was standing behind them in the doorway. He motioned with his head to the other room. "Come here."

Shaw and Cooke walked around to the other room while Mike and Ohio took stock of the items on the table and gathered them into large black bags. In the next room, Slausen and Massey were kneeling on the floor, placing bandages on a trembling body lying in the fetal position on the floor. Dalonna nodded to them as they stood in the doorway, then he just shook his head. Hagan whispered something Shaw couldn't hear. It looked like Slausen and Massey were having a hard time keeping the body on the ground, so Shaw leaned forward to help. His hands hit cold, trembling flesh. Wild eyes darted up toward him from a mass of tangled black hair on the floor. It was a boy, stripped of all his clothing except for a white pair of briefs with a dark mass smeared on the bottom.

Massey wore latex gloves and ran his hands over the boy's face and hair. His fingertips came away bloody and streaked with black residue. The boy was thin and slight. Fragile. He had a metal clamp around his neck chained to a concrete block in the center of the room that kept his head close to the floor. His knuckles were bruised and bloodied, and swelling had set in so thick it was impossible to tell where the bones separated from flesh. His coal-black eyes darted about the room and his body tensed and flexed. He looked like a trapped animal and the medics were doing their best to soothe him like an old scared horse trapped in a stall. Massey and Slausen were light with their movements, gentle. Small, flaky white bits of something that looked like oatmeal or vomit, maybe both, peppered the boy's hair. There was a small puddle of dark, grainy fluid on the floor where he sat. A harsh smell grew stronger the longer Shaw stood in the room. He realized the boy had shit himself.

"Donna, cut him," Shaw said.

Dalonna nodded and Hagan gestured to his pack. Dalonna

grabbed bolt cutters from Hagan's pack and opened the pincers, setting the chain between the teeth. He squeezed and the chain fell loudly to the ground. The boy's eyes grew wide and he stared at the chains and lock on the floor. He tried to stand up, but Slausen held him down. A small bubble of spit formed on the boy's lips.

"I don't think I can cut the thing around his neck," Dalonna said.

"Don't worry about it," Massey said. "They'll take care of him at the FOB."

Massey had the boy's mouth open and ran his fingers inside it, tracing the jawline and looking for broken teeth. His fingers came away bloody. Shaw wondered what the boy's breath smelled like.

"He's missing some teeth," Massey said. The boy's eyes were darting around the room, but Massey kept his head still. Slausen rubbed the boy's back with his big gloved hand. "Anybody got a blanket?"

Hagan nodded. "I've got an extra top in my pack."

He gestured to Dalonna again, and Dalonna brought out the top and gave it to Massey. Massey took the top in his hands, looked at the boy, and mimicked putting the top on. The boy took the top in his hands, rolled it into a tight ball, and held it tight against his bare belly. He started rubbing it back and forth, hard. Massey shrugged and Slausen just kept rubbing the boy's back.

"All right," Shaw said. "Let's go. Bring him on the bird."

They took what they needed from the compound. The tech devices, papers, checkbook, IDs, and the three phones, along with other stuff they weren't sure about but figured might've had some value. Shaw held the black bag over his shoulder while they walked to the exfil. He'd put the slimline cigarette holder in one of Tango1's shoes, thinking Intel could run it for DNA and maybe get traces of other HVTs. They gathered the car parts, the electrical wiring, and the bags of white powder into a big pile a hundred meters west of the compound and dumped the cups of glue and bags of metal pieces on top of the pile. Then they set a charge to detonate and blew it while they waited for the birds. There was a bright flash of orange and white and a loud crack that made the wind shift and the ground tremble beneath them. The boy nearly fell over, but Hagan steadied him. Then everything was black again and thick smoke clouded over their heads.

Massey and Slausen led the boy over the ground to the exfil, their arms around his shoulders. They gave him an extra pair of socks and he trampled over the earth with the baggy, too-big socks flapping on the ground like a second set of feet. He had Hagan's top wrapped around his shoulders and his ribs were sharp and cast jagged shadows on his stomach in the moonlight. He had a Snickers bar in his hand, not yet open.

Hagan walked next to Shaw and gestured to the boy.

"What'll they do with him?"

"I don't know. Hopefully find somewhere and someone for him."

Hagan nodded. "Chained to the floor to shit all over himself."

"Yeah. Fucked up."

Shaw looked around. The night was as beautiful and quiet as it had been when the birds first left them. He watched Slausen and

Massey walk the boy over the uneven ground. He'd seen the same look in that boy's eyes when rabbits got their legs caught in the steel traps his grandpa used to protect their garden. He'd stopped eating the rabbit stew he loved as a boy after a certain age.

"You think he knows he can eat that?" Hagan asked.

"Eat what?"

"The Snickers."

"Probably, Hog."

Hagan nodded and looked south. "Man. I could sure as hell eat that. I'm starving."

"Why don't you ask him for it?"

"Really?"

"No, of course not. Get a hold of yourself, you animal."

"Man," Hagan said. "Chained to the floor. Poor kid."

The teams all took a knee and waited for the birds. Shaw looked back at the compound, at the bodies they'd left outside. The six corpses lay next to one another like firewood or cigarettes in a pack. The operators left them so anyone who cared could bury them in the morning. They tried to be mindful of local custom, even in death. When the birds started touching down, a team huddled around the boy and Slausen and Massey took the boy's hands and lifted him into the cabin. He didn't look comfortable, the big metal collar around his neck weighing his head down, but he wasn't fighting back, either. He sat between Slausen and Massey and they put their big arms around his young shoulders. The boy nearly disappeared between them, he was so small. Eventually he propped his elbows on their thighs. He held the Snickers bar rigid, propped straight up on his knee like a trophy.

. . .

The birds flew through black clouds of burning trash on their way back to the FOB. Shaw's nostrils burned and he felt a stinging heat in his throat. Those dark clouds were what the government reps talked about if the men ever got sick and were owed government compensation. They were probably breathing in their own deaths.

The birds touched down on the tarmac and the muffled chuckles and drumming of snuff cans filled the air as they whined and shut down. It wouldn't be light for another couple hours, they could still get spun up for follow-ons, but everything felt quiet and light despite all the noise. Peaceful. The guys walked slow and calm and Shaw let his shoulders sag and relax under the weight of his kit. Massey and Slausen took the boy off the tarmac and around the gravel barrier separating the dirt from the airfield. Then they disappeared behind the concrete blast walls. Back at the war room, Hagan took off his helmet. The pads left indented rows of honeycombs in his blond hair. Dalonna kissed the picture of his girls and sat down on his footstool with his kit and helmet still on. He let out a deep breath. Cooke set his weapon in his locker and took off his helmet and kit.

"Good shooting," Cooke said. He stretched to the floor, touched his toes. Shaw took off his helmet and placed it in his locker. He took off his kit and let his head rest against the wooden locker.

"I would've been aiming at kneecaps if I'd seen that kid," Hagan said.

"Hell, that would've just wasted rounds," Cooke said. "None of 'em are breathing anymore."

Hagan unwrapped some tape he had coiled around his knees. "You guys hear the kid screaming?"

Dalonna shook his head. He glanced at the pictures he'd put up of his little girls.

"I heard someone screaming when we breached," Shaw said. "I heard Mike and Ohio shooting and then some screams."

"That was a death scream," Hagan said. "Sounded like an old woman getting beaten to death with a stick or a club."

Cooke took off his kneepads and tossed them in his locker. "Well, he was gonna get blown up in a market or police station, and we came in and killed everyone around him. So that sounds about right. And a stick or a club, Hog?" Cooke unlaced his boots and rested his elbows on his knees. "Colorful. Very precise."

Hagan shrugged and they were all quiet for a while, taking off their equipment piece by piece. Shaw sat on his footstool and grabbed an empty bottle from under his locker and put in a big chaw. He let his head rest against the wooden walls of the locker and started feeling the sweat in his bottoms getting cold and wrinkling the skin of his ass and legs.

Hagan got to his feet, stretched his arms above his head, and clapped his hands. "Well, all right. AAR in ten or fifteen. I'm gonna go take a shit."

Cooke said he'd join him, and the two ran out of the war room together.

Shaw disassembled his weapon and started cleaning the bolt and upper receiver of the rifle with a bore brush, Q-tips, and some CLP. Dalonna stayed in the war room with him and neither one said anything. Dalonna was holding a full mag in his hands and unloading and reloading the rounds.

"Donna. You all right?"

"Yeah."

Dalonna answered quickly, glancing at Shaw and then back down at the mag. He kept nodding, even though neither one of them said anything after that, like he was listening to his own private music.

"Okay."

Shaw left him alone. Seeing a kid all messed up like that on his first mission of the hop probably wasn't the best thing for him. Take the kid out of the equation and it would've been business as usual. Shaw looked at Dalonna's girls taped on the wall. The gap-toothed smiles and Cheetos lipstick. Guys came into the war room quietly or talking privately among themselves, and they exchanged hellos and head nods. Some guys made their way to the briefing room or the TOC, still holding their weapons and all kitted up. Most grabbed coffee or spitters and ate energy bars. Shaw finished cleaning the bolt and set it on a clean rag. Dalonna kept his head toward the floor. Shaw wondered if he'd fallen asleep. He watched him, moved his head around to see if he could see his eyes. Then Dalonna looked right at him.

"Fuck it," Dalonna said. He got up off his footstool and left the war room.

Massey came in as Dalonna was leaving.

"What's up, Donna?"

Massey watched Dalonna leave and then he shrugged. He turned to Shaw with his hands on his hips and stretched his back.

"The doc up at the CASH said the kid probably has Down's. But he's not sure."

"Isn't that something he should know right away or not, being a doc and all?" Shaw asked.

Massey shrugged. "Not sure."

"The kid looked comfortable around you and Slausen."

Massey smiled. "Yeah, I don't know. Maybe. Probably not. I don't think he knew what to make of any of it, to be honest. Pretty fucked, huh?"

"Yeah, it is. What'll happen to him?"

Shaw grabbed the upper receiver and ran a bore brush through the barrel. The black, ashy carbon pushed out of the barrel onto the white swab came from rounds that killed a man. He thought about that for a second. Then he looked at the swab, thought of the kid in the chains, and let the swab fall to the floor.

"No idea," Massey said. He rubbed the back of his neck with his hand. "The doc I left him with said there isn't any kind of orphan system in operation or anything around here that can guarantee his safety. And finding any relatives is unlikely. If he has any." He looked at his hands. "Is that the kid's blood?" He spit on his hands and rubbed them on his pants and shook his head. "Sick. I told the doc they should see if they can't fix him up with a job serving food or something around one of the bases. Give him a job he can do. That'd keep him alive for a lot longer than sending him out on the street would."

"That's a good idea," Shaw said.

"Yeah, it is. Be a hell of a lot better than the job he was chained to the floor for, anyhow."

Shaw put his weapon back together and cleared it. The bolt slid smooth and the metal sang.

"You ready for the AAR?" Massey asked.

Shaw nodded.

"That motherfucker was gonna strap a bomb to that kid and blow him up," Massey said. He raised his eyebrows and looked Shaw in the eyes. "And that kid would've walked out into a market just happy to get away from those guys. No idea what he was wearing." Massey nodded to himself and then slapped his hands on his kit, took it off, and put it back in his locker. "Let's go to the AAR and then throw some weights around."

They had their after-action review in the TOC. Guys wore baseball hats, T-shirts, and sandals while the kill TVs showed live footage of other raids. Some of the men had their boots and kits off, while others were still all kitted up and weapons slung. Ready to go back into the dark. Guys held coffee and spitters in one hand and printouts in the other. Shaw was breaking in a Cardinals hat for Massey. With the playoffs running full blast, Massey was getting superstitious and wanted Shaw to rub as much dirt and CLP on the cap as possible. He didn't say why and it was starting to stink. Shaw felt like a wrench monkey.

Their CO was hands-off during planning and execution, but the AARs were his property. He leaned forward and his eyes narrowed. He spoke fast.

"Describe the layouts of the first and second floors."

"What did you have to avoid on your movements?"

"What did the rooms smell like?"

"Were they hot or cold?"

"What kind of metals did you find? Anything you hadn't seen before?"

"What would you change?"

"What surprised you?"

It was a debrief, not an interrogation, and the teams would answer in as much detail as possible. Shaw could almost see the information taking the CO inside the objective as his eyes widened, the nuts and bolts of his brain moving overtime. Putting puzzle pieces together and saving others for later. Everyone, everything, had patterns and trends that could lead to the next target. So the men tried to describe a smell as closer to a tulip than a rose if it would spark a trend and a follow-on raid. A shade of brown more Hershey's than Godiva. After his questions, the CO leaned back, relaxed, and they discussed strengths of the raid and lessons learned. They agreed that the strengths of the raid were the speed and precision of violence, and minimizing their time on the objective. They agreed that the surprise afforded by walking in instead of roping onto the roof or landing right outside the compound outweighed the risks of being compromised on the infil and taking casualties. They didn't mind the walk. The men inside were armed and likely to shoot it out if they had heard the birds approaching.

The CO rubbed the tops of his knees with his hands.

"Good shooting. Good movement."

He nodded to himself and looked toward the kill TVs flanking the walls, at the other raids and possible targets.

"No follow-ons tonight," he said, watching the screens. "Get some sleep."

He looked like he could've used some.

The operators got to the war room and changed the batteries in their NODs and lasers. They emptied stale water from their reservoirs and filled them up again with fresh new bottles. They reloaded mags and adjusted their kits and then left for their tents. Outside, the sun would soon be up. The Intel teams would dissect the files and tech devices while the men who took them off the objective slept. The next targets would be waiting for them when they woke.

The machine was up and rolling.

Hagan pointed his horseshoe at Cooke in the sunlight.

"You know what I like about you, Cooke? You just suck. You know that? Literally suck and are the worst at everything in the whole world. Don't know what the weather will be like in the next week or two, but one thing's for sure. Cooke's gonna keep on sucking."

Hagan let his horseshoe fly. It missed the stake.

Cooke laughed and pointed his horseshoe at Hagan.

"Hog, listen carefully." He aimed the horseshoe at the stake and spit at his feet. "Your single greatest accomplishment in life," he said, letting the shoe fly, "is being a sometimes invalid whose mouth makes him a genuine all-the-time one." He ringed the stake. "Now bend over real nice like your mother."

Hagan stood upright with his hands on his hips. "What the hell is an invalid?"

"Look it up," Cooke said. He gestured with his fingers for Hagan to turn around.

"I will look it up," Hagan said. Then he flicked Cooke off and dropped his pants. Cooke rubbed his boot in the dirt and kicked Hagan in the ass.

Dalonna laughed, squinting in the bright sunlight. "Hog, why do you keep offering your ass up so much? You're worth at least double what he's paying you."

Hagan turned around to face Dalonna, his pants at his ankles. Then he flicked him off and turned back around to let Cooke kick the other cheek as they had agreed.

It was late in the afternoon, still hot though the sun was getting lower. Dalonna seemed to have cheered up from the night before, and they'd eaten and lifted as a team after getting a few hours of sleep. Shaw had gotten up before the others. He grabbed his ruck and walked around the FOB for a while. Birds flew overhead every now and again and the *salat al-'asr* echoed throughout speakers from the mosques. Even though the air seemed to be on fire and the dirt was blowing in his face, it still felt good to move around.

They got a 4 while Hagan had his ass hanging out of his pants. Cooke was ready to give him another boot and both he and Hagan paused mid-kick and looked at the beepers clipped onto their belts. Shaw looked at his and so did Dalonna. Massey had marked that he was at the CASH, so he'd be making his way over shortly. Hagan stood up. He pulled up his pants and tightened a fake tie, lifted his chin and put on a snooty face.

"Gentlemen. I am going to masturbate. Do not bother me. See you at the brief."

It was early for a brief, 1800 hours.

Like the night before, satellite images were tacked to the thin cardboard strip on top of the whiteboard and individual printouts sat before each seat at the tables. Unlike the night before, the satellite images were of a sprawling city. Clusters of concrete dwellings seemed patched together like the cloth of a quilt, ten or twenty dwellings per block. By the time their CO walked in, nearly forty men had gathered—teams from both squadrons. Guys walking in loose and joking saw the images and got quiet, sat down stiff.

"We traced a number from one of the Tango1 phones found last night to this house," the CO said. He pointed to the sixth of ten structures running north to south in a crowded neighborhood. "Lots of buildings. Lots of people in the buildings. So we'll have a few more men than last night. At least double, with options for conventional attachments."

The men crossed their arms and shifted in their seats.

"The exiting squadron monitored numerous HVTs operating in different al-Ayeelaa cells throughout the city. Three of them travel together—Scar1, 2, and 3—and we've got reason to think one of their numbers is the one we traced to this house. They're not soldiers or button pushers. They're former academics. Scientists. They're from the bombing-operations wing of al-Shabaab and rumored to build bombs for Tango1. None of them live in the house, so we believe they're holding some kind of meeting or clinic. Maybe coordinating with others to distribute their operations throughout different parts of the country."

He ran his tongue around the inside of his lower lip and pointed to the three headshots on the printouts. "Snatch and grab tonight, boys. We want to get these birdies chirping, so do your best to get them alive."

He was quiet for a little while then, and put his hand on the back of a chair.

"You guys know the risks of areas like this. We want to get these guys without taking unnecessary causalities, our own or civilian, but it can get messy. Watch your sectors and pull out if things get too thick. I'd rather scrap it on the ground than have news crews running in after we leave."

He paused and nodded to himself.

"As soon as one of these guys pops we'll be getting a 1. So no one at the gym. It's too crowded for the birds tonight. Get the GMVs up and running."

He left and the men broke into their respective teams, clearing up team-specific issues and then delegating responsibilities and coordinating with others. Shaw and his team drew support. They'd be attached to sniper units on the roofs or staged on the street for immediate insertion on the target.

The city was waiting for them.

2

Ahmed was nearly eleven. In the pass where he'd been born, lived every single day of his life, that was nearly a man. He'd worked the fields of the valley since he could stand on his own. When he was little his mother would carry him down the sharp rocks and boulders to the irrigable land where a small patch of almond trees sprouted. The walk from their village, nested high in the rocks, took half the day. Sometimes more. They would gather what they could in sacks wrapped around their shoulders and then spend the night on the valley floor. In the morning they would pick again until the sun hit its meridian and then they would climb home. They gathered roots and almonds, whatever they could find. They didn't trade or sell. It was sustenance.

That was years before. The land wasn't the kind of place to get stuck in alone during the dark hours anymore, if it had ever been. The foreigners had flooded through the passes for years and some had even married into the rock. Ahmed's father told him not to play near the villages the foreigners had settled in. Some were farther away and separated by huge rock outcroppings, but most could still be accessed if one climbed in the right spots, took the right trails and tunnels. Eventually the small trails all funneled into a larger village that seemed busier than it had at any time in recent memory. Ahmed was to avoid the large village without question. The foreigners spoke their strange languages freely there and seemed to run the land. They rounded up the able-bodied men until there were just small pockets of families and clans left living among themselves in the rock. Sometimes there were murders. The foreigners had long eyed boys like Ahmed for sexual conquests or conscription, and he was nearly the age where both could be realized. Some might have thought him past it. Whether Ahmed's older brother had joined the foreigners on his own or was taken, it didn't matter. He was gone.

Ahmed's parents worried about him. The tension between husband and wife had built since their son's death. They argued over what to do with Ahmed as the war raged on. He couldn't follow his older brother's path, his father insisted. He should go to school. The son of a respected, hardworking religious man with a well-known uncle would surely be accepted. Maybe he could even go out west. But not to the madrassas. Absolutely not. His mother never said it, but she might not have thought it such a bad thing if Ahmed followed his older brother's path. She still had framed pictures of her dead son in the home, after all. She was the one who kept putting them up after her husband took them down. Ahmed's father blamed his own brother, Ahmed's uncle, for the death. His wife blamed the Americans, shook her hand at their warships when they flew by. Regardless of blame, word reached their village that their daughter-in-law remarried after the death of their oldest son and now lived in the city—at the insistence of their dead son's uncle, no less. It was scandalous. Word had it that the arrangement had been fast, but they had not been consulted or even invited to the wedding. It had been a trying year for Ahmed's family. A test of family and faith.

Ahmed's family didn't have to merely survive. They could thrive by the standards of their country. His uncle was a respected construction worker. Sure, he had a reputation from the war with the Soviets, but most men did in the region. Some good, some bad. Ahmed's father and his uncle had had a falling-out, which had started years before and been sealed by the death of Ahmed's brother. The beginning of the feud was a matter of religious principle, and neither Ahmed's father nor his uncle would acquiesce. The death of Ahmed's older brother did not make things better. The uncle made it known that he was open to reconciliation. He made it known that he missed his nephews and nieces as well. Family was everything.

The family was originally from Oman but had moved so long ago that the pass was home. All the sons of their family had traveled to the region to fight the Soviets in the 1980s. Ahmed's father had been a supporter and brave fighter during the struggle, but that jihad had been carried out within the confines of a defensive struggle—fought against an invading, unprovoked army. What happened now was not jihad, he insisted. It was gangs battling over turf and drugs. Murder. Ahmed's father had made it known that if airplanes were crashed into his home, killing women and children, he would hunt the aggressors down and hang them himself. It was grounds for *takfir* and the perpetrators were *kafir*s. The Prophet would not approve. He'd told his own brother this. When his brother spread his hands before he left for the city and said, *They'll be hunting us in our lands. In our homes. They'll be in the very air we* *breathe,* he had agreed. And then he thrust a steady finger in his brother's face and said, "And it is you they are hunting. Their bullets will fall like rain, and you summoned the storm. *Inshallah*, may they find their mark." And then Ahmed's father turned his back on his brother.

Ahmed. You'll come with me today?"

It was the first time Ahmed's father had asked him something he could have simply told him. Ahmed hadn't even finished eating. He still had his fingers in his mouth. Goat milk and wheat on his fingertips. He swallowed fast and wiped his hand on the table. His father had taught him not to rub anything on his clothes. Keep them clean. He wanted to be a proud man, after all. Didn't he? It starts with one's clothes and works inside to the flesh and bone. The heart.

"Yes, Father. I will."

He smiled and his younger siblings looked up at him from the floor, eyes wide. As if he were flying in the air and might hit the ceiling. His mother shook her head from under a framed photograph of her dead son. She clubbed the wheat in the mortar all the harder. There'd be one less hand to help. His father had an old wooden rifle resting over his shoulder as he stood in the doorway. A bolt-action, cherry-stocked Mosin-Nagant. It took a 7.62 shell and his father had a pocketful. He walked out of the home and Ahmed ran after him while his brothers and sisters finished his breakfast.

"We're hunting," Ahmed said, out of breath. He chased his father into the rocks surrounding their village.

"Yes."

"What will we find?"

"Whatever shows itself."

"What if nothing shows itself?"

"Then we find nothing."

"Why would we hunt then?"

"Why so many questions?"

Ahmed's father turned around, a few rocks above his son. He looked like a giant. He had a smile on his face.

Ahmed shrugged and they carried on.

They climbed the rocks, father in front of son, pockets full of finger-length rounds and almonds. They drank cool water from young streams. Ahmed gripped the edges of the hard rock with his toes through the thin pads of his sandals. His feet were so rough he probably didn't need the leather he would wrap in rabbit fur in the coming weeks when the snows came. His father often went barefoot. But Ahmed would need the rabbit fur when the snows came. No doubt. Even his father would.

Rabbit. Lynx. Ibex. They were all in the rocks of the pass but stayed hidden. Hunting was banned in the land during the wars, but that was mainly for the foreigners—the Arabs and the wealthy Saudis who came with their falcons and Land Rovers. Ahmed and his family were locals and the government wouldn't enforce the laws. They could hardly keep themselves alive, besides.

The two walked for the better part of the morning. They chased elevation, trading warmth for sunshine and better views. If they looked behind them as they climbed, which they didn't usually, they would see the ice and snow forming at the mouth of the pass on either side of the rocks they called home. The sun brought warmth, and when it ducked behind the clouds the air felt drastically colder. It was strange land. The rocks would have a light blanket of snow on their shoulders for long stretches of the year. Sometimes the green-and-black rock would never show and other times the snow would melt in the sunlight and one might find himself passing through different seasons in the same day.

"Here," Ahmed said. He looked around at the jagged rock leading up to a steep escarpment. He seemed unimpressed.

"Yes."

"Why here?"

"Because we shouldn't be here."

Ahmed felt the rocks under his feet. They gave way and crumbled apart when he rubbed his heels in the dirt. Small pebbles ran off the sides of the escarpment and plunged to the sharp rocks below.

"Why shouldn't we?

"Look down."

His father pointed to the valley thousands of feet below. Ahmed followed the finger to the sharp blanket of drab rock and earth that seemed to stretch on forever.

"Would you want to fall?"

"No," Ahmed said.

"That wouldn't be good."

"No, it wouldn't."

"That's why we are here. Because we shouldn't be."

"We'll fall."

"No. We won't."

His father climbed on his hands and knees across the loose

rock, up the escarpment and onto the narrow base hanging over the rocks below. He took the rifle off his back and crawled forward with it in his hands. The pack on his back looked like a child holding on for dear life. There was a heavy wool blanket in the pack, and the thick warmth rubbed against his spine through the cloth. When he took off the pack he would have a wide patch of sweat across his back. He crawled a few meters out onto the narrow escarpment, then looked back toward his son. A fall wouldn't be good.

Ahmed watched him and licked his lips.

"I'll fall."

"No. Same as me."

His father waved him on and turned away, out onto the escarpment and above the valley and sharp rocks below. Ahmed crawled with his face touching the rocks. He could feel dirt on his face and chips of rock clawing at his skin. He closed his eyes and kept moving. Rocks traded places with the dirt beneath him, and after a few moments his head hit his father's foot.

"Okay?"

Ahmed opened his eyes and looked at his father. He nodded and smiled.

His father took his hand and dragged him gently forward. Beside him. The two of them could fit side by side but wouldn't be rolling over or making sudden movements.

"How do we hunt?"

"We wait."

"How long?"

"However long it takes."

"And if we don't find anything?"

"Then you climbed a big rock all by yourself. You can brag to your brothers and sisters."

Ahmed smiled.

His father took out the 7.62 from a cloth pouch he carried on a string around his neck and tucked against his chest. He loaded the rounds into the rifle and closed the bolt. He looked at the rifle, then back at his son.

"This will be loud."

Ahmed nodded.

"You mustn't jump or fright."

Ahmed nodded.

"Have you ever shot?"

Some of Ahmed's friends had boasted of firing their fathers' guns. Some even claimed to have brothers fighting in the war. On both sides.

"No."

"Okay," his father said. "Another time, then."

His father looked over the edges of the escarpment and spit. The sparkling glob disappeared into the rocks below.

"Do you know how to spot?"

Ahmed shook his head.

"We can't speak," his father said. "It'll frighten them away. So we point."

His father held the rifle in one hand and extended the index finger of his other hand into the air. He pointed to the sky and tapped his finger on the tops of the clouds. *Tap. Tap. Tap.*

"We look for movement. When there's none we look for changes in color or patterns. Brown rocks where there should be only black. White where there are only brown. You point. I fire. Okay?"

Ahmed nodded. He held his hand out like his father had done. He tapped the air where he saw fluffy clouds and his father smiled. While he pointed, the bracelet on his wrist loosed from his kameez. The red specks of the cloudy marble rock twinkled in the sunlight. The leather band was tied into two holes expertly drilled into the base of the rock by his uncle's hand.

"That was your brother's."

Ahmed looked at his wrist. "Yes." He ran his small fingertips over the leather straps as if rubbing a pet dog or cat.

His father smiled. He patted his son on the head, ran his hands through the soft black hair.

"Now what?"

"We wait."

They settled into the escarpment, pack and blanket laid over sharp spots in the rock. They waited and talked quietly. Ahmed's father might have thought of the son settled next to him and the one who had been killed months earlier. He might have compared the characteristics of the two and wondered if they would turn out the same, or if the one beside him still had a chance. While they waited for the elusive animals of the rock to show themselves, American fighter jets flew gracefully overhead after their bomb runs. They seemed to cut through the clouds effortlessly, knife the air like falcons.

3

The teams got the three Scars alive from the quilted city raid without having to fire a shot. Shaw and Dalonna posted up on one roof with Barnes while Hagan and Cooke did the same with Bear. Mike and Ohio led the raid. Slausen and Massey entered after them, rendering aid to a little girl with a bad fungus on her leg and an older woman who had gotten knocked around some during the entry.

The morning after the raid Massey woke up Shaw in their tent.

"Rocks," Massey said.

Shaw was lying on his bunk with his hands over his eyes. Massey had his hands on his hips and blocked the door of the tent from view. Shaw could hardly see anything. Then Massey kicked the door open and light flooded the tent. He repeated himself. When Massey said *rocks* the second time, Shaw remembered the two boys. He hoped he hadn't hurt them. Blinded them for life or anything like that. Brain damage.

The boys had been on an adjacent roof, just a stone's throw from Shaw, their hands straddling the lip of the parapet. They kept raising their heads and watching the target house. At first Shaw thought they might be combatants, holding rifles and RPGs, maybe strapped with a vest. He'd had his safety off and his laser painted over their little heads. They were a couple pounds of finger pressure from having their hair and skulls and futures split all over the roof in the humid air. But he'd taken a gamble. He had a feeling they were just kids horsing around, but as he'd gotten into bed after the raid, he'd been troubled. He wondered if he'd let himself hope for that scenario without good reason. The neighborhood was run by dangerous cells and the civilians were known to shoot at foot patrols from their windows or roofs and then go back to their magazines, TV, meals, or prayers. A warning shot might have been more appropriate. But he saw two kids horsing around. So he flicked on the safety, had Cooke cover the spot with his own laser from another roof, and grabbed a handful of gravel and rocks. Then he flung the handful at the boys and they disappeared. They had sharp cuts on their soft foreheads, but they were alive. If the boys had worn suicide vests, the target house and the men inside it—not to mention the sniper teams and their attachments—could've all been killed. They could've detonated before the rocks hit their heads. Guys could've died. Still, Shaw had been right.

"You threw rocks."

Shaw sat up. "Yeah. I feel kinda bad about it."

Massey sat on the edge of the bed. "Hell, those rocks could've been rounds. They wouldn't have had sore heads to deal with this morning. Nice throw."

"Hopefully I just hit the bigger one."

Massey raised his eyebrows. "There were two of them, right? You played short in high school. Don't kid yourself. You hit them both."

Shaw thought about the smaller head. The boy was probably not even ten yet.

"Aw, hell. Want to feel good about yourself?"

"I'm not going into a bathroom stall with you."

"Get fucked," Massey said. "Follow me."

The sun was up, but it wasn't too hot. The sky was blue, the clouds cotton balls. The two of them kicked up dust clouds with their boots and scattered gravel with each step. They watched birds flying overhead on gun runs between outposts and the FOB. They walked outside their compound, over the gravel arteries linking their compound to the conventional ones, and came to a large concrete structure with a façade decorated with bullet holes. A large wooden sign nailed to posts set in the ground declared *Combat Support Hospital.*

Massey looked at Shaw.

"You been to the CASH?"

"No. And I kinda hoped to keep it that way."

"It used to be a school. Maybe a factory. I don't know. Now it houses most casualties in the region before sending them out of the country or back home."

"Hell, Mass. It's a little early to see anyone blown apart." An Apache screeched overhead and then sped off on its gun run. "Not the best field trip."

"Not too early to be a wiseass, though?"

"Fair. My apologies. I'm enjoying myself. Truly."

"Don't be a pussy."

Massey opened the door and they walked up three wooden

planks making a half-decent effort at being steps. They entered a small waiting area. Metal folding chairs spanned one wall half the width of a football field and the receptionist's desk manned the wall opposite. The lights were bright and the air smelled of rubbing alcohol, hand sanitizer, and packaged gauze. Tear-drained screams and muffled cries were creeping through closed doors down multiple hallways. Shaw felt a headache coming on, a rumbling in his stomach. He thought of the little girl in the poppy fields and the one he saw on the news.

"Mass, I don't feel like seeing any kids all blown to hell."

Massey shook his head. "We're seeing our friend. He'll be happy to see us."

A tall blond in fatigues and a crew cut guarding the hallway nodded to Massey and pointed down the hallway. He carried a rifle and wasn't shy about pointing it at them. They followed his finger down the hall.

"Third door on the left from the end," the guard said.

There were ten rooms on both sides of the walk. Instead of doors, there were stained bedsheets hanging down from the frames to the floor. Most of the sheets were pulled aside and brown streaks ran the length of the floor. Blood or mud. Likely both. In one of the rooms there was a boy asleep with bandages on the stumps that used to be his legs. In another, a bearded man staring out the door with ragged hair, tubes coming out of his legs and face. Other doorways led to a girl sitting up in bed staring at a wall and a grown man and woman huddled over a form Shaw couldn't see on a table. He noticed the loudest screams were coming from entryways with their sheets drawn. The sheet doorways did not muffle the cries very well.

"I'm gonna get something sent over for all these kids," Massey said. “This place is too depressing.” He stopped at an entryway with the sheet drawn, third on the left from the end, just as the guard had said. “Here’s our guy.”

He pushed the sheet aside and motioned for Shaw to walk inside.

The walls of the room were made of thin wood and were unpainted, so the notches and rings of the cut stood for wallpaper. A light shined bright from the ceiling and there weren’t any windows. The room was hot and stuffy. On the bed was a boy in oversized, mismatched hospital scrubs. He wore bright green bottoms and a blue checkered top. He stared at Shaw, his head never moving off the pillow.

“Looks better with clothes on, doesn’t he?” Massey said.

He entered behind Shaw and waved at the boy in the bed. The boy had red welts around his neck and wrists where the chains had been. When he saw Massey he smiled and raised his hand off the bed slowly. It was a good smile, slight and without teeth, but genuine. His eyes were partly closed. He looked relieved, like he’d gotten good news after getting mostly bad for some time.

“They gave him a job.”

Shaw looked at the boy. He was looking only at Massey. Someone had washed him. His black hair was glossy and bright and his skin looked clean.

“Who did, and doing what?” Shaw asked.

“Here at the CASH. He’ll clean up for them. Wash the sheets, sweep the floors, and stuff like that.”

Shaw nodded.

“They said he could sleep on a cot in the main bay.”

The boy never took his eyes off Massey.

"That's good, Mass."

The boy shifted in the bed with his head on the pillow. His mouth tightened and his eyebrows rose. He took in a breath of air, like he would speak, but let the breath go, and the smile crept out again on his lips.

The Scars from the city raid were more valuable than any bomb materials that might've been found. All three of them were in fact former members of al-Shabaab. This they freely admitted. Each Scar was from a different region of Africa, one even had British citizenship, and the tentacles of their networks within those regions spread deep into the terrorist lifeblood. The information gleaned from the raid could spark raids on nearly every continent of the globe.

Intel had grilled the Scars continuously since the night they were picked up. Nearly three days and nights without sleep. Scar1 and Scar2 hadn't spoken a word, but Scar3 started talking. Scar1 and Scar2 got sent to an off-site center for further questioning, but Intel kept Scar3 around. They promised to let him see his daughter, the girl Massey had treated with penicillin for her leg fungus—apparently he traveled to the meeting with his wife and daughter—and he started talking about a small village in the mountains. He said he'd used the village to smuggle in new recruits and refit old ones.

After the teams had gotten the 4, the CO told them about the area. It was an isolated sustenance area, full of goat herders and mountain folk, which meant the only traffic coming and going was temporary. Not a normal part of life. Scar3 told Intel he'd personally used the area to pick up and drop off people and supplies twice in the last year. Apparently foreign fighters mixed with the local population and it wasn't clear where allegiances lay or what kind of balance the two groups had struck up together.

"Intel thought it was worth finding out," the CO said. "So you're here."

Sitting in the briefing room, Shaw thought about Scar3. He'd probably hung his head over a table after he'd been kept awake for days without sleep. Shaw wondered what Intel had said that had gotten him to spill his guts. Shaw had sat next to Scar3 in the GMV. His tank top had sagged loose on his frame and his chin touched the overgrown hairs on his chest. One of his nipples hung flaccid and sad from his chest, like that of a mother who'd nursed for too many years. He was an orchestrator of suicide bombings. And a father who just wanted to see his daughter again.

The op would be a ball-buster.

There were only the ten of them in the brief. Shaw's team and Mike's. The CO stood in front of them, blown-up images of the mountain pass printed on sheets and tacked to the whiteboard behind him. He had a red laser pointer in his hand. He highlighted multiple possible insertion points to the village, narrow trails breaking off the main pass, but there was only the single pass to get through and then a single exfil point. The pass started high in the rock and the trails splintered off like fingertips of lightning. They lost elevation until they funneled into the large village. In the village there were smaller structures with thatched roofs made of straw, mud, and tree limbs.

"We'll need rucks packed for four days," the CO said. "But keep in mind the choppers can't get to you after the infil until the exfil. The pass is too narrow. Unless we pull out."

Shaw wrote down "food for five days" on his printout. "Batteries, ammo, and water for eight."

"The village and surrounding area is to be considered hostile. Intel's let me know some of the fighters likely have families settled there, so we can't count on getting a welcome. The bird will drop you off a couple klicks south of the draw leading to the pass. We're not sure how the comms will hold up in the narrow straits, so you're freed from command decisions. No checks or need to confirm. We'll keep an eye on you from the sats as long as we can. Just get to the village and the 47 will grab you for the exfil. We can try supporting fire in the pass, but any brought in will be danger close. Regardless, we'll have a Spooky circling the entire movement and we'll get to you if we can. We'll pick you up right in the damn village unless it's too hot."

Hagan had a whole horseshoe of dip in his lower lip. He looked like he had packed too much and had a nicotine crash, or didn't like the thought of walking fifty to sixty klicks to the village. It was probably both. He looked like he might get sick all over the printouts.

"I could use a walk," Cooke whispered. "Damn GMVs are coffins."

Dalonna had a question.

"Sir, women and children?"

"Yes. Likely."

Cooke raised his hand.

"Sir. What are we looking to accomplish?"

The CO took his time. He nodded to himself with a hand curled into a fist, propping up his chin. The men all shifted in their seats.

"Recon, then capture or kill. Intel's let on that recent foot traffic corroborates Scar3's claims. There's a good deal of movement and we could be tapping a major access point from neighboring countries. If we can find HVTs or FAMs there, we will want to talk to them. If we don't, we don't. Regardless, you guys are cleared to engage as necessary." He traced the village on the map with his hand. "Scar3's been the first target to mention the village but Intel dug through past findings from SSEs and was able to link numerous HVTs to the area. This could be a major hub for numerous cells operating in-country. Transparency? This could be big. We don't know how big, but it's got potential. We need eyes on before we know what we've got."

The CO let the operators digest what he'd told them and the teams sat studying the map printouts. The rocks looked like some of the canyons of Utah and California they'd been through in the summers on training hops. No one had any more questions.

"There's no popping hot on this. We're moving out in three days, regardless of the weather. If we're lucky, the weather will be shit and no one else will be out. Rain or snow would be nice. We're off the green until then so the days are yours."

The room was quiet.

"All right. It'll be a bit of a walk, but mostly downhill. So there's that."

Then he left and none of the men did for a while.

. . .

The few days they had off preparing for the walk flew by in a flash of day and night shoots, rucking around the FOB, and sweating out in the gym. Coverage on the increasing bombings in the region spanned the news among reports of the World Series, and Hagan put up 375 on the bench a few times. The guys made him stop there because he was prone to bullheadedness and they didn't want anyone hurting himself before the walk just to hit 400. The teams pored over satellite images of the area. They had at least a guy or two on the drone feeds watching the village around the clock. There was movement in the area—heavy at times, with women and children walking the mountainsides and village grounds. Other times movement was sparse or nonexistent. It seemed like the whole village would wash over the area like a flood one moment and then disappear into the rocks the next.

On the night of the walk, Lou Reed played softly over the speakers in the war room while Velcro was getting strapped and refit. Hagan stood smiling in the middle of the lockers. He looked at Shaw, raised his eyebrows, racked his weapon, and checked the chamber. The metal slid smooth and echoed sharp.

"Hey, babe," Hagan said. "Take a walk on the wild side." He winked and put his helmet on, brought his NODs down, and turned them on. Then he switched them off and raised them. "Good shit. Lou Reed's badass."

"You know what that song's about," Massey said. "Don't you, Hog?"

"Nope. Don't tell me, either. You guys ruin my life."

Shaw smiled. He was thinking of filling any extra space in his ruck with food or extra rounds. They could get stuck out there for a lot longer than they'd planned. His ruck weighed in at sixty-eight pounds and the nylon fabric stretched so much he could identify items by their bulge. Extra batteries. Extra mags. Extra rounds. Extra batteries. Extra CLP. Dip. Hide site cover. Extra batteries. Extra rounds. Extra strobe. Lemon pound cake. Shaw looked around the lockers and got on the floor. He would kill himself if he ran out of ammo or batteries but had extra pound cake. He saw three more clips of 5.56, a few more batteries, and a black plastic speed-loader under a footstool. He grabbed them and threw them in his ruck, taking out the pound cake and his toothbrush.

"Hog, you should bring your deodorant," Dalonna said.

"Donna, you know we're going native, right?"

Hagan looked concerned, like Dalonna had forgotten something important that needed remembering and it worried him.

"Yes, I do. And I stand by my statement."

Hagan looked at the ground and then up at Dalonna with fire. "Oh, dammit, Donna. We're all gonna stink like shit together."

They all laughed and Hagan tried to get in a jab or two while they started funneling out of the war room.

"You smell like a dead cocker spaniel that fell asleep in his own shit! You hear me, Donna?"

Dalonna had a deep, rich laugh and it drowned Hagan out.

They grabbed their rucks and headed out into the night.

The 47 was up and burning holes on the tarmac when they got to the airfield. The length of two school buses, the helicopter had rotors on the head and tail and was trusted to climb the highest elevations. It was cooler out on the airfield and the clouds were so low it seemed like the men could just grab a few and push them out of the way to let the stars breathe a little. Hagan pulled on his cold-weather top after setting down his ruck and sitting in his canvas seat closest to the gunner on the back ramp.

Cooke sat next down next to him. “Hog, you gonna wear that on the walk?”

Hagan looked at him and raised his eyebrows. “No. But I’m sure as hell not gonna freeze my nuts off on the flight up there.”

“All right,” Cooke said. “Smart. And I got a sports bra and some tampons in my pack, too. When you need ’em, just give me a holler.”

They all laughed and buckled in, metal snaps echoing down the line. A gunner strapped himself onto the back ramp of the bird and sat on the floor with his legs straddling a minigun that poked aggressively into the night. The 47’s rotors slapped hard at the sky like oars on water and the aviation fuel soured the air. Their bodies trembled on the roar of the engines.

“This’ll suck,” Massey said.

Shaw laughed. “Probably.” He pulled a balaclava over his head, his mouth and eyes finding the holes. “I’m nervous,” he blurted out.

Shaw looked around to see how many guys heard, but only Massey looked at him. His white teeth seemed to glow.

“Fucking-A right you are. This is gonna suck ass. I don’t wanna die in some shit valley reconning some piss village.”

The rotors found their lift and Shaw watched the tops of the clouds melt away from the bird and drop beneath them over the gunner’s shoulder. The stars came out and spread across the sky like pebbles on a shoreline after the tide washes away. He watched them shine until the pilots voiced their approach.

. . .

The bird dropped them off about a klick from the mouth of the pass, in a shallow draw. Before they started walking they all took off the cold-weather tops Cooke had given Hagan so much grief for wearing. After a few minutes in flight they'd all put them on and Hagan had had a big shit-eating grin on his face.

"I'll grab that sports bra from you when you're through with it," Hagan whispered to Cooke while Cooke stuffed his top in his ruck.

Cooke smiled and blew Hagan a kiss.

It was cold in the draw. Their breaths steamed in front of their faces and froze in icicles on their beards. The rocks and dirt had a shine glossed over them, and Shaw made sure his footfalls were balanced, sturdy. The air was clear and cool. Breathing it in felt like tapping into good drinking water. Massey slipped and landed on his ass as soon as the birds flew through the clouds, and they all dropped to a knee and scanned the ridgelines with their lasers. Shaw lit up a bunch of jagged rocks with pebble runoff spilling from either side, but the sound of Massey slapping hard on the ground didn't bring anyone out of the rocks. Massey got to his feet and keyed into the comms.

"Anybody planning on getting shot?"

No one said anything for a while and then Slausen came over the comms.

"That's probably a negative, Mass. Generally frowned upon in our profession."

"Good," Massey said. "Then I'm gonna throw this goddamned Skedco off a cliff."

The big plastic stretcher was rolled tight on his back and he'd strapped it over his ruck. It looked like he was humping a bazooka. Shaw smiled and scanned the rocks and boulders knifing up before them, steep and jagged like ice in the mouths of winter caves. Slausen came over the comms again.

"Well, let's see if any of the dumbasses are stupid enough to get shot on the walk, and if not, we don't need the Skeds. We can throw them off a cliff when the bird picks us up."

With that their teams split a laugh and then split up for the walk on separate trails. Mike and his team took a shallow trail north and Shaw and his team moved south of them, keeping the elevated rocks of the pass on their left. Mike's team would keep the same rocks on their right and they'd funnel into the large village together from either trail.

Shaw led their movement. They kept Massey in the middle to even out the distance he'd have to cover if they took casualties, and Hagan and Cooke fanned out on one side of the pass. Dalonna and Shaw took the other. They walked slow, aiming for fifteen to thirty klicks a night and then they'd pitch hide sites and squat during the day. Every turn in the pass was lit up by lasers from either side and breached like a doorway. They picked their way over sparse patches of dead, wind-chapped grass and around large boulders and weather-beaten trees and shrubs. It was quiet and the overhanging rocks of the pass kept the moon from lighting the way. They kept their NODs down until the sun lit the cliffs and then they hugged the boulders, pulled out camo tarps and blankets. They slept two men at a time, the other three awake and watching the rocks for movement. Then they'd wait for the light to fade so they could move again.

The first night Shaw watched a large cat or mountain goat bound up a cliff outcropping and fade into the mountains where the horizon hit the rocks, but that was it. Hagan had some nice, deep blisters on the sides of his feet and Cooke kept saying he saw a boy on the rocks but no one else ever saw him. Shaw's mouth was feeling grimy already, so he tried to keep a chaw or Skittle in at all times. He regretted leaving his toothbrush, should've offloaded another tin of dip or pouch of chew. The comms between teams stayed clear but faded in and out with their CO, Intel, and the air support back at the FOB or circling above. The men reeked of sweat.

The rain and snow held the first night. They watched clouds gather overhead in the morning, hoping for some moisture to beat down and smooth out the tracks they'd left behind, and it came in the early afternoon. They had buried their MRE wrappers or stuffed them back into their rucks, empty of their contents after they closed in on twenty klicks the night before. They sweated through their tops and bottoms in the cold dark during the movement and changed into dry ones in their hide sites during the day. Shaw picked at the crumbs from the crackers that landed on his top and sucked the peanut butter dry from its package. Then the sleet came. The tarps and covers of their hide sites sank under the weight of the water and ice, and water streamed through the sights thinned into the fabric for concealed viewing. Shaw shivered in his site. His dry top and bottom were soaked before he even lifted a foot for the night's walk. He had dug a shallow hole to piss and crap in under his cover and it filled up and overflowed so the fluids he'd released found their way back to him. Their tracks were smoothed out but their limbs were freezing and soaking wet.

During his time to rest, Shaw didn't sleep as much as stop thinking. It was welcome rest even if it wasn't sleep. He grew dizzy from scanning every crevice of rock or sliver of irregular earth. It was all irregular after a while. His pants and hands were too cold and wet to free himself when he had to piss, so he just let fly through his bottoms and enjoyed the warmth for the little while it lasted before the cold and misery crept back in. He looked at the extra food he'd packed into his ruck and wished he'd brought a good pair of thick gloves instead. But he didn't. So he shadowboxed with small, choppy jabs when the cold got to be too much.

Hagan came over the comms a few hours into the sleet.

"*National Geographic* would hate us. There's a falcon circling at eleven o'clock."

Every head of the team strained through their hide sites to get a better look. Shaw angled his head up through the recon slits and sure enough, to their northwest a big dark bird arced in lazy circles around a peak out of reach. Watching the bird's graceful arcs let him forget about being wet and cold for a while, and he acknowledged the dramatic expanse of the surrounding cliffs and jagged rock. He watched the falcon circle and swoop, paying no mind to the water getting in his eyes, until after some time it came to a dead stop in the air and dove at something in the rocks below. It was beautiful, it was gone, and it didn't come back.

Then they were alone with the cold again.

That night either the fog settled in high on the mountains or they were walking through the clouds. The movement didn't bring much warmth, but it kept the deep-setting cold from clawing at their arms and legs. Shaw changed underwear before they moved, so at least his nuts were clean and warmer than they'd been in a while. They all changed socks and kept the wet tops and bottoms on because they'd be soaked after the movement anyhow. Visibility was at a rifle barrel's length, and Mike's team radioed in that they'd just shot two men.

"They walked right past us down the pass," Mike said. "We put a couple through them after they'd passed. We nabbed a wood-stocked PRK with a Soviet sickle in it, but we'll probably drop it. It's heavy as shit."

Cooke came over the comms. "Don't toss it. That's a keeper. I can offer Hog for it when we get back to the FOB."

They laughed quietly as they picked their way through the rocks and Hagan radioed over that Cooke and him weren't friends anymore if anyone was looking for a new best friend. Shaw asked Mike if they were going to continue down the pass or radio in and request an exfil back at the draw.

"They're dead, so we're not compromised," Mike said. "Yet, at least. We'll push on. Whoever sent them out is gonna come looking for them anyhow, so we'd rather meet them than have to watch our ass for twenty to thirty klicks."

Shaw told them to keep an eye out and Mike radioed back the same.

The next day, while they were set in their hide sites, a boy appeared on the rocks.

Cooke came over the comms in a whisper.

"There he is."

The sun was out and the pass had softened and evened out some; the nest of dark boulders and rocks surrounding them had brightened in the light. They were under the tan tarps and covers of their hide sites. The boy stood on a large rock not fifty meters from Hagan, who'd taken the lead of their movement. The boy was facing them and raised his hand. Then he pointed at each of their hide sites as if he were counting birds in a park.

"We're compromised," Hagan radioed in.

Shaw radioed over to Mike. "Rook1, this is Rook2. Come in, over."

"Go ahead, Rook2."

Shaw watched the boy. "Did you guys see anyone else with those two you nabbed last night? A boy, maybe?"

There was a pause that lasted longer than Shaw was willing to wait.

"Rook1," he repeated. "Did you guys see a boy?"

"Negative," Mike said. "The men were alone."

Shaw let out a slow breath and Hagan came over the comms.

"He's looking right at me. No weapon, but he's staring bullets."

Shaw keyed the comms again. "Rook1. What were the two wearing?"

Another pause.

"They both wore salwars and one had a vest and the other a coat," Mike said. "Not a field jacket, more of a windbreaker. They both wore black taqs on their domes. We just balled them up and left them in the rocks."

The boy was standing like a statue in the light, straight and tall. It looked like he had a few wisps of early beard that added a little smoke to his jawline. He had light brown skin, as if he'd gotten suntanned permanently. He wore a dark brown kameez and a white salwar that left a couple inches of bare skin between the hem and his sandals. He didn't have anything in his hands or on his head.

"There are shepherds around here," Dalonna said. "Goat herders."

"Yeah," Cooke said. "Where's his staff or flock?"

Hagan keyed in.

"He's looking right at me."

He was trying to speak slow and calm, but he sounded edgy.

The boy stood on an outcropping at the head of a bend in the pass. Shaw couldn't see what was behind him.

"Hold, Hog. Can you see anything behind him?"

Hagan came back quick and short.

"Negative."

Shaw keyed the handset. "Cooke. Is he the same one you saw a couple nights ago?"

Cooke came over slow and even.

"Can't tell for sure. Hope so. Otherwise there's more than the one looking at us."

"How old do we think he is?" Shaw asked.

Massey came over the comms.

"He's got fuzz on his jaw, so teens."

"Teens," Dalonna agreed.

"Fuck his age, he's staring right at me," Hagan said.

Cooke came over slow and even again. "He's short, but I'd say scouting age for sure. He could be strapped with a vest."

Shaw rapped his fingers on the trigger guard of his weapon. He licked his teeth and cracked his neck. "So he's either following us or just happened on our way."

"You'd think a kid that just happened upon us would act a little surprised," Cooke said. "Not count us out."

Shaw nodded and swallowed dry air. He was thirsty. He radioed in again.

"Anyone see any goats or other shit that walks?"

"Negative," Dalonna said. "Just the boy."

When Dalonna finished keying the comms, Shaw felt a weight rolling around in his stomach. It seemed like his intestines were knotting themselves into a monkey fist. He felt like he had to take a spine-bruising shit. He keyed the comms.

"Kill. Capture. Let go."

Silence won out for a little while and then Cooke keyed in.

"Well, it's not like we can ball him all up and throw him in our rucks."

Dalonna came over next.

"You'd think he'd have run if he wasn't comfortable seeing us."

"Which means he sees us as a threat and doesn't give a shit because he's a threat, or he doesn't give a shit because he's a friendly?" Shaw asked.

"I don't know," Dalonna said. "Could be either."

Shaw waited awhile in case anyone had anything else to add.

No one did.

"Cooke's right," Shaw said. "We can't take him with us. So leave him alone or take him out?"

Hagan came over again. "I swear he's getting closer to me."

The boy hadn't moved. His feet gripped the lip of the rock with his thin sandals, and his salwar blew light on the wind passing through the pass. He had a tuft of black hair that rose above his head every time the salwar moved, and the sleeve of his kameez brushed the leather bracelet he wore. He hadn't been standing there a whole minute.

"He's not, Hog," Shaw said. "He hasn't moved."

Massey keyed in.

"He sees us, so why doesn't he do anything?"

"I don't know. Take him or let him go?" Shaw repeated.

Cooke came over first.

"We've gotta take him."

Hagan agreed.

"Donna?" Shaw said.

Dalonna keyed in but didn't say anything for a few seconds. "He's comfortable," he said finally. "Definitely not afraid."

"Mass, what do you think?" Shaw said.

"Hell, I don't know," Massey said. "Everyone's right."

Hagan was closest to the boy and Shaw saw his cover shift slightly. The boy hadn't moved since first counting them out like he had right away. Like ducks on a pond or friends for a game. He might not even have known what he was doing.

The suppressors screwed onto the barrels of their rifles would catch the pressure of the fired rounds and expand the area out of which they escaped from the barrels. The sound of the shots would be muted to more of a cough than a sharp crack. The boy would be down before he heard the slightest whisper of the bullets. He would never be able to see them, even if he'd been looking to. Shaw closed his eyes and shook his head. "Shit." He thought of guys he'd known who had gotten ambushed after getting compromised. He'd known their wives and seen the kids they left behind grow up after the funerals. Then he looked back at the boy. He'd already memorized his face forever. "Hog, take him out."

The wind blew softly, and instead of the shots, Shaw heard his own breathing and a harsh pulsing in his head. It felt like his eyeballs were throbbing with each beat of his heart. The boy seemed to crumble off the rock in slow motion, almost gracefully. He landed on the ground with one of his sandaled feet propped on the rock, pointing up toward the sky. The sun was bright and had made its way directly over the short gap in the pass. Oddly, Shaw felt warmth. He realized that for the first time in weeks he hadn't smelled the stench of burning shit for the last few days. And his clothes were dry. They could've been camping in their backyards or in a national park on a holiday weekend.

Hagan keyed in. "He's down."

There was a long silence in the valley. The sun was so bright Shaw had to strain his eyes into slight slits. "We need to move the body behind the rocks," he said. "And cover him."

It was quiet again for so long that Shaw wondered if he had spoken the words out loud or been speaking to himself. Then Hagan came over again.

"I'm not moving him."

Shaw moved the boy himself.

He got out from his hide site and walked up the pass while the team covered him. The sky was clear and the sun warm. Any clouds in the air moved fast, racing toward the mountains and then covering them briefly before passing on and disappearing out of sight.

The boy had two holes in his chest, not a finger width between the two entrance points. The salwar was raised to his knees and the sandal not propped on the rock rested in a pile of mud unearthed by his heels. The blood spread in a large dark patch in the middle of the kameez, from his shoulders to his waist. The sun gleamed off the wet fabric like it was gold panned from a stream. The boy looked unimpressed, like death hadn't fazed him. He looked young. He had some mud and dirt splashed up under his chin that had looked like a beard. Shaw could rub it off with his fingertips. A thin river of blood ran from the corner of his mouth to the ground and colored the earth around him in tones of rust. He was surprisingly heavy, lean but broad-shouldered. He had probably worked in the mountains his whole life.

Shaw set his hands under the boy's armpits and dragged him into a tight spot between the loose rock and boulders on the opposite side of the pass. The rocks were shaded and it was cool, the moisture not yet dried by the sun. It would be a nice place to rest after a jog. The boy could fit between the rocks if he nestled him on his side, so Shaw knelt down and tried to place him on the ground gently. He saw the bracelet the boy wore, the red rock shining in the sun, and the boy's body pressed against Shaw's kit and he felt a stinging in his chest from the agate necklace. Shaw moved any shards of rock or loose dirt away from the boy's face and folded the boy's hands gently over the wound in his chest. He tucked his cover around the body tightly, folding the edges around the boy so the cover doubled as a body bag and his own personal hide site. Then Shaw walked away. The boy's blood was on his gloves, on the sleeves of his top. He couldn't see any of them through their hide sites, but he knew the team was watching him. He keyed into the comms.

"Who's got room for another in their site?"

There was a pause and then Massey came over.

"I got some space."

Shaw walked past Hagan and his old site, and Massey opened his cover for Shaw to crawl under. Massey had dug in between a large pair of boulders on a sharp rise. He had a shithole dug into the low ground.

"Watch your step."

No one said anything over the comms for the rest of the time the sun was up. Massey offered Shaw some diet pills to keep him cranking and Shaw told him Hagan could probably use some as well. Hagan accepted the offer and Massey threw a pack into the rocks toward him, but it fell short. Hagan left his site when a cloud passed over and retrieved the pills, then covered up again. The team covered him, and when the sun dropped the comms opened.

"Rook2, this is Rook1, come in, over." It was Mike.

Shaw answered.

"This is Rook2. Go ahead."

Mike's voice was light and the transmission spat static.

"How'd the situation with the little one go?"

No one said anything.

"Rook2," Mike said. "You there?"

Shaw let out a heavy breath and Massey watched his face in the failing light.

"We're good, Rook1."

"Okay, then," Mike said slowly. "Stay up. Razor1 out."

"Two out."

Shaw couldn't see the tarp he'd used to cover the body from

Massey's site, but on the right side of the pass and wrapped around the boy, the tarp, Shaw knew, was doing its job.

Intel broke through that night as they walked. They reported that a group of three FAMs had left the village shouldering weapons and disappeared north into the rocks. The teams acknowledged the movement and added that weight to all the rest. They moved heavily, picking their way through the hard rocks with soft feet on their final approach to the village. They were tired, and Shaw watched the stars and clouds trade places. No one joked over the comms or said much of anything. The pass rose sharp and then fell flat at the entrance of the village. Cooke, leading the last leg of the movement, halted them when he thought he saw something in a shallow inlet off the main pass. Their lasers painted the opening, but it was nothing, just some earth that'd broken away from a larger piece of earth at some point. Like the rest of the rocks in the pass they walked through.

Mike came over the comms and announced they had eyes on the village.

"Waiting on you, Razor2," he said.

Shaw could see a section of the first dwelling's roof off to his right, over Cooke's shoulder. Cooke was on a knee, painting the dead space behind the first dwelling. The village was set between a group of large boulders in a clearing some size bigger than the pass. The clearing emerged from the pass like the head of a tadpole. In some cases the dwellings used the sides of the boulders and pass at large to form their fourth walls. Three dwellings inhabited the outermost ring of the village, nearly flush with the mouth of the pass. There were nine huts in total, the three at the mouth of the pass and the other six trailing off the first ones like scattered raindrops. Shaw and his team were responsible for the three huts immediately to the front and Mike's team would take the northernmost three. Whoever was able would take the remaining three huts in the southeast sector until all had been searched.

"Check, tape, and tie down," Shaw said over the comms.

He ran his hands along his ruck, made sure all the straps were tied off or taped in rolls. Then he checked the mag in his well and those snug in his kit. He synched the ruck down tight on his back and the shoulder straps bit into his back and chest. He cracked his neck and squatted up and down a couple times.

"Good to go," Cooke and Hagan said.

"I'm good," Dalonna said.

Massey said he was as well and Shaw radioed over.

"Razor1, we're set. Moving on your mark. Over."

"Roger that, Razor2. Moving now," Mike said.

They broke off and flowed into the village.

Hagan and Shaw approached the first dwelling. It was made of hard-packed mud, and long strands of straw and tall grass lined the walls. Dalonna and Cooke took the next in line and Hagan brought his boot up fast and hard and kicked in the clapboard door. The door splintered in the middle like kindling and collapsed on the dirt floor. Shaw stepped over the splintered pieces, and the room was empty except for a garment thrown over the dirt in one of the corners. Hagan lit it up and Shaw checked beneath it. Nothing. They left the hut and lit up the door of the next dwelling while Dalonna and Cooke made their way to the next line of huts. Shaw could see the other teams checking the remaining huts at different points in the head of the tadpole. Again Hagan brought his boot up and crashed it through the door. Again they stepped through the doorway and over the broken wood.

Nothing.

Shaw walked outside the hut and painted the surrounding rocks and other dwellings, expecting targets, or even goats. Anything. Hagan pointed at one of the dwellings in the distance. Then one of the Razor1 teams emerged from the doorway. Soon enough all of the men stood outside the empty dwellings, scattered in teams of twos, shrugging and kicking aside clumps of earth. Guys painted the rocks of the pass surrounding the village or lined up against the huts and took a knee. The comms came to life.

Nothing.

No one.

More voices came over with the same response.

Shaw radioed over to their CO.

"This is Razor2. Objective secure. The village is empty. No one in the huts. Requesting exfil."

"Roger, Razor2," the CO said. "The bird's en route. ETA forty-five mikes."

"Roger ETA," Shaw said. "Holding for exfil."

The comms quieted down.

"Nothing, man," Hagan said.

Shaw shook his head. He spat on the ground and closed his eyes. The village smelled like trampled earth and livestock. The pass smelled fresh where they had killed the boy. He wondered where the people of the village had gone, if the boy had lived in one of the huts. Then Mike came over the comms.

"We got tunnels," he said.

The teams searched the surrounding rocks while they waited for the bird to pick them up and found nearly twenty different tunnels carved into the rocks surrounding the village. Some were large enough for a grown man to walk through standing up, while others could be accessed only at a crawl. They radioed them into Intel and were told not to enter. The 47 came in and landed in the dead space between the dwellings, its rotors blowing the roofing off some of the dwellings and throwing rocks and dust into the walls of others. The teams climbed on board while the gunners of the 47 kept the visible openings of the tunnels painted.

No one came out of them, and the captors flew away.

Shaw took his helmet off on the flight back. The cool air passing through the cabin from the open gunner's perch in the rear felt good, cleansing. He looked around the bird and everyone was asleep. The metallic scent of the bird was harsh compared with the earth they'd just left. A soft red glow lit the inside of the cabin and their faces looked gaunt and haggard, tired. They looked like shadows and ghosts. Then the light went out, or Shaw fell asleep, and he could hardly see his hand in front of his face. The 47's drone and the *thump, thump, thump* of the rotors rolled into a steady stream of white noise. His ears popped and the pressure lifted. He felt light. Weightless.

Back at the FOB they did their AAR and told the CO about the boy and the two other men they'd killed. The CO didn't comment much on it one way or another, but Shaw saw him wince for a moment after they said they had killed the boy. Then he caught himself and said they'd done well, what they had to do, and that

Intel would monitor the pass and the village around the clock. Future activity in the village would open the possibility for air strikes and they probably wouldn't get boots on the ground for the tunnels. JDAMs would fit in better.

Dalonna said he was going to call his family. The rest of them got to their tents and collapsed into their beds. Shaw dreamed of the boy. He was standing on the rock and waving at them, not pointing at their positions. A soft light from the sun brought warmth to his body and he looked like a stained-glass window churches put up. He seemed to glow. Then Shaw woke up and the tent was cold. And there wasn't a light anywhere.

Hagan yelled out in the dark.

"Oh, fuck off!"

Shaw shot out of bed, startled. He hadn't even felt the beeper vibrate in his pocket. It glowed with a 1 and headlamps started popping off in the tent. They hadn't been in bed for more than a few hours. Shaw looked at his watch. Not even 0900 hours yet. He still hadn't brushed his teeth from the long walk. He could taste too many days of chaw and dirt and Skittles and filth. His breath smelled like something had died in his gut.

"Interdiction," Cooke said in the dark. He sat up straight on his bed, his headlamp on and the glow hiding everything but his mouth. "Ten bucks."

"Of course it's an interdiction," Hagan said. "Screw your ten bucks. I want to sleep. Fuck you, interdiction."

They ran out of the tent and into the sunlight.

Cooke was right. Resting at the foot of their lockers were laminated cards of a white pickup and a clean-shaven man with a crescent-moon strip of hair standing guard over the rest of his balding head. The man wore small, circled glasses that looked like wire Easter-egg droppers. He seemed like a professor, or maybe an accountant. The CO pointed to the images on the laminated cards and spoke while the men strapped on their gear. His voice peppered the straps of Velcro and snaps of helmets, the weapons racking.

"There are two guys in the truck. The driver's a courier for the Scars and we're not exactly sure who the other guy is, yet. Get them and bring them back."

The operators ran out to the pickups and sped to the airfield, tires slinging gravel and kicking up clouds of dust. Two Little Birds sat spitting fuel on the tarmac and shaking under the rush of their wings. The helicopters looked anxious, trembling on their skids, as the sun beat down on the tarmac. The engines screamed and sent waves of fire blasting into the air. The heat and the smell of burning fuel and trash were dizzying. Shaw was sure he'd be sick. Cooke threw in a chew, sat on the bench, and offered him one. Shaw waved it off. They clipped in and plugged in their comms, and Dalonna, Hagan, and Massey hopped on the other side. Mike and Ohio did the same with their team on the other bird. Slausen was the last to sit down and clip in. He ran to the bench with his helmet snugged between his arm and chest. His boots were untied and he was buckling his bottoms. They were already sweating, even though it was getting cooler during the days. They had rolled their sleeves and bottoms up to their elbows and knees. Hagan wore no top save for a T-shirt. Their hairy legs glimmered in the sunlight. The pilot asked if they were clipped in and ready, and the birds rose off the ground before they finished a response.

"Well, Baldy's fucked," Cooke shouted over the wind.

The birds dipped their noses and charged straight ahead. They headed west.

As the birds flew on, Shaw had to piss badly. Before running out of the war room he'd felt the piss coming on, so he'd grabbed an empty Gatorade bottle and thrown it into one of his cargo pockets. His bladder weighed heavily in his stomach and felt like it would drop out of his skin if he stood up. He knew if he didn't let loose soon he'd probably piss himself on the hood of the pickup during the interdiction, so he grabbed the empty Gatorade bottle from his cargo pocket and tightened the sling of his weapon around his chest. He undid his bottom buttons and edged up off the lip of the bird. Cooke watched him.

"Cooke, I gotta piss."

Cooke shrugged. "So piss."

Shaw closed his eyes and tried to relax, hung himself limp inside the bottle. Nothing came out. He opened his eyes. Cooke was still staring at him.

"Cooke, what the hell?"

Cooke laughed and yelled over the wind, "I'm just messing with you. Go on and piss."

Shaw clenched the bottle and looked at Cooke, then at the other bird flying next to them. Mike and Ohio sat on the bench across the sky. They waved. Shaw looked back. The CSAR birds trailed behind them, small and black, a few klicks to the southeast. They looked like black flies in the sky. Shaw closed his eyes, tried to relax, then tried to blast and push it out. Nothing came, so he swore and threw the bottle. It fell to the earth, tumbling end over end, the orange cap fluttering on the wind and the sun flashing bright in the plastic.

"Shouldn't litter," Cooke yelled. "We're trying to rebuild this country."

The Little Birds hugged the earth as miles of dry flatland sped under the operators' feet. Clouds of dirt and packed earth thrown into the air by the white pickup stretched across the empty land like smoke.

"Target ahead," the pilot said over the comms.

The dirt trail from the truck spread over hundreds of meters and their bird banked to the left side of the trail, the other bird hopping onto the right. Shaw couldn't see the truck yet. Then the piss came. He swore and undid his pants, whipped out and let fly. He pissed all over his bottoms and sent a trail along the bench and tail of the bird.

"You're a savage," Cooke yelled, laughing.

Then the white pickup broke through the clouds of dust and the lead bird throttled forward. The other bird decelerated as Shaw's shot past them. They sped in front of the truck and cut hard ninety degrees to the north, cutting the vehicle off. The truck slammed on the brakes and the operators were on the ground before it was in park. The men were hidden in dust.

Shaw had his sight on the driver. He wore dark sunglasses and had an overgrown face that dwarfed his nose. Fat folds dripped from his chin and his mouth was frozen open. The birds were screaming behind them and it sounded like the world was blowing itself up.

Dalonna and Shaw led, yelling, *"Motar sakha raa wudzai,"* and *"Barah."*

Then a pressure wave hit and the lights went out.

The sky was beautiful, blue and vast. Shaw opened his eyes. Black smoke curled and flexed across his face like passing clouds, dark fingertips. He lay on his back, on the ground, dizzy. It felt like his head had caved in. Massey stood over him, his mouth moving, but Shaw didn't hear a thing. A loud drone rang in his head, spreading from ear to ear like a siren before settling in the middle and drowning everything out. Everything echoed or muffled and he blinked slow. Then fast. His limbs tingled and felt impossibly heavy. He could see the tips of his boots and a black mass of clouds. Red-and-orange flames danced in the wind over the ground. He smelled gasoline and fire. Burning metal.

Massey helped him up and Shaw saw Dalonna on a knee a few feet away on the ground. Slausen, Hagan, and Cooke were holding him upright by the shoulders. Dalonna spit out some blood and what looked like a couple teeth. He took his helmet off and let it tip over onto the ground, then he collapsed onto the dirt and stared up at the sky. Clots of blood were matted in his beard, shimmering in the light like beads of sweat. Mike, Ohio, and the rest of their team stood around what was left of the truck, kicking up pieces of burnt metal and rubber, sifting through the wreckage and what was left of its inhabitants.

There wasn't much.

There was a blackened piece of leather sitting just beyond Shaw's feet, skin melted into the stitching. It was the top half of a sandal. Next to it was a hand cut at the palm, missing all its fingers. Hagan saw Shaw and ran over. Hagan's eyes were wide and he pointed at Shaw's crotch, the veins in his forearm popping like little snakes. Shaw was dizzy. The burning tires and metal had stirred up his guts. He looked at the fingerless hand and saw the blackened bone sticking out of the charred flesh. It looked like a burnt piece of char-broiled chicken. He felt faint and nauseated and then he got sick, threw up all over his boots. There were grains of rice stuck between his laces. He couldn't remember having eaten anything in hours. He felt Hagan's hands rummaging around his crotch, the fingers fluttering between his legs and grabbing bare skin. Then Hagan stopped and patted him on the back, and the black took Shaw away.

That night the five of them sat around the TOC, watching the monitors together.

"I thought you'd lost your nuts," Hagan said.

Shaw had a cold pressure wrap tied around his head and he offloaded some of the chaw from his mouth into a foam cup. Spit streaked his beard. He probably didn't need the nicotine. He was dizzy enough from the painkillers. Hagan looked over at him, his feet propped on another chair. He spoke through a thick horseshoe, drooling into a white foam cup.

"That's why I was molesting you. Why the hell was your fly open, anyway?" Hagan rested his hands on his thighs. He balanced the cup between his belt and his stomach.

Shaw shrugged.

Dalonna lost his front teeth and had his mouth and cheeks cut up some. Shaw didn't remember the blast or the flight back, just Hagan feeling his nuts and seeing body parts lying next to charred metal. Both Shaw and Dalonna were diagnosed with concussions. The two of them were off mission status until their concussions cleared, and the rest of the team was given the option of continuing on as attachments or waiting it out with Shaw and Dalonna. They chose the latter and the five of them watched the monitors together, the birds flying out to an objective like dragonflies on the screen.

Shaw had a metallic smell in his nose and a headache ever since the blast. It reeked of hot metal and sawdust, pennies and blood. His brain felt like it was trying to breathe but couldn't through the thick walls of his skull. The cool wrap wasn't doing much, but without it he'd probably be sweating and miserable. Massey and Cooke stood behind the other three, facing the monitors, arms crossed over their chests like bandoleers. Dalonna sat next to Shaw, his face puffy with gauze. He had holes shaved into his beard for the stitches. The black sutures looked like hairy moles. He smiled at Shaw.

"How are the nuts?"

Shaw looked down at his pants.

"Donna, the nuts are good. No nut problems. Dandy nuts, guys."

"It was piss," Hagan said. "You had piss all over you. The dirt and all from the explosion made it look like blood. That's why I was checking down there."

"You're good, Hog," Shaw said. "Thanks for looking out for my nuts."

Hagan nodded and turned to the monitors.

The birds hovered over the target building long enough for fast ropes to drop and then two teams rode the ropes to the roof, entering the dwelling from a protruding doorway while another entered from the ground. The kill TVs weren't tapped into any sound, so the team watched the screens like a silent black-and-white movie. White flashed on the screen from the doorways as the teams threw in bangers, and then all the screens showed for a while were the teams pulling security around the compound. They scanned the surrounding buildings with their lasers, waved a few neighbors back inside their homes, and then a few more operators entered the building. Minutes later the teams exited the objective, leading four men with hands bound behind their backs. Then all of them walked a ways to a clearing and the birds swooped down and carried them away.

"Good shit," Cooke said. "Hey, Hog. What were his nuts like?"

They all laughed, and Hagan's faced turned red. "I explained myself, Cooke. I was worried about his nuts."

Cooke didn't say anything else, and Dalonna winced and brought his fingers to his mouth. The stitches were raw and part of his lip had split like he'd gotten caught on a fishhook. Smiling made him bleed.

Massey got up.

"Glad you two are good," he said. "Donna, have you told the lady yet?"

Dalonna shook his head.

"I don't think I will." He ran his hands across his face and touched the stitches. "She wouldn't be able to sleep."

"Yeah," Hagan said. "Probably better if you didn't."

. . .

The docs told them to stay out of the gym for a few days while their concussions cleared, so Dalonna and Shaw loaded their rucks and walked around the base for hours. They walked at night and during the day. They walked under the stars on the cool desert dirt and against the sun and dust storms and the heat. It was a good distraction. Dalonna got a fake set of teeth made up and never told Mirna about the blast. He'd just come home with a few more scars. She might not even notice. During one of the days they were off, Mike and Ohio came in to check on Dalonna and Shaw and told them about the courier and the professor.

Intel had watched the courier, the driver, for nearly a year. He was thought to run for all three of the Scars at one time, but he'd stopped doing so for the last couple months. The change made Intel wonder what he was doing instead—whether he was dead, running for someone else, or had come to the light—so they increased the surveillance on him and put out requests with other foreign agencies. It turned out he'd been coming in and out of the country often, five or six times in the last four months. He utilized two different safe houses on his trip back into the country and the houses were hundreds of miles apart on the same border. Intel let him continue without bothering him to see who he might lead to, and after his second trip in a single month they started watching him full-time. He was busy. He'd get across the border without any issues and then drive all over the country, picking up women, children, and older men. Intel started calling him the Mayor for the way he made his rounds. When he stopped using his phone Intel really perked up on him. Then one day he picked up a balding man with glasses in a white pickup truck.

The balding man was the holder of a Jordanian engineering doctorate. He'd taught at a London university and was asked to leave after his name popped up on a list of donors to a charitable organization that had laundered money to associates of a known bomb-builder. The story had been printed in *The Times*. He entered the country legally after losing his post, and international intelligence services kept tabs on him for years ever since, letting him move freely and make acquaintances but watching him still. When the Mayor picked him up in the truck, Jordanian intelligence services following the bald man contacted Intel. Intel beeped through the 1 immediately, and the Little Birds were sent out to meet him.

The trunk of the truck was full of packaged fertilizer, hair spray bottles, batteries, five-gallon drums of gasoline, and other white powders in addition to two prototype vests the professor had developed. He saw the birds in the rearview mirror and riffled through a duffel bag in the backseat, arming the vests just as the truck came to a stop. He was a brilliant mathematician, but miscalculated by inches. Intel figured he didn't want to be taken alive and decided to try to kill as many of the operators as possible.

"We couldn't question the shoulder or wrist we found," Mike said. "But at least they didn't blow in a market or busy street."

He wore a black ball cap and T-shirt with his bottoms and a pair of shower sandals. He rubbed his hands over his knees and picked at his kneepads with his fingernails. Then he started mumbling softly and no one could hear him over the air conditioners running in the tents. He shook his head and his voice trailed off for good and no one said anything at all. He rubbed his eyes and held his head in his hands. When he looked up again his eyes were red.

Close, he whispered. *Close.*

. . .

Dalonna and Shaw passed their concussion checks six days after the blast. Dalonna trimmed the ends of his sutures to keep them from catching on anything and Shaw walked around during the day in full kit and helmet for hours to see if anything felt off. The kit felt sown to his chest and shoulders and the pads of the helmet found their slots in his skull and hair. Everything felt good. Tight and right. They were on the green again.

The sun was dipping into the horizon and cool air blew on the wind. Fall had left summer for winter during their week off the green and the cold had crept in. The men wore zip-ups, long-sleeve tops, and winter hats to their briefs. They left their tents more during the daylight hours to shoot and play Wiffle ball, and some of the shit stench seemed strangled by the colder winds. They were pitching horseshoes when they got the 4 and Shaw was glad for it. He hadn't ringed a shoe yet and started getting a headache after concentrating on the stake for so long. He didn't want to start having second thoughts whether he should be greened or not. He needed the distraction, saw the boy in the pass whenever he closed his eyes.

"We should grab Donna," Hagan said.

Then he ringed a shoe. Probably the first anyone had ever seen him land.

"He's on the phones," Massey said.

Hagan looked off toward the phone tent. He didn't seem to have noticed his shot.

Shaw stood up from the ground where he'd sat staring at the gray mass of clouds overhead. A long gray wall spanning the entire sky. "I'll grab him."

Hagan nodded and spat in the dirt. "He told me to leave him alone a while ago." He threw his other shoe and ringed it again. "I think he's messed up."

"All right. I'll get him," Shaw said. "Thanks, Hog."

Cooke pointed to the stake. His mouth was open and his dip had settled untamed in the gaps of his teeth. He pointed to the stake, at the two horseshoes Hagan had ringed.

"Hog, you've never ringed a shoe as long as I've known you, and you just ringed two. What kind of shit are you pulling?"

Dalonna was sitting outside on the dirt with his back propped against the wooden shitter shacks across from the phones. He wore a zip-up and a watch cap pulled low on his head. He had an old pipe in his hand and smoke curled in thick leaden tails from his lips. The clouds were gray and heavy, low in the sky. The same color as his smoke.

Shaw walked up with his hands in his bottom pockets. "Nice pipe."

Dalonna acknowledged Shaw with his eyes and threw the pipe to his side. It landed in the dirt, the tobacco spilling out on the ground. "It was my granddad's. It's supposed to calm."

"Does it?"

"Nah. Mainly just tastes like shit."

Shaw nodded. "You all right, Donna?"

Dalonna's stitches were clipped so close that one or two had broken free from the skin. Shaw could make out small dots of dull red blood that had dried to his face. Dalonna looked at him for a brief while and then shook his head. He let out a heavy breath.

"Little Danny isn't doing too good."

Shaw tried to picture a Danny they knew. Couldn't find one.

"Who's Danny, Donna?"

Dalonna smiled. "Daniel Dalonna. My boy."

Shaw said the name in his head a few times, mouthed it with his lips. Daniel Dalonna. Danny. Danny Dalonna. It rolled well. Sounded good.

"Danny Dalonna. Daniel. That's a good name," Shaw said. "I hadn't heard his name yet."

"Hadn't told anyone yet." Dalonna smiled.

"What's wrong with Danny, Donna?"

Dalonna spat at the pipe, missed. "Abnormal nuchal fold."

Shaw raised his eyebrows.

"It's a fluid buildup in the neck," Dalonna said. "They can see it on the ultrasound and measure the levels. They have safe levels, averages, and then levels of concern. Mirna had an ultrasound today and Danny's levels aren't good."

"Not good or bad?"

"Bad."

"And what does bad mean?"

Dalonna sighed and raised his hands. "Not sure yet. They stabbed Mirna with a needle and took some samples from Danny's neck to test for issues with chromosomes."

"They took samples from his neck? How the hell do they do that?"

Shaw imagined Dalonna's Danny, the little guy squirming in his mom's fluids and getting tapped with a needle. He probably wasn't even the size of an acorn yet.

"They stabbed Mirna in the stomach with some big-ass needle

and took samples from his neck," Dalonna said. "Maybe his body. I don't know. He's the size of a fucking plum. A lime."

Shaw looked at his hand. He imagined a small fruit that could sit in his palm. "Damn. Donna, I'm sorry."

"The needle could've killed him to begin with, and Mirna said it hurt like hell, but the doctor said it was necessary. If we wanted to know if he'll live or not." Dalonna rubbed the heels of his boots in the dirt.

"Live? Why wouldn't he live?"

Dalonna shrugged. "That's what the tests will say, I guess. Larger nuchal folds can mean Down's syndrome and trisomies, or other disorders that can kill him before he's even born."

"Can mean isn't a sure thing. Right?"

"Yeah, that's what I told Mirna. But apparently the doctor was freaking her out. He told her to consider her options for the pregnancy."

"Options as in?"

"Termination."

"Because of a fluid buildup in his neck?"

"Yeah. He gave Danny a twenty percent chance of living. Less than ten for having a normal life. Based off his experience."

"His experience." Shaw spat. "Twenty percent? Because of some fluid. How much experience does this doc have?"

"I don't know. At least thirty or forty years. He's a gray-hair. Mirna said he's some expert in the field. He's not her normal doctor. They called him in when they saw the nuchal-fold levels."

"Screw him, Donna. Gray-hairs don't even know how to drive."

Dalonna laughed and wiped his hands in the dirt, rubbed them together slowly. He locked his fingers together and looked at his boots.

"Man, I want a boy. I love my girls. But I want a boy."

He sat propped against the shitters with his shoulders slack and deflated. His neck hung exposed and limp to one side like he was waiting for a blade to take his head off. He looked scared and young. Fragile. Then he brought a hand up and started picking at his stitches. He took one out, and then the others. Blood started to trickle down his face in slow beads that left behind thin trails.

"Mirna almost lost one of her boys a couple days ago and Danny could be waiting to die inside her." His hand disappeared into one of his pockets and he pulled out the beeper. "I got the 4."

"You can get out of it, Donna. No worries."

"I'm good. Just need a few minutes."

"Donna—"

"I'll be fine. Meet you at the brief."

Shaw nodded because he didn't know what to say. He turned around and left Dalonna. Then he turned back and Dalonna waved him on and Shaw walked to the briefing room. On his way he kept opening and closing his hands. Shaw imagined the smooth skin of a plum nestled in his palm. It would be so easy to break.

The men ate frosted Halloween cookies sent over from Massey's niece, Penelope, as they waited for the brief to begin. Dalonna came in after the others had already gathered. He grabbed a cookie and the laminated printout in front of him and studied both of them for a while. Then he put down the printout, ate the cookie, and rubbed Hagan's head and patted Shaw on the back. There were twenty of them in the room. Four teams.

"We're getting off the Scar intel for a while," the CO said. "After the village and the car bombing we're going to develop the intel a little more before moving on any more of it. We'll be heading up north tonight. There's already some snow up there." He shrugged. "So it'll be a little cold."

The men were already wearing long sleeves, zip-ups, and winter hats. The real cold might've saved itself for the night in the south where the FOB was, but it had already crept into the daylight throughout the rest of the country. The mountains were full of snow. A couple of the southern boys had full jackets on.

"Our target's with one of his wives tonight," the CO said. "They loaded into a black SUV with a few other FAMs and left the city in the morning. Not sure if they're making a run for the border and just squatting for the night or just dicking around, but we can't risk it. As you can see"—he pointed to the satellite images—"they're completely isolated. Not another building for at least a klick in any direction, and most of them are goat-herding squat shacks already abandoned for the winter."

They went over the target and his accomplices during the brief, their reasons for catching Intel's attention. The FAMs were given the moniker Pup1–4 for the way they followed the target, Lion1, around like his puppies. Lioness1 was the wife.

"She might talk more than any of the men," the CO said. "We don't usually get a chance at the women if little kids are around, so getting her alive will be priority one."

Lion1 was a Saudi in his late forties, an old man for the region he was from. He grew up in a centuries-old village carved into the side of a mountain, and as a boy he was rumored to have killed his own father for abusing one of his sisters. Apparently he ran away to a madrassa for refuge and found his fire. He was a leader from an early age and he'd grown tall and crooked at the hip from a round that had found his legs during the war in the region with the Soviets in the eighties. He was known to hack off the legs of those who fell out of his favor and he kept the de-legged alive to spread fear among his ranks, forcing them to act as runners in firefights. They'd wheel ammo carts tied to their middles and have to crawl around boulders and rocks. He walked with a limp but carried no cane and was known to shave his peppery beard when he planned on making a move. He hadn't been seen in four years and then a CIA asset on the ground had sent pictures of him with his beard shaved just the day before and Intel pounced.

Lion1 had formerly led an al-Qaeda cell the squadrons had decimated. In the first years of the war his network owned the western regions of the country. If a bomb blew or a body showed up missing its head in an irrigation ditch west of the capital, Lion1's network had a hand in it. At the height of his power he even had his name thrown in on the ballot for election to the position of Ministry of Defense for the rebuilding government. But he didn't win and the political move poisoned his network. Captains in his cell alleged that he was straying off the sect's polarized path of sharia, getting too Westernized with his political aims, so there were assassination attempts. One day his car blew up as it idled next to a fruit stand in a bazaar. He'd gotten out to look at some clothes for sale across the street when the bomb planted in a melon stand next to his car by one of his exiled lieutenants detonated. The blast killed the driver, liquefied the seats, and twisted the metal skeleton of the vehicle. But Lion1 didn't die in the blast, so he killed the exiled lieutenant and his family and left the bodies in an irrigation ditch off a dirt road. Then he started getting paranoid and killed off his other officers. His cell leaders showed up bound on the sides of busy roads with bullets in the backs of their heads. Weeks and months passed and the killings didn't, so he lost his clout and his followers. Other cells took over his network while it was reeling, killing those who refused to switch allegiances, until there was nothing but scraps left. The Pups were his oldest living son, his nephew, and two cousins of one of his three wives. The shaved beard and trip up north were reason enough for Intel to move, so the 4 came through.

The CO leaned against a table.

"He's not with al-Ayeelaa. At least not to our knowledge. But some of his ex-lieutenants that are still alive are rumored to be. Every squadron and coalition force has been looking for this guy for years. Intel figures he's a bad egg worth talking to. A drone tracked the SUV to the compound and hasn't reported any activity since they arrived. This is a live feed."

He pointed to a black-and-white image on one of the kill TVs. The camera circled slowly with the arc of the drone while the compound sat still in the middle of the shot. The CO looked at Dalonna and Shaw.

"You guys feeling okay?"

They nodded.

"Good. Welcome back."

They got the 1 at 2242 hours.

They were all sitting in the war room, debating whether they should play blackjack or a game Hagan had made up called tittyspank. Blackjack was winning out, even though Hagan was campaigning pretty hard for tittyspank, and Dalonna wasn't talking a whole lot because of a new set of stitches he had to replace the ones he'd torn out. When the beep came through he folded an ultrasound picture into halves and put it in his top. Then he racked his weapon as the claps of metal mags and bolts slamming home walked the men into the night.

After they clipped into the birds they flew north to the snow. The cold bit at their faces first and then settled heavily into their legs. It hurt to breathe. They flew fast and low, nap-of-the-earth. Shaw could dip down a couple feet and scoop up snow on his boots. The dried, wind-chapped earth gave way to rolling fields of snow and the moon shined bright. The wind blew snow off the tops of the hillsides and the plumes came off the crests as if the land were breathing deep breaths. Their NODs weren't needed, the world lit up instead by the light of the stars caught in the blankets of ice and snow. They saved their batteries and lifted the NODs.

The *Five mikes out* call came over the comms and they continued riding the hills until the land flattened and the birds dropped them off two klicks from the compound, where the hills of snow would strangle the noise of their approach. The goat-herder shacks were set up every couple hundred meters and they stood out from the land like tombstones. Like thumbs on the earth's hand. With NODs down and lasers fired up, the operators painted the world green. The snow was a couple inches thick and crusted over with a thin film of ice. Shooting stars cut the sky and the wind blew snow across the countryside. After they had walked for a half hour, the perimeter teams radioed in *Panther1 and 2 in position* and the operators could see the objective. Banks of windblown snow draped the target building. It looked like the compound was driving itself out of the snow or trying to hide in it.

The assault teams moved in and Shaw led them to the front door. There weren't any lights on, the compound set back in the snow and the dark. As they posted up alongside the house Shaw noticed how cold the walls were, how dark everything was. Not a single light escaped from the dwelling, and he wondered if Intel was right and people were sleeping inside. Living inside. He watched Hagan run his hands over the lock, his breath pluming in front of his face, and imagined kicking in the door and finding a bunch of freezing, scared-to-shit goats cuddled up in blankets.

"We're blowing it," Hagan whispered over the comms.

He set the charge on the door, and as it blew Shaw noticed the windows were simple, whole sheets of thick metal. The door blew in and bright light from inside the compound flooded out into the dark.

The lights were on.

Bangers started popping and Shaw entered the doorway over the scraps of the blown door. He followed the wall left and Dalonna turned right. It was warm and bright inside and smelled of baharat, wood smoke, and old blankets. Two men stood behind a waist-high table, a third in an open doorway behind them. They'd been eating. Their forks were closer than the rifles settled on the tables, but they flinched forward. The man standing had his thumb looped through the sling of a rifle as if he were resting his hand on a pair of suspenders, his nose and eyes scrunched together like he smelled something off. Dalonna's rifle popped and coughed before Cooke and Hagan had fully entered the room, and Shaw heard the shots and continued down the wall. He and Dalonna pushed through to the next room while Cooke and Hagan checked the bodies. There were footsteps overhead as Mike's team cleared the second floor, and then a loud *crack, crack,* and then more shots. They sounded like coughs muffled by a fist. Then Mike's voice calling for another medic to come upstairs came over the comms.

"Two wounded. Two EKIA."

Massey left the three bodies in the first room and ran up to the second level. Then Mike came over the comms again.

"Second floor secured."

The whole house was cleared in minutes.

Shaw and Dalonna stood in a dark storeroom, scanning the shelves and dusty corners with their tac lights. It smelled of rotten grains and burlap musk. There were half-empty hemp bags of wheat and oats and jarred vegetables covered in dust, the labels nearly faded off. In the corner of the shed were two long wooden rifles that looked like they could hardly fire a shot, and on a nail by the backdoor, a set of car keys.

The black SUV was parked right outside the storeroom. The paint had been chipped and faded, beaten by the countryside for years. It looked like it was shedding its skin. A man could cut himself simply running his hand along the doors. Shaw opened the trunk and found it full of black duffel bags. Inside the bags were false passports, a couple thousand American dollars in crumpled wads, and extra clothes. A loaded Glock 9mm and a Makarov with three loaded clips. The clothes were mostly male tops and bottoms with a few colorful items and silk hijabs sprinkled in. The clothes were not folded. The front seats housed a full bag of almonds and a nearly empty pack of Marlboros. There were two plastic lighters. One yellow and one orange. Shaw radioed in *Objective secured* and then they left the car and searched the layout and the bodies inside.

The place was tidy, ordered and neat. Shoes were lined up at the front door and low moans and short, strained language came through the ceiling. It sounded like furniture was getting shifted around upstairs. Carpets blanketed every inch of the floor and there were prayer rugs rolled into tight cylinders and stacked against a wall flecked with drops of blood. Elaborate floor lamps with beaded tassels on the covers stood in a corner of every room on the first floor and there were books on shelves and old *Time* and *National Geographic* magazines on a small table. A fireplace with ashes in its hearth occupied most of one of the walls, and a large black pot of rice was set on the table between the dead men who had fallen off the chairs and were lying on the floor. Cracked yellow plates of unfinished food were on the table, rice and animal bones with greasy gristle and fat still on the bone. It looked like goat. Partially opened bags of fertilizer lined the walls.

Shaw walked over to the men who had been shot at the table. They lay crumpled on the floor next to their overturned chairs. Their fingers were oily and they had black and green spices stuck in their fingernails. They wore dark jeans with light stitching on the hems and had ashy skin and dark beards. Their blood was settling in the carpet. Dalonna had gone for the face. The two men had holes in their cheeks and foreheads.

"Donna," Shaw said. "Headshots?"

Dalonna shrugged and leafed through their pockets, set what he found on the table. "Nuchal folds on my mind."

Shaw looked back at the bodies. Their faces were sunken and

cracked where the rounds had entered. The flaps of skin were jagged and the flesh and bones broken. The features—eyes, noses, and mouths—contorted into shattered glass doll masks by the lead. Blood had settled behind the heads and made mops of their hair, and their skin seemed to be taking on the same yellow, sickly glow as the lamps. One of them wore a white kameez with a dark vest and the other wore the same but had a khaki coat with cargo pockets instead of a vest. Shaw went through the cargo pockets of the khaki coat. There was nothing but crumpled tissues in two of the four pockets. The other two were empty. Neither man wore shoes. Shaw smelled something harsh while he was kneeling and noticed a dark bloom on one of the guy's pants. His bowels had relaxed after he was shot.

"Dude was packing heat," Dalonna said.

He threw two lighters on the table and three packs of cigarettes. The packs were all opened.

"Were those all in his jacket?" Shaw asked.

"No. He had one in his pants." Dalonna shrugged. "Dude needed his fucking smokes. Beat cancer at least."

The man who had stood with his thumb in the sling of his rifle lay on the floor between the first room and the storeroom. He had a white dress shirt buttoned to the collar and black pants with no belt. He wore a ratty old green jacket that was frayed at the collar and waistline, and he had a bushy black mustache that reminded Shaw of the one his father wore in pictures he'd seen as a kid. Two red flowers bloomed at the man's breastbone where the rounds had entered before splintering the wall behind him. Dalonna had spared the man's face and made his way across the floor and was checking the body.

"Phone," Dalonna said.

He held it up for Shaw to see and threw it on the table. They bagged it. Then they took pictures of the bodies and fingerprints.

"I think this is sugar," Hagan said. He had his hands in one of the bags of fertilizer running the length of the walls.

"Taste it," Cooke said.

"After you, sweetheart." Then Hagan shrugged and licked his fingers. "Yeah. It's sugar."

Shaw and Dalonna walked over to the bags, and Hagan tasted the other bags along the wall.

"All sugar," Hagan said.

"What if it had been fertilizer, Hog?" Cooke asked.

Hagan shrugged again. "I don't know. Wouldn't have tasted as good, I guess."

Then a sharp inhale came from behind them. There was a whimper, like a puppy stepped on in the dark. Massey was struggling down the stairs, carrying a short, wide woman over his shoulder. She was wearing a long, dark chador, and the back of her head was exposed. She cried out every time Massey took a step. Her long black hair was braided and wrapped in a bun. It shined in the lamplight. One of the braids trailed behind her and bounced off Massey's back with each step. She had a large mass of white bandages wrapped around her middle, and Slausen walked down the stairs behind them. He was growing his beard back in and the mustache was overpowering the new hair. He carried Ohio over his shoulder, wraps and compresses snaking thick around one of his legs. His face bounced against Slausen's shoulder with each step and his eyes were open but glassy. He didn't say anything. Massey walked out of the door with the wife, and Slausen gave them a thumbs-up and followed with Ohio.

"He'll be fine," Mike said. He made his way outside, following behind the medics. "Took one in the leg. In and out."

"And the wife?" Shaw asked.

"Took a few in the gut." His voice started strong, booming through the warm house. "She probably won't make it."

Then the wind swallowed his voice and there was quiet and Shaw looked at his hands. Small tracks of blood had made their way into the creases and wrinkles of his gloves. He didn't know which dead man it'd come from. Then Hagan came over beside him and tossed him a red apple. He held another, half eaten, in his hand. Shaw caught the apple and looked at him. Hagan was nodding to himself, eyeing the books on the shelf, a hand on his hip.

"This place is like my grandma's cottage."

Shaw held up the apple.

"Where'd you get this?"

"On the table next to the goat plates," Hagan said. "I found a phone right next to it." He held up the phone in his hand.

"And you're eating it?"

"Yes to the apple, no to the phone. This isn't fucking *Snow White*."

He laughed and Shaw threw the apple back at his chest.

"Man, it's hot in here," Hagan said. "My nuts are swimming. What's with all the sugar?"

Shaw brought his hands to his nose. "No idea."

He could still smell the apple on his gloves on the flight back to base.

They took the duffel bags from the trunk. After destroying the weapons and ammunition while waiting for the exfil, they left the rest of the compound relatively intact and stacked the bodies outside neatly. They got all four of the Pups. One was killed on the second floor along with Lion1, and the others were the ones Dalonna tapped with headshots and the man with the blooming breastbone. Lion1 was upstairs in bed with his wife, an AK loaded and lying between them. He got two shots off on Ohio before Mike killed him, and then the wife picked up the rifle and Mike had to put two through her middle. It happened fast. In the air Massey pounded her chest, but got back on the tarmac with blood all over his hands and arms.

"She bled out," he said.

He opened his hands and let them fall to his sides.

Intel found numerous SIM cards sown into the inside flaps of the duffels taken from the black SUV. The techs analyzed the cards and phones immediately and pored over the data. Spiderwebs formed in major cities and mountain complexes from the networks spun by the plastic chips no larger than a child's thumbnail. There was also a zip drive wrapped in a teal hijab, balled and tucked inside another black one inside one of the duffels. They found documents and drafts, copies of e-mails saved from various accounts. Those could be tapped and traced.

They were.

Massey and Shaw were sitting outside the tents days after the Lion1 raid. They rolled a baseball across the dirt in the daylight. The heat had left for the year and the clouds hung low and wide, heavy and sinking with snow. Dalonna heard Daniel was okay after advanced testing and they were all happy about that, relieved. He passed out sugar cookies with light blue frosting that Mirna had sent over, and they were good. The men demolished them in a single sitting.

Massey and Shaw rolled the ball back and forth and the cool air felt good. Fresh. The temperatures were more comfortable now outside during the day than at night. They'd been running nonstop since they landed more than a month ago and their op tempo was charging ahead. Intel gathered at the objectives was analyzed immediately and follow-on targets were identified and hit just as fast. Sometimes within hours. They'd hit a target at night and then have a follow-on target the same night heading back to the FOB. A vehicle interdiction during the daylight hours. Then they'd continue the cycle all over again the next night. Their ops had nearly doubled their days in-country. The machine was alive and working. They'd been busy.

Shaw told Massey he was tired.

"Me too," Massey said. "Lot of blood. Lot of intel."

He had the last of the Halloween cookies Penelope sent over in a tin beside him sitting in the dirt, and he threw Shaw one. It was a sugar-cookie ghost with black and white frosting. The ghost was black and its features white. It had teeth with little red blood blobs on the ends.

"Dark child, Mass. And when did ghosts get fangs?"

"Penelope is into scaring the shit out of herself now. She loves Halloween."

"She's probably scaring the hell out of your brother, too. He'll think he's raising a psychopath."

Massey laughed and nodded. He rolled the ball toward Shaw and ate some crumbs from the tin, squishing them on his thumb and sucking them off. It had been nearly a week and Penelope's cookies were still highly sought after. Massey took to hiding them under his bed after the men had devoured Mirna's cookies. Hagan was especially aggressive, eating nearly half the Halloween tin within the first two days. He'd been bugging Massey about when Penelope would send along more and Massey lied and told him it would be soon. Around Christmas, maybe. Hagan got impatient and asked for Penelope's address, so Massey gave him the address of an old girlfriend. Hagan hadn't gotten a response yet, but the men were all eagerly awaiting one.

"Up for heading over to the CASH again?"

Shaw took a bite out of the ghost's side. The light and fluffy base had turned hard and sharp, stale. He thought the frosting might have cut his lip.

"No, Mass. Again, the CASH isn't somewhere I like to hang out. What's with you medics? Morbid and bloodthirsty bastards."

Massey threw what looked like another cookie at him, but it hit like a rock. "No, man. Candy." Then he smiled real wide and wild. "I got a shit ton of it."

They carried plastic shopping bags full of Snickers, Reese's, Kit Kats, Hershey's, and a bunch of other brightly colored happy shit, and walked to the CASH the same as before—over the gravel and dirt, and across the various perimeters and checkpoints sectioning off the base.

"How exactly did you get all this sent to you?" Shaw asked. He felt the plastic lining of the bag straining under the weight of its contents. There must have been five pounds of candy inside.

"Well, it wasn't all sent to me. Exactly."

"Exactly. *Exactly* meaning what?"

"Exactly meaning I might have gotten a couple smaller bags in the mail sent to me and then got inspired to find some more." He winked at Shaw.

"I don't want to know. If I don't know I can't get burned."

"Well, that's probably not true," Massey said. "For starters, you're holding the hot merchandise. But I'll save you some grief and say its initial owners and nation of origin are classified. There. You can't be charged with aiding and abetting a fugitive."

"Fair. Don't go breaking your clearance for me."

"Never. You're not worth it."

The rickety front steps of the CASH had a few more nails in them and felt a little sturdier than before, but Shaw's stomach didn't. He felt his guts moving around. They entered the CASH and Massey nodded to the same blond guard as before and the guard nodded back. Then the guard nodded at Shaw and Shaw returned it and lifted the plastic bag. The guard smiled and eased the barrel of his rifle down to his belt. The pair made their way through the corridor and Shaw leaned toward Massey.

"Security sucks in here. A smile and a nod and you're in? We could be lugging live grenades and demolish this place."

The sheets covering the doorways had been replaced with real wooden doors. There wasn't as much screaming as before, but low moans, muffled and steady like an air conditioner running in the summertime, were still audible from inside the rooms.

"We don't have grenades and Matty is security," Massey said. "He doesn't suck. Matty knows me. Now us. If he didn't he'd throw that rifle in your face and knock out your damn teeth. He had the safety off and the barrel smiling at me the first time I came in."

"Well, that's good. Good for Matty."

Massey nodded and stopped in front of a doorway at the end of the hall. He entered the room and Shaw followed. Lines of beds spanned the entire floor. The crinkling of plastic bedsheets, a sniffle here and there, and their boots rubbing on the tile floor were the only noises. A kid coughed and it echoed across the entire ward. Small children sat upright and against pillows. Some were lying down, asleep, with covers pulled up to their chins. Others didn't have covers at all but rather white bandages stained black and red from their amputated arms and legs. The sheets looked like they might irritate the fresh bandages and wounds. Shaw hoped none of the kids were cold.

"The wards are separated by age," Massey said. "These are the youngest."

The room was full of dark hair and dark eyes. Bandages. The walls were painted gray and the sheets were a soft blue. Shaw counted ten beds on either side and only one of them was empty. A TV showed *Sesame Street* running on mute, subtitles rolling over the bottom of the screen. Some of the kids looked at them and others stared at the wall or watched their stumps. There was a young boy with half his hair shaved off bald and fresh stitches spanning the length of the bald spot on his head. He'd lost an arm above the elbow and was staring at where his hand must have been just days before. His eyes were complete glass and he had a little drool slipping onto his pillow from his mouth. They must have had him on some serious shit. Morphine or something heavier. Very slowly, he was wiggling what was left of his arm.

"Hi," Massey said.

Massey held his hand up and waved it back and forth slowly. A little girl with white bandages on her arms and her lower half covered by a blanket sat propped up in a bed in front of him. She smiled a little, had a dimple on the right side of her face. She was missing some hair but cute, a really pretty little kid. She had some green in her eyes, same as Penelope. Massey dug into his bag and pulled out a big fistful of candy, set it by her hands. The girl watched the bright colors come out of the black bag and then she chirped back excitedly, like a little bird. She held the candy in her bandaged hands and ran her fingers over the wrappers. She probably liked all the colors, the sound of the plastic wrappers rubbing between her fingers. She smiled at Massey and then at Shaw.

They walked around the ward and stopped at a boy's bed. He propped himself on his side and smiled. He put out his hand and said, "Hi." Shaw gave him some candy from the bag and then the boy nodded and said, "Hi," again before putting the candy in his pillowcase. "It'll melt," Shaw said. He pointed at the case and rubbed his fingers together, made a disgusted face. The boy nodded and said, "Hi," again. Then he smoothed his pillowcase, the candy hidden beneath it, and Massey patted his bed and smiled, let him be. The boy was missing both of his legs.

Shaw and Massey made their way around the room for a long while. Some of the kids were scared or shy, so Shaw and Massey would just leave some candy under the pillows. Other kids tried to speak English. They said things like "Hi," "Basketball," and "Real Madrid." One girl even said, "Snickers, please," real soft and quiet. Most smiled or were probably too drugged up to decide on their reaction. Shaw liked being around all the kids. It was nice to see some happy faces in the depressing place, and he even made funny faces to bait smiles out of the ones who didn't warm up to them. It made him feel good. Then he thought about how both sides dropped bombs and he figured the kids had a right not to smile at them if they didn't feel like it.

When a nurse came in, Massey hid his bag behind his back, so Shaw did the same. They waved at her and she smiled and inserted an IV into a sleeping girl by the door, brushed the girl's hair, and then left. They gave out all the candy and put the empty bags in a trash can filled with needles and bloodied compresses and walked back in the failing light. Shaw was going to ask Massey if he ever brought Dalonna to the CASH, thinking that all the kids would make Dalonna happy, but when they left Shaw looked back and saw all the kids in the beds watching them go. Their bright smiles stood out sharply against their dark hair. Even the ones they couldn't get smiles out of watched them leave. The boy without legs who had propped himself up on his side and said "Hi" to them held a hand up, and Shaw felt good and like he might get sick at the same time. Seeing all the kids torn up would break Dalonna.

"Mass. Won't they get sick from all the candy?"

"Nah. They're blown up, not malnourished. The starving kids are in a separate area of the CASH." He looked at the sky for a while and put his hands in his pockets. "They monitor that ward especially close. These kids just need to get used to living without their limbs. Some candy is small potatoes."

Shaw thought that made sense and then asked about the kid they'd found chained to Tango1's floor. Massey said he was cleaning up the wards, resupplying some of the medical materials. He'd gotten his cot and room, and Massey said he seemed happy. Shaw thought he might like to see him.

"What was his name?"

Massey stopped walking and his eyes narrowed. He looked up at the sky. "You know what? I don't even know his name." He laughed and shook his head.

"Do you think he'll get some fake teeth?"

"I don't know," Massey said. "I hope so. But it's probably not a priority."

They walked on a ways, and Shaw was enjoying the light breeze and the fading light, the quiet. He smelled dust and rain and it was nice.

"You know what?"

Shaw looked at him, then at the moon switching spots with the sun. "What's that?"

"People are messed up," Massey said.

Shaw had just put in a chew. The juices were warm and rushing hard. He didn't say a thing.

Massey shook his head. "Cute kids. All blown to hell."

Just then the wind kicked up and blew cold and Shaw wished he'd brought a jacket along. He hadn't, though, so he put his hands in his pockets and set them in deep, reaching for warmth.

They didn't get spun up that night, so they watched feeds of other raids on the kill TVs in the TOC. Shaw watched Dom, the Belgian Malinois, run into a room before an assault team and then the screen flashed white. The team outside the door moved back with the blast—except for Stephens, who ran into the room. The teams radioed in a casualty and Shaw thought about the white flash and the pressure that moved the team backward. He knew Dom was gone. He thought about Patch then, how Patch used to sit next to him on hot days when he was a kid and pant and pant all day long. Patch liked to lick the salt off Shaw's knees, and Shaw would rub the crown of Patch's skull between his thumb and forefinger. Patch would fall asleep against his legs, stomach rising and falling quick. Then his grandma would come outside and they'd both pet him together. Shaw missed him, wanted to feel the soft white fur on his fingers.

The rest of the raid went well and they got their guy alive, but everyone was quiet in the war room after they got back. Dogs and their handlers were closer than most team members. They slept in the same beds, jumped out of planes together, and even showered together. Shaw and Massey sat against the lockers with Stephens after the teams got back. Stephens held one of Dom's tac vests in his lap and ran his fingertips over the bristles of the toothbrush he kept looped into the vest at all times. He brushed Dom's teeth three times a day, was hoping to get the Belgian Malinois to live twenty years. He was convinced that keeping the plaque from forming in Dom's teeth would keep the dog's arteries and intestines clean, assuring a longer life. He talked about it endlessly.

Stephens rifled through his pockets slowly and took out a bright green tennis ball. His eye sockets were puffy and his cheeks shined bright in the light. He spoke real soft, barely made a sound. "Can someone get rid of this for me?" He released the ball and it rolled under the lockers. Then he seemed to sink into the wall lockers, his upturned hand resting on the ground and his fingers extended. A single tear from each eye fell down his cheeks and disappeared in his beard.

Shaw grabbed the ball and walked out of the war room and put it in his tent. He figured he'd give it back to Stephens in a few weeks. He probably didn't want to let it go, just didn't want to have to look at it for a while.

The men gathered in rows and had a service outside for Dom that night. The sun was just setting and the sky was clear. Stephens had cut up some leather from one of Dom's collars and tied it off around his wrist. Shaw asked if he could have one, too, and Stephens brightened up and said he'd get working on it. After the service they got a 4 on their beepers and in a few minutes the briefing room was full of guys shifting in their seats. Stephens was there, even though he wouldn't be on the op. He had an Orioles cap set low on his face, only his beard visible below the brim, and Ohio sat beside him with his bandaged leg propped on a chair. He wouldn't be on the op, either, and he rested his hand on Stephens's shoulder. The CO stood in front of them and began the brief.

"To start. That was indeed sugar in the fertilizer bags from the Lion1 raid. Intel's been digging through the finds from the SSE for the past week, night and day. Most of the e-mails they've breached are written in code. They've been able to break some, take good guesses on others, and are working on the rest. We didn't think he had anything to do with al-Ayeelaa, but he did. From what Intel can gather, they think Lion1 and his caravan made a deal with al-Ayeelaa. They might have agreed to provide a hundred pounds of fertilizer in a remote compound in the hills in exchange for safe passage out of the country. We didn't find an ounce of fertilizer, but we did find enough sugar to supply a small bakery for weeks. Add in the fake documents, the money, the packed bags, and shoot-it-out firepower they had, and I'd say that's a pretty good guess. Lion1 was probably planning on giving al-Ayeelaa a final *Fuck you* before you guys ruined it for him."

There were more operators in the room than there were during any other brief thus far, and the teams seated around the tables seemed to notice. They kept looking around the room at one another while they listened to the brief. Shaw couldn't help but stare at the images tacked to the whiteboard. They showed a compound nearly a block wide dropped into the middle of a cluttered neighborhood of dust-colored shanty homes, small storefronts, and narrow alleyways. It was the same quilted spread of urban patchwork as the night with the rocks, only spread over a larger area. Shaw thought of the boys and the rocks he threw at them and wondered how they were doing. If they were good boys or bad, and where he'd draw the line between the two. He wondered if they were still alive.

The CO said multiple correspondences had been traced from the zip drive they found to a single IP address originating in the compound pictured on the whiteboard and printouts. Frequent contributors to a jihadist website had the same IP address.

"We also have two different numbers that have popped hot in the compound today. Both were recently dialed from phones in the Lion1 compound. The phones have popped in the Scar network as well. We're attributing the numbers to a Pike1 and 2. The compound is formerly a school. It's not anymore. Sources on the ground can't verify a specific use, and based on its size it could be a lot of things. It could be a bomb factory. It could be a meeting or housing area. It could be a damn daycare or an urban training ground—we know they're not using the mountain camps anymore like bin Laden used. Or it could be nothing." The CO shrugged and opened his hands. "But take the IP address and the two phones and it's worth checking out. If Lion1 was dealing with someone in the compound, they're likely a big fish. Even more if the Scars had anything to do with them. Any FAM should be taken in for questioning. All tech devices are to be bagged, no matter how big or outdated."

Shaw thought of the maze of classrooms his schools had had in his childhood. There were lots of blind corners, open spaces, and places to hide. The room seemed to tense and hold its breath the longer the CO spoke.

"You all know the laws around here," he said. "One weapon per household, and there's a hell of a lot of houses. The GMVs make the most sense. It's too risky to bring birds into the neighborhood, so we'll drive out and hope the whole city doesn't decide to come out and mess with us. They shouldn't, they're smart enough. Intel's received hits within the past three hours, but they haven't gotten one in an hour and a half. We're not hauling until we know they're still there. Expect a 1 as long as it's still dark out. The objective's barely an hour away."

He asked if there were any questions and there weren't.

"Stephens." The CO swallowed, his Adam's apple rising and falling sharp in his throat. He ran his tongue around the inside of his cheek. "We're sorry about Dom."

Ohio rubbed Stephens's shoulders and Stephens stared straight ahead, nodding along slowly. He didn't blink or look like he'd heard a single word the CO had said.

. . .

After the CO left, the teams stayed in the briefing room to plan movements and flow patterns. The compound looked to be at least two stories high, maybe more. Cooke was squatting and wringing his hands, rocking on the balls of his feet.

"There's probably a basement, too," he said. "Places like this always have a lower level."

Every wing of the compound would be neutralized by one of four different assault teams, while the same number of perimeter and sniper attachments would try to keep any potential combatants from entering the compound. After a while the planning got redundant. The scenario on the ground would likely blow all the plans to hell, so they agreed to keep their flow patterns flexible with an emphasis on section isolation and containment. They figured they'd settle the rest out on the objective. Then all the teams split up and went their separate ways. Hagan got up and wiped stray flecks of dip off his pants after packing his lip.

"Well. This'll be an interesting night. I'm gonna go take a shit."

"Poetic," Cooke said.

Hagan looked at him and smiled. "Cooke. I love you." Then he paused. "But, and this is a big but—Donna's wife's ass big butt—should you get your nuts shot off tonight . . ." Then he paused and took a bow. "I think the world would be a more peaceful, happier place."

He winked at Shaw and Massey, and his voice carried him outside.

"That's my security plan," Hagan said. "Neuter Cooke, increase the peace."

"Low, Hog," Dalonna yelled after him. "Mirna's ass is sanctified."

The night stretched through endless cups of dip spit and the war room got noxious with all the gun oil and farting thrown into the air. Nicotine highs peaked and adrenaline burnt off after the hours passed. The men were bored and falling asleep. They'd passed 0200 hours, and bets were getting put down whether they'd even roll that night. Shaw put down money that they would, but was hoping they wouldn't. He reconsidered his bet after sleep crystals started stabbing the pockets and corners of his eyelids. Cooke was lying against his ruck and looked at his watch at 0245 hours and then again at 0330. Dalonna was asleep and Massey seemed to be as well. Hagan was pounding diet pills to stay awake, buzzing pretty hard. He'd yell every few minutes.

"Come on, 1. Beep, you beeper-bitch bastard!"

Then it did and the room came alive.

The operators turned into a sleep-strained mass of swearing and flailing arms and legs. Shaw jumped to his feet and knocked over a cup of spit. The thick spit and dipped tobacco got all over Dalonna's legs.

"Brutal," Dalonna said, wiping off his pants with the backs of his hands. "Nothing worse could happen to me."

Shaw laughed, apologized, and said he hoped that was true. He draped his kit over his head and snapped it in. Checked his watch. It was 0437 hours.

"Damn right," Hagan said. "How much did I win?"

"Twenty-three dollars," Cooke said. "Big winner."

Cooke had fallen asleep in his kit and helmet, so he just stood up and racked his weapon. He gave Dalonna a towel to wipe off the spit streaking his ass and thighs. Some guys flipped down their NODs right away, while others left them up, but they all racked their weapons and stepped outside. The GMVs were motored up and waiting for them, growling on the gravel and spitting out fumes. The clouds were low and moving fast. The teams settled into the cabins and the driver and gunner keyed into the comms, asked the teams if they were good to go. They said they were.

"All right," the driver said. "Closing the coffin."

The gears of the doors whined and clicked, then hissed on the frame and sealed shut. Everything went black. A voice yelled out in the dark.

"The sun will be up."

The GMVs surged forward and chewed up the roads. Shaw and his team split up with Mike's, so two carriers held half of both teams. If one carrier got separated or neutralized, members of either team would still be able to hit their part of the objective. Mike and Bear sat with Shaw, Dalonna, and Barnes. Hagan and Cooke were in another carrier with Massey and Slausen and the newbies in Mike's team. Shaw cracked his knuckles over and over again until they wouldn't pop anymore and he felt pain in the joints. Every set of legs bounced as if the GMVs were driving over rough ground even though the wheels rolled on smooth highways. The men kept checking their watches and shaking their heads.

The GMVs were armor-plated beasts, half the size of a school bus, with tires taller than a man and bomb rails lining the sides. Everything about them was loud and large. The .50-calibers mounted on the roofs saluted the sky, their thumb-sized rounds waiting to breathe. The operators sat in the cabin with sections of collapsible ladders at their feet, disconnected and ready to wear on their backs. The snipers would post up on ladders inside the wall and man the perimeters after the assault teams had climbed and entered the compound. Shaw sat next to Dalonna and Bear. Barnes sat on the other side with Mike. Bear was grinning, his hands dancing up and down the stock of his rifle. He was blowing bubbles with his gum.

"Careful or you'll get dirt in that bubble," Dalonna said.

Bear looked at him. His eyes were milk white in the dark. "Donna, I've had dirt in my mouth for the last decade." He blew another bubble. "I like the dirt."

Dalonna and Shaw laughed.

"When does the sun rise?" Barnes asked.

"Soon," Mike said. He chewed a granola bar slowly and cracked his neck. "We'll be out in the light unless we turn back."

After a while the gunner opened the top hatch and fresh air flooded into the GMV from outside. A soft light lit the cabin. With the hatch open it was easier to figure out where they were, and the traffic and city noises gave way to silence soon enough. They'd cleared the limits of one city and were racing toward another. The vibration from the wheels marked their speed and progress—slowing down meant less bouncing but larger bumps, while speeding up was more bouncing but smaller bumps. Shaw felt the changes in speed in his ass and face. Air started moving around inside the cabin and he thought he could smell some plant life. Then someone took out some dip and he could only smell Copenhagen. They bounced along and Shaw turned to Dalonna.

"How're the little lady and the littler ones?"

Shaw spoke soft, didn't want to put Dalonna in a tough spot. If things with Mirna were rocky and he didn't want the whole cabin knowing about it, Shaw would feel like a dick.

"You know," Dalonna said. "Not bad, not great."

Dalonna looked at his wrist and smiled. His girls had made him a pink bracelet and he had it wrapped around his watch.

Bear leaned in.

"I hear you got some sausage cooking in that oven finally, Donna."

Dalonna smiled. "You bet. And finally is right. Now I'm done. Cut my tubes."

"Congratulations," Mike said. "Little dudes are the best. I love my girls, but the little guys are just fearless. It's awesome to watch."

"Good for you, Donna," Bear said. "Congratulations."

He offered his gum and Dalonna and Shaw shook their heads. Barnes spoke up and said he'd take a few. Bear handed him a couple pieces and Barnes unwrapped them all at once and chewed them all together. Then he took out a pouch of his tobacco, grabbed the gum out of his mouth, and wrapped the gum around the plug.

"Barnes," Bear said. "You're fucking up my gum."

Barnes smiled and shook his head.

"Nah, just making it work a little differently than it's used to."

Mike laughed quietly and shook his head and soon the only noise was the rumbling of the engines, the slides of the mounted

.50-caliber scanning the road ahead. The moon's pale light came softly through the open hatch, casting shadows and hard angles on the men's faces. Their faces appeared sharp and blackened. They looked like ghosts in the dark.

All the men were fidgeting. Shaw ran his gloves together. They used to be a deep glossy black but were bleached ashen by all the sun and foreign earth over the years. They fit better than any pair of socks he ever owned or ever would and formed so well to the grooves and contours of his hands he could see his own ribbed veins and enlarged tendons in the fabric. Notches in the fingers of the gloves allowed for airflow and a hard plastic ridgeline spanned the length of the knuckles. The ridgeline was good for bracing against concrete and keeping the knuckles fresh, although some guys just liked it because it delivered a hell of a blow to anyone who needed a little push along.

After a while *Five mikes out* came over the comms and elbows flared out and gloved hands fingered straps, tightening buckles and fasteners. Velcro straps loosened and then sealed shut, spreading dust into the air. Shaw refastened his gloves, cracked his knuckles, and made sure he had a round in the chamber and fingered the safety. He turned on his NODs and the world turned green. Then he turned them off. A mag clicked into its well and Mike and Barnes checked their comms. Bear, Dalonna, and Shaw did the same on their side.

"Good to go?" Shaw asked.

Everyone gave a thumbs-up.

Mike looked around, holding onto the straps of his kit with his hands.

"The Cowboys play tonight."

"The Cowboys suck," Bear said. "And you're from Alaska. Why the hell do you care? Who're they playing, anyway?"

"Alaska isn't exactly a desirable sports market, Bear, and we don't suck. We're focusing on the future. And I don't know. The Falcons, maybe? Cardinals? Some shit poultry."

The whole cabin laughed.

"It's Dali's birthday," Dalonna said softly, looking at the floor. He smiled. "She's three today."

"Happy Birthday," Shaw said. He clapped Dalonna on the knee with his gloved hands.

Mike smiled and congratulated him and then his face hardened a little. Bear slapped Dalonna on the back.

"Three," Barnes said, nodding from across the aisle. "Three's a good age." He put his hands on his kneepads and smiled at Dalonna. "Wish I was three again. Happy Birthday, Little Donna."

Mike smiled and nodded along with the bumps in the road. He looked at his watch.

"Sun's up."

Then it started to rain, the large drops splashing loud and hard against the metal sides of the carrier. It seemed every face in the cabin peered down at their watches at the same time and then the gunner on the .50 started shifting sides on the mount in jerks, practically throwing himself from wall to wall. He came over the comms, talking fast.

"Engaging targets on the roofs."

Shaw recognized the rain as incoming rounds and the .50-caliber on the roof started spitting its thumb-sized rounds, *woomf, woomf, woomf,* out into the streets. The men racked their weapons and tightened their helmets and kits.

"Well, this is nice," Barnes said. "The whole city'll be out."

Dalonna made the sign of the cross with his fingers and Shaw bit his lips until blood came thick, tasting like rust. Bear had his eyes closed, the back of his head resting against the side of the carrier. He looked asleep.

The carriers slammed to a halt and the door dropped to the ground.

Shaw jumped off the ramp first, into a cloud of dirt and exhaust and a city on fire in the sun.

Shaw brought his sight up to engage targets before his boots hit the dirt. He saw Hagan and Cooke run out from their carrier just a couple meters ahead, then two large women came into view dressed in long black chadors. Their faces were visible, so Shaw looked for the husbands. He saw only the women herd some kids back inside, so he ran through all the dust thrown up in the air by the GMVs. He threw his weight against a wall that looked like it couldn't hold him, and it didn't. Brick shifted at the base of his back and then dust and pieces of the wall landed on his shoulders.

AKs cracked their 7.62, and the .50s from the carriers answered with their *woomf, woomf, woomf,* while 5.56 started spitting around the alleys and streets as the teams hit the ground. Cooke aimed at a blind spot Shaw couldn't see—behind the house the women had just herded the kids into—and squeezed off a few rounds. The casings ejected and glittered in the sunlight and then settled in the dirt. Cooke and Hagan and Dalonna ran across the road with ladders on their shoulders, weapons up and scanning with one hand. They settled into the wall behind Shaw.

The air snapped, pinged, and buzzed around them. The GMVs raised their doors, stayed put, and the .50s continued sending rounds into the buildings, storefronts, and rooftops. The men moved toward the compound, and targets that popped up on roofs were dropped down onto the street. There wasn't a lot of screaming, but the fire was total, the roar of weapons deafening. Rounds came from all over and were sent out the same. Shaw led the two teams hugging the wall down its length and turned when it ended in front of a storefront with yellow fruits and vegetables spread out on a ledge. A gangly male wearing a white T-shirt, dark green pants, and flip-flops was leaning out of a doorway in front of the stand, his back turned. He sprayed rounds down the street and his back rippled with the AK's kick. When Shaw raised his sight and dropped him, his head snapped and his long black hair caught on the wind. He twirled and face-planted, settling between the doorway and the street. They ran past him and Shaw heard a *pop, pop* as Hagan put two in him to make sure he was down. The air smelled of burning metal and tires. Calls of fire came in so fast they were jamming the airwaves. The comms were useless.

Fire to the east fifty meters, on the rooftops.

Storefront ahead one hundred meters.

Alleys.

On the roof.

South one hundred.

West seventy-five.

North fifteen meters.

East one hundred fifty.

Shaw shot a man wearing sunglasses and propping a rifle on a third-story windowsill, and the man fell back inside the room.

Then a woman stuck the muzzle out the same window and he put her down, too. She was wearing a hijab with her face exposed and had strands of black hair cobwebbed over her face from the wind. He could've sworn he saw her eyes light up as the rounds hit her chest. He turned a corner and saw the compound on the next block, the walls the color of sand and smoke. Rounds chipped away at the concrete, sending puffs of rock and dust into the air. Black smoke from tire fires rose on the sides of the compound and started blotting out the sun. Apaches had already been called in over the comms and were speeding to the area.

Hagan and Dalonna sprinted across the street ahead of the rest and threw the ladders at the wall. They climbed the rungs and hopped into the compound without pause. The rest of the teams followed suit and dragged the ladders over the walls and inside. Barnes and Bear immediately climbed the rungs and engaged targets. Brass from their fire started raining on the concrete inside the compound. Shaw breathed heavily, scanning the surrounding rooftops and the walkway in front of him that led to the doors and stairwells of the compound. His sight was shaking, bobbing up and down with each rapid breath, so he tried to steady himself. He held a couple breaths and let them go slow.

"Hog and Mass. First floor with me," he said.

Cooke and Dalonna ran up an exposed stairwell bisecting the first floor to the second level. They didn't need to be told. Rounds tore through the compound and over the walls, embedding into the walkway that led to the rooms and against the sides of the first level. Shaw heard shots coming above them. *Pop, pop, pop, pop, pop, pop.* Then the rounds landing in front of them stopped. He and Hagan started down the walk slowly, Massey watching the surrounding rooftops and following behind them. They crept over chips in the walk and spent casings. Hagan and Shaw tac-lighted the rooms and found empty carpets spread out on the floors and sham cloths hung for doorways that led to more carpeted empty rooms. There were bookshelves lined with scattered paperbacks and knickknacks, and a couple pairs of shoes but nothing else. Massey fired at targets outside the compound from the doorways and Hagan and Shaw cleared the rooms and made their way to the next one. It sounded like the world was burning itself down.

The sky was a beautiful blue and the air swarmed with helicopters, lead, and smoke. The Apaches leaked streams of brass shells onto the streets below. Massey changed a mag and Hagan and Shaw cleared another empty room. Massey brought his rifle up and Shaw saw a man in a loose red T-shirt across the street on a third-floor rooftop shoulder a weapon, then fall back as rounds tore through his front. The casings from Massey's rifle hit him in the face and Shaw brushed the burning metal away from his collar, the skin already blistering.

Shaw pressed on to the last room in their sector and walked into a windowless space, dark except for the light coming through the open door. His tac light lit up a dozen pale faces huddled into a corner. Boys and girls of knee to hip height with snot and tears crusted on their faces stood bunched together behind a single woman dressed head to toe in black. She had her arms flung out to her sides. She was short but cast a wide arc. He lit up her face and she squinted in the light. Full, wrinkled cheeks and thick, dark brows. A wide nose and deep black eyes.

"Erfa yadayk," Shaw said. *"Dasthaa baalaa."*

He tried to say it softly, but she winced with each word. He saw her arms trembling and could smell her breakfast on her breath. Fruit and some type of cornmeal. Her chador twitched and her breast heaved.

"It's okay," Shaw whispered. "Show me your hands."

Shaw's throat was dry and thick. It felt like he'd swallowed a whole apple. The kids were whimpering and staring out from behind her. Some of the kids had their hands raised and others had them cupped around their ears. The noise had been deafening.

Shaw dropped the light from her face a little.

"Erfa yadayk," he repeated. *"Dasthaa baalaa."*

Her arms trembled, but she raised them in the air.

"Good," Shaw said.

Shaw let his sling hold the weight of his rifle. He brought his wrists together, gestured toward her. She mirrored him, held her hands toward him.

"Hog. Cuff her. But light and in the front."

Hagan stepped in front of him and placed the flex-cuffs around her wrists. An RPG impacted the wall somewhere outside and large blocks of concrete peppered the walk inside the compound. Gravel scattered into the room from the open doorway. The kids recoiled with the blast and the woman started to cry. Hagan patted her on the shoulder and then ran the backs of his hands along her body. She avoided his touch and Shaw shook his head.

"She's good, then," Hagan said.

"Okay," Shaw said. "Okay."

They were all quiet for a while then, standing in the room together while the rest of the world erupted behind them. Shaw heard sniffles from a few of the kids, and the woman's breathing had slowed and then softened. The comms were crackling and voices were rushed and shouting, but it was all white noise, faded voices from far away. The kids studied the operators' beards and the bearded men studied their hairless faces. The woman never moved her hands from her front. She stood rigid and upright and stopped crying after a while. Shaw felt bad about having to cuff her. He'd been at it long enough to recognize the hate in her eyes. They would never win over people with eyes like that.

A small girl placed her tiny hand on the woman's side, and the smooth, pale skin on the black cloth stood out harsh in the beam of Shaw's tac light. The hand looked skeletal, ghostly. Shaw radioed in that they had their sector secured, and Cooke and Dalonna came down to the first level and gathered outside the room with Massey. The three of them kneeled on the walkway and scanned the perimeter, popping off single shots at targets Shaw couldn't see. He heard a call for exfil over the comms even as the calls for fire kept coming through. Birds swooped over the compound and their miniguns buzzed like chainsaws and the shells rained down on the streets and dwellings and *plink*ed, *plink*ed, *plink*ed on the streets and rubble below. Rockets *whoosh*ed and hissed and shrieked, crashing into walls and storefronts. Then there was a loud crash and the outer wall caved in on itself where the rear of a GMV plowed through the crumbled stone. The hatch dropped right in front of the room with all the kids.

Massey, Cooke, and Dalonna ran in and Hagan and Shaw turned away from the kids.

"Hog," Shaw said. "Cut her loose."

Hagan let his rifle hang on his sling. He took out a knife longer than his hand from his kit and walked to the woman. She raised her chin. Some of the kids tried to hide behind her. Hagan brought the knife to the cuff and sliced it. Then he sheathed the knife, patted the woman on the shoulder, waved to the kids, and ran past Shaw. He ran into the carrier and sat down. Shaw looked at the kids and the woman and held his hand up in the doorway. The woman stared back at him and then turned her back, covering the kids with the cloth of her chador. Shaw saw their little faces start to press through the fabric of her black cloth and then he ran over shells, chipped concrete, and wall rubble and jumped into the carrier. The door sealed shut behind him and the GMV lurched forward and accelerated up the streets.

They bounced over the wreckage and through the chattering gunfire. The gunner opened the hatch in the roof. Sunlight and stale air came through. A loud blast filled the streets as an IED blew nearby and pieces of earth and the blast fluttered into the carrier like snow. Then the gunfire faded away as if the whole world had run out of ammunition at the same time. The only sound was the GMV's engine and the shift of its gears. Shaw took off his helmet and set it at his feet. Everyone looked around the cabin, eyes wide. Flecks of the IED blast peppered the men's boots.

"What the hell was that?" Hagan said. He shook his head, looked at his boots, and spat on the floor.

"Seven," Dalonna said. "I got seven."

Cooke put a big chaw in his cheek and rubbed his pants. "Yeah, that didn't go over right, did it?"

Shaw let out a deep breath and set his head against the wall of the carrier. His hair was wet with sweat and he closed his eyes. He wondered what their CO was doing then and how many calls were getting made. Secure lines must've been firing up the world over and reporters would be speeding to the scene. He opened his eyes and took off his gloves and dropped them at his feet. He ran his hands over his face, through his beard.

"Mass," Hagan said. "Did we take any hits?"

Massey shook his head. "I didn't hear of any over the comms."

"Christ," Hagan said. "We must've dropped hundreds. That was totally fucked. Am I right? What the hell was that all about?"

"Got caught in the daylight," Cooke said. He shrugged and swallowed his spit. "News crews will be in soon."

It took hours to get back to the FOB, the carriers bouncing along and getting stuck in traffic jams in the bazaars. Shaw watched the sun shining bright through the hatch and imagined the street vendors swarming around the carriers, hawking their fruits and clothes. Making their living around those who'd left so many dead. He thought of those kids and the woman with the flex-cuffs on her wrists.

They started nodding off in ones and twos. Then Hagan's voice broke through the quiet.

"Hey. Did we even get any of the Pikes?"

Shaw looked at him and opened his hands. He let them rest on his thighs and shrugged. Everyone else was asleep.

"What a cluster," Hagan said.

Shaw watched him close his eyes and unbuckle his helmet, rest his head against the carrier. Hagan breathed deep and raised his voice.

"We're gods."

4

The head of al-Ayeelaa sat in his upstairs bedroom, with the window open, puffing on an American cigarette. He'd seen footage of the raid in his city, in the very compound he owned, on the TV from his house nearly an hour away. Had he looked out the right window at the right time, he might have been able to see the smoke rising into the sky. He rubbed the bridge of his nose between his fingers. The smoke of his cigarette trailed out the window, reaching toward the morning sun.

"Should we be worried?" his wife had asked him earlier.

Images of explosions and screaming masses flashed on the TV behind her. He knew many of the faces on the TV. She had her hands on her hips.

"No," he said. "We shouldn't."

"You're sure."

"Yes."

"You're positive."

"Yes."

"Okay."

She walked out of the room and tried herding her three children outside to play on the tire swing in the front yard. He had left the TV and climbed the stairs, sat on the edge of his bed.

He smoked only upstairs and had chosen Marlboros exclusively for the last decade, no matter how hard it was to get them. When he'd fought the Russians he smoked only Sobranies. He sat with his legs crossed, a wrist balanced elegantly over his knee. He looked at the leather bracelet on his wrist. A hunk of marble mountainside blasted by a Soviet rocket that had literally landed in his lap was fashioned between the dark leather straps. Pieces of the rock had lodged in his legs when the rocket hit, nearly killing him. He'd packed the rock in his sack and steeled his men and they held out and the Spetsnaz retreated. The man had called it a victory, though he probably knew it just hadn't been a defeat. He had bracelets made up from the hunk of rock for his nephews and nieces, and their eyes lit up when they saw the flecks of ruby in the smoky rock. It made him smile. One of the nephews he'd given a bracelet to—his favorite and the only one who'd fought with him—was dead and another was missing. He vowed to care for the dead nephew's wife, so he had her remarried to one of his top lieutenants. He hadn't made it to the family pass yet to speak with his brother and formally grieve. Make peace.

The morning's fight in his compound would complicate things. He and his wife had talked about what she would do if he was ever taken by the Americans. There would be one call from the phone buried in plastic in their compost pile out back. The family would wait, he hoped he'd return, and then they would have to go into hiding. They hadn't had to yet, but he knew that probably wouldn't last.

Most of the other cell leaders were arrogant and dead, or soon to be. They made videos claiming responsibility for attacks, and doing so restricted their movements. Meanwhile, he had been able to walk around, live a normal life with his family. His oldest daughter was even in the West, of all places, studying at university. It was his suggestion, helped with appearances.

Then the family phone rang and he heard his wife's voice. She called him downstairs. He closed his eyes, took a deep breath, and rose off the bed. He turned and smoothed the bedspread with his hands, his cigarette stuck to his lips. It was his wife's side of the bed. He stood upright, left the window open. His children's rooms weren't far down the hall. He wet his fingertips and squeezed the lit tip, then he left the cigarette on the windowsill.

He walked downstairs, picked up the phone. A man's voice. Speaking fast. He cut him off.

"You called my home. Still, you called my home. Did they find anything? No. You're sure. What happened to the computers? And everything was moved. You're sure. Slow down. It's okay. No, I'm not mad at you. It was a matter of time. Yes, the mountains. I don't know. Could be tonight, could be weeks. Years. No. I'm not mad. Yes. I'd leave right away. Yes, we'll have to leave soon. This is your cell? How many cards do you have? Get rid of them. Yes, all but the one. Yes, theirs, too. Yes. All of them. No throw them away, you should have long ago. Good-bye. See you."

The call took only a few minutes, the man's voice on the other end rushed and breathless. It was the last time the two would speak and the man who received the call likely knew it, for he would put everything in motion. The ambush would buy him and his family time, but at the expense of the lives of others. Those decisions had been made so many times now that he probably didn't even think twice as he said good-bye to the man who would soon be dead.

His two boys were at his side when he put the receiver back in the cradle. He hadn't seen them enter from the yard. The call was distracting. They tugged on his pants with their little hands. His shirt. They pointed outside to the yard and he looked through the living room window. His wife stood at the tire swing with her arms held out, palms turned up. She shrugged and laughed. She couldn't push as high.

"Okay," he said. "Grab your sister. She likes to fly, too."

The boys ran off, babbling excitedly. They screamed for their sister to come out of her room while the sound of an insect buzzing came from the kitchen. He walked over, craned his neck over the kitchen sink, and looked out the window. Helicopters flew overhead lazily in the sun. They looked like the pair his men had put down just a month or two before.

5

When the operators got back to the FOB, news of the raid was already streaming through the international news outlets. Video of the streets and bodies all torn to hell flooded the different broadcasts. Crowds were rioting and burning American flags, holding the Koran up and spitting in reporters' microphones. The teams gathered in the TOC for the AAR and watched the news feeds, looking at the streets they'd been on hours before through the eyes of Al Jazeera, the BBC, and CNN. A reporter held up a teddy bear and talked about possible civilian casualties. One of the techs watching the raid in the TOC pointed at the bear. "Ten bucks they placed that in the street after we left," he said. "I've seen it before. And civvies don't tote weapons. What the hell, CNN?"

During the AAR, guys watching the raid on monitors back in the TOC told the teams people were running toward the compound like water rushing into a sewer. People were hopping rooftops and sprinting from storefronts and alleyways carrying AKs and RPGs, anything that threw fire. People came forward in waves and the men dropped them all as long as they carried weapons. Men or women, it didn't matter. Their CO looked gaunt and exhausted. He held a cup of coffee in his hand during the meeting and it shook gently during the whole brief. He looked like he hadn't heard a single word the teams had said. He kept rubbing his forehead, running his hands through his hair, and nodding along even after they'd stopped talking.

The whole squadron was put off the green for a week so command could sift through the blowback and decide how much to release to the public. The phones would be locked down and the men's families would see all the news broadcasts and think about the calls that weren't coming, and the smart ones would connect the dots. The two governments would posture with each other and make demands and accept political apologies in public, exchange partial truths and come to commonsense understandings in private.

While they were off the green, the men lifted and ate and shot at the range. They read books and watched feeds from other countries and targets. The news broadcasted reports on the raid for days and the men pointed out discrepancies during meals and between sets. Some tallies had hundreds of deaths while others had them as low as forty-six. After the AAR, they came up with eighty-three. But the birds couldn't verify the kills like the men could. Regardless of the reports, a lot of people weren't breathing anymore. The guys felt confident they didn't drop anyone who didn't have a weapon and Shaw knew he didn't, but the men still didn't paint the mission a success. They didn't find a single device, let alone a single FAM. The family men in the squadrons took the news reports calling them murderers of children especially hard. They ran until they puked and wore their hats down low on their faces.

Shaw dreamt for a few nights about the woman he and Hagan flex-cuffed, and decided he didn't need the sleep bad enough. He packed his ruck and walked around during the day and night, logging more than a hundred miles during the week. He would watch the clouds pass and blot out the sky and let the wind bat his beard. In one of the dreams Hagan used the knife to slit the woman's throat when she lifted her chin. It was a bloody mess. In another, her face was covered by her chador and then she ripped it off and it was Shaw's grandma. She smiled at him with bloody teeth.

He and Massey had a catch every day. They talked about the raid and others that had passed and about Penelope. The leather struck leather for hours in the sun. It felt good. Like home and childhood. One afternoon Shaw was wearing one of Massey's Cardinals hats for him again and Massey told him not to mess with the brim.

"You told me you wanted me to break it in."

"Break it in, yeah. Not fuck it up."

Shaw gave the brim a tug and Massey winced.

"How're you a Cardinals fan and a Bears fan?" Shaw asked.

"What do you mean?"

"Well. You're from Illinois. So you got the Bears, I'll give you that. But what about the Cardinals. Why not the Cubs or the Sox?"

"We're closer to Saint Louis than Chicago."

"Then why aren't you a Rams fan?"

"The Rams were in L.A. when I grew up," Massey said. "Plus, I don't like the AL and I'm not a martyr, so being a Cubs fan is a definite no-go."

"Got it."

"You giving me shit about my teams? You've got the Vikings and the Twins. Don't get me started on hockey. You couldn't even hold on to your damn team. Or basketball. You don't want me to get started on basketball."

"We've got rivers and lakes and Mother Earth. You can keep the Cards and the Bears."

Massey laughed.

They were really hitting the leather well. The sun was starting to dip and Shaw felt good. He went into his chest pocket, took out the envelope holding his grandma's necklace.

"Do you think Penelope would like this?"

He held it up by its silver chain. It looked beautiful in the light. Every shade of blue was crisp and clear, the lines of white thin and pure like silk or diamond threads. The sun cast its blue mass in the dirt. It even made the dirt look nice.

"That was your grandma's."

Massey wasn't asking. Every man in the squadron had probably seen Shaw's grandma wearing it in the picture taped to the locker. She was beautiful for her age and the necklace hinted at royalty. Guys passing by might have thought Shaw was related to some foreign queen or duchess.

Shaw nodded.

"Why would you want to give it away?"

"Not so much wanting to give it away as hoping it would get better use than sitting inside one of my pockets," Shaw said. "My kit'll crush it."

"Penelope would love it. You're sure?"

Shaw nodded. He was. "Just give it to her in person. I want to hear about how excited she is. And I don't trust the damn mail."

"You've been wearing it under your kit?"

Shaw nodded.

"In the envelope?"

Shaw nodded. He walked over to Massey, put the necklace in

the envelope, and handed it to him. Massey held the envelope up in his hand.

"Must've brought you some luck," Massey said. "That blast should've killed you and Donna. And I won't put it in the mail. Maybe it'll bring me some luck, too." He put the envelope in his cargo pocket and closed the flap.

They threw the ball over the dirt for hours, stopped talking for a while. The only sound the ball striking mitts and the birds that flew overhead. Then their arms got sore and they forgot about it in time. Shaw hadn't had a catch that long in his whole life. He felt weightless. Then Massey spoke.

"You think we're killing more than we're making?"

"What? Who?"

"Terrorists. Al-Ayeelaa. Bomb makers. HVTs. Resident dickheads. Whoever."

Shaw caught the ball and ran his fingers over the stained off-white leather. "I hope so. We're killing a lot."

Massey nodded to himself. "I think I'm glad I'm getting out. The war's changing."

"Changing how?"

"Drones. Kid suicide bombers. Al-Ayeelaa. No one wants to shoot it out anymore. We're barely going after key guys anymore because we already killed them. UBL. Zarqawi. Saddam and his sons. No one even knows the structure of the damn cell. Nothing but wannabe dons and kid lieutenants left and we're wasting them before they get big."

"You want to let them get big? You don't have to be big to blow people apart."

Massey nodded for a while and then threw the ball back. "I got six of them the other day, Shaw. How many of them were innocent? We got what, eighty-three?"

It had gotten cold out. They could see their breaths rising in front of them.

"Angles and opportunities, Mass. And you didn't hit anyone that wasn't trying to hit you. Did you see anyone get hit without a weapon?"

Massey spat on the ground and caught the ball. He shook his head. Then he was quiet for a while. The ball smacked the leather for a few more throws, neither one of them saying much of anything. "But that was a lot of people. We didn't get any of the Pikes. They weren't even there. No computers. No phones. Nothing."

"Yeah, they must've ducked out after popping hot," Shaw said.

Massey looked at the sky and shrugged. "Or they were never there."

The clouds were moving fast and disappearing over the mountains, tiny teeth of the earth in the distance. Massey fired the ball. It hit the meat of Shaw's palm, stung hard.

"You ever feel like a murderer?"

Shaw dropped his glove to his thigh. "That's a hell of a question, Mass."

Massey shrugged.

Shaw thought about it and rifled the ball back at him. He tried to make it hurt. Massey didn't let on, but Shaw thought it marked his palm pretty good.

"Probably not. Maybe. No. No. We kill people, but that doesn't mean they were murdered. You hold a weapon, you can only be killed. Not murdered."

Massey let his hands fall to his sides. "That boy in the pass wasn't holding shit. And that little girl in the poppy fields? Whenever I see Penelope I see that little girl. Smell those damn poppies. Hell, I can't hold Penelope's hand without feeling the hand of that little girl. I'm fucked if I ever have a daughter."

Shaw thought of their last deployment, the night their team hit a river hamlet in a field of white and pink poppies and three squirters fled the objective. Two men had weapons and a woman looked to be strapped with a device, so the team took them all out. Shaw walked up to the bodies with Hagan, Cooke, Massey, and Dalonna, and they began checking the dead. Then there was an animal shriek, a high squeal coming from the dirt that sounded like a fawn Shaw had hit with his grandpa's truck when he was learning to drive—the fawn's legs had gotten all wrapped up in the Ford's axle like a barber pole. Shaw rolled over the dead woman and there was a little girl lying trapped beneath her. The woman had been carrying the little girl like a backpack. The girl was wailing and pulling at the dead woman's black hair and Massey freed her from the corpse and walked her back to the house while the team finished searching the bodies. They found out the woman was the girl's mother and one of the dead HVTs the father, so they had orphaned her. Shaw watched the little girl standing at kneepad height, holding Massey's hand while he walked her away from her parents. She had leaves and little poppy petals in her tangled black hair and she kept looking back at her mom and dad lying dead at Shaw's feet. In Shaw's dreams, her cries had turned to laughter.

Shaw had a big dip in and it was getting stale, not settling right. His stomach started fighting back. He spat it out and ran his tongue over the stray flecks, gathered them together and started spitting them out in bursts. He shook his head.

"I hope he was a lookout, maybe for those two guys Mike put down the night before. If that's the case, then it was operational security and just part of the knife."

"And if he wasn't a lookout?" Massey asked.

"Then yeah, I think we could've murdered him. But I gave the call and it's on me, then. And that girl—" He shook his head. He saw her eyes and her face with the poppy petals in her hair. Always. He saw Massey holding her hand and walking her back to her home while he searched the mother and father. Always would. "She was a mistake. We shouldn't have killed her mom."

Massey caught the ball and took off his glove and rubbed the ball between his hands. "A mistake."

"Yeah. A mistake. A bad one."

Massey nodded to himself and tossed the ball back. "Hell of a mistake. She doesn't have parents anymore." He rested his glove under his armpit and rubbed his hands together again. "My hands are sore. And I think we murdered her."

"We didn't do anything. I gave the damn order and Hagan took the shot. It's on me. And if it happened once or twice it doesn't mean it's a habit or an identity. Who we are."

Massey smiled at him and nodded. He held his glove out like a serving platter. "I'm worn out, I guess. Over the war. And one of us would've taken that shot with or without you saying so. You're a good shit, Dutch," he said. "Not sleeping for shit, though, huh?"

"You watching me sleep?"

Massey laughed. "Nah, I'm not that creepy. Eyes and ears, you know?" He walked to Shaw and slapped him on the back. "Part of the job."

Shaw spat and rubbed his beard. Then he took off his hat and rubbed his eyes.

"There's no shame in it, Dutch. Hell, we all sleep like crap."

Everyone was losing it being off the green. The teams walked around the compound loaded up with hundreds of pounds of gear and shot on the range until trigger fingers blistered over and popped. If the days were theirs to do as they pleased, they spent the nights together watching feeds from other raids as if it were required. Hagan decided it was okay to start whacking off in the tent, so he just put a blanket over himself and pretended no one else was there, grabbed a *Playboy* or a *Hustler* and went to town on himself. Dalonna told him he was disgusting and Hagan just called him a prude and started asking for pictures of Mirna before he propped up his whack tent. Dalonna picked his battles, though. He didn't split Hagan's lip or mash up his guts. He waited.

Then the last night they were off the green he got Massey, Cooke, and Shaw to leave the tent when Hagan said he was too tired to shoot, ruck, or lift. Dalonna told the three of them to wait outside the tent and then he ran off to the other tents and rounded up the other teams. Somehow nearly twenty guys crept into the tent without Hagan hearing them. Sure enough, Hagan was huddled under a blanket, his hairy white ass sticking out bare and naked in a gap of the cloth. The blanket was rocking back and forth and a dim bulb of light was visible through the blanket. The men could hear the crinkle of magazine pages being turned. Dalonna slapped Hagan's bare ass and Hagan let out a high yip and they all grabbed ahold of his arms and legs. They carried him out into the night screaming and ass naked, his hard-on slapping his thighs and belly. Then they taped him to the railing of one of the shitters and his hard-on drooped in the cold air like a limp flag on a dead wind.

Dalonna called their CO and told him Hagan wanted to speak with him, said he didn't look right. It was Shaw's idea. He was sure every CO worried about their guys and suicides, so they hid behind the shitters. They watched their CO come stomping out of the TOC, his long hair blowing behind him on the wind. He walked with a purpose, quick steps and shoulders tight. Then he saw Hagan and his shoulders dropped, his feet started slipping out from beneath him. He was laughing so hard he had to sit in the dirt. He pulled out a camera from one of his pockets and took a few shots, then hollered for them to "come cut this filthy Hog loose!"

So they did.

And everyone seemed to feel a little better after that.

Stag1 had no known ties to al-Ayeelaa, but Intel flagged him the entire week the city raid was jamming the airwaves and the squadron was off the green. One of the Pike phones monitored after the failed raid popped briefly at his house and then died off. Stag1 lived in a small two-story house with a red clay roof sitting at the end of a long dirt path lined by trees on either side. It looked like a desert home in Nevada or Arizona. There was an iron gate cutting off the front of his house from the road and a large man-made wall spanning the other three sides of the compound. A child could slip through the posts of the gate and the wall could be hopped with a decent effort. It was a perimeter meant to slow down and control visitors, not necessarily avoid them. A lone tree stood inside the walls a few feet back from the gate and there was a tire swing hanging from a branch in the front yard.

Every weekday Stag1 would get picked up by a silver piece-of-shit van and take the same route into town. The drive crossed two major roads and numerous improvised ones. Altogether, about an hour's drive. He made a few stops in the bazaars every now and again to inspect melons and other fruits and run his hands through clothes he never bought. Then his driver would take him on a circuit of thc neighborhoods. He'd stop off at different buildings for different lengths of time on no particular schedule and in no particular order. He visited his mosque regularly during the three prayer periods in which he wasn't at home, but after those he could be anywhere at any time. A local intelligence source on the ground let Intel know the drop-off points were cafés known to attract the occasional warlord and cell leader, but these instances were rare and the shops were mostly full of youths too young to fight and village elders discussing community issues. He visited families in the neighborhood, and everywhere he went people came outside to meet him and welcome him into their homes. None of these families were known to operate in cells, but they were mostly academics and business owners, people of influence. That was interesting.

Besides the cafés and friendly homes, he would stop in on his cousins and their children and then his silver piece-of-shit van would drop him off at home, and if it wasn't the weekend, he'd do the circuit all over again the next day. One time his van stopped on the side of the road and the driver got out to check a tire and Stag1 joined him, put a hand on the driver's back, and then they both got back in the van and carried on. Stag1 had gotten on his knees to check under the car with his driver.

He was from Oman and wore a white turban and a dark sport coat over a white salwar kameez. He'd take off the coat before entering the mosque but leave it on during his errands and neighborhood visits. He was a father of four and hadn't gotten his hands bloody directly since the jihad with the Soviets during the 1980s. He led a band of valley locals from the NWFP then and would shift allegiances with every new paycheck. He was known to be courageous and ruthless, and remembered for always having a cigarette in his mouth. He would switch sides at will but prohibited his followers from doing so. He demanded loyalty from his followers and would cut off the right arm and left leg of defectors so they wouldn't have an intact side for the rest of their lives. He also had a change-of-heart life story primed for the movies. The year the war ended, his wife got pregnant and he decided he didn't want to vie for control of the country. Instead, he decided to test a war friendship that promised a safer life over the border and he began construction work. He was smart and lucky. All the other warlords who stayed in the fray jockeying for political position would be dead within six years.

Without a formal education he learned on the job and developed a good reputation, started making a living off small government projects that turned into larger ones. Then the American war started and, oddly enough, he came back. Left his new life behind and moved his whole family to a war zone. Intel figured a man versed in putting up structures would probably be equally knowledgeable about bringing them down, so they kept tabs on him for years with cooperation from local intelligence networks. It was odd to move a family into a place where a war was pushing most of the peaceful population away.

He was clean by all accounts, never associating with known cell leaders or members, but once Intel noticed he'd been in-country for years and hadn't built anything, they got suspicious and started following the people he met with. Sources on the ground couldn't confirm a specific occupation for him other than some kind of consultant, and then his nephew turned up dead in a mountain ambush with another squadron and Intel decided to start monitoring the dead man's house. Stag1 never visited the place after the death, even though it was a known home of a relative in the neighborhood and grieving was a formality. Not to mention a familial and neighborly responsibility. He continued visiting other families and neighbors as he normally would but avoided the nephew's house. Intel didn't see that as so normal. Add in the Pike phone popping hot right after the raid and Intel decided it might be wise to pick him up and ask him some questions. So the teams got the 4 early on a Saturday night.

They debated whether they should take his van on one of the lesser-traveled roads or in his home, knowing his family would be there. The CO sat in front of them with his elbows on his knees. His hands were clasped and resting on his chin. It looked like he was praying.

"We want to talk to him. The van brings another FAM into the picture and groupthink leads to aggression. We don't want to put holes in him if we can help it."

"And us being in his own home wouldn't lead to aggression?" Cooke said.

"Maybe," the CO said. "Or maybe he's smart and would play the game to keep his family safe." He looked around at the circle of men. Shaw was picking dirt out of his fingernails. "He might not have a lot of fight left in him after the eighties. Plus he's smart enough to still be alive. Maybe he's moved past the gangster phase and embraced the provider role—likes being a daddy. We're just going to talk with him."

"I don't know," Cooke said. "Someone comes into my home, I'm fighting. We can scare him out on the road all alone."

Everyone was quiet for a while, shifting their legs over their knees and cracking knuckles and necks. Then Hagan spoke up.

"The last interdiction didn't go too well, Cooke."

They agreed to take Stag1 at home.

The teams erected tape layouts of Stag1's home on the gravel outside the war room and ran tape drills over and over and over again until they knew the layout in their feet and could turn the corners on step counts in their sleep. Intel hired a second-degree source to approach the home and see if she could get inside selling herbal remedies, but the wife didn't bite. The source got to the front door, though, and reported lots of walls and blind corners leading to a stairwell. The teams marked those off on the tape layouts. Along with Stag1 and his wife, there would likely be at least two young boys at waist height—neither at FAM status yet—and a girl of roughly ten years of age. His oldest daughter was in her twenties and off in Europe at university.

They'd head in slow and smooth, hope for a silent breach and push in carefully. Two assault teams would enter the house and they upped their perimeter teams to three to keep as much attention away from the house as possible. The CO told them to expect the 1 at around 2300 hours, so they checked weapons and batteries, topped off water, and then settled in to wait. Dalonna went off to the phones and Cooke said he was going to rub one out. Massey and Hagan and Shaw sat on the concrete roof of the war room.

It was cold out but clear, so they grabbed jackets, winter caps, and gloves and watched the sun set. They rubbed their hands together and blew into their palms and packed their lips full to the brim, got a good juice flowing. The sky was on fire among the full clouds. Vapor trails from fast-movers crisscrossed the sky and oranges and pinks painted the horizon and swallowed all the blue that was left. It was beautiful.

"Sky's pretty," Hagan said. He spat over the lip of the roof. "Too bad the rest of the country is such shit."

Shaw looked at the sky and thought of the palm trees they flew over on the banks of the rivers to the south. The ancient ruins half swallowed by sand and the royal palaces with their deep green marble walkways. The gold-domed blue mosques that caught the sun and winked back into the sky. They seemed to fly over postcards at times.

"It's not shit, Hog," Massey said. "Dumbass cell leaders and pricks just crap all over it and then we come over and piss on it some more and then everyone wonders why it's such a shit country. It's not. You could get some Manhattan contractors out here and they'd get hard-ons looking at all these cliffs. They could blast the holy shit out of these rocks, throw up some stockbroker towers, and then call their cousins over in Aspen. You'd have another Dubai surrounded by world-class ski resorts. Thousand-dollar whores would be running around with their executive pimps for long weekends. This isn't a country. It's a place full of people that wipe their asses with the land for God, oil, or country—whatever the fuck—and wonder why it stinks so bad. The land is beautiful. We're shit." He shook his head. "I'd want to be buried in a country this beautiful."

Hagan stared at Massey, his eyes wide and his mouth open. Dip was falling out of his lip.

Shaw laughed at Hagan and shrugged. "You've offended him, Hog."

"Damn, Mass," Hagan said. "You want to be buried here?"

Massey smiled and shook his head. He threw some pebbles off the roof. "Hell, no. This country is a shithole. I'm speaking out of my ass. Sky's beautiful, though. You're right about that."

Shaw laughed again, and Hagan sat with his eyebrows raised to his hairline. Hagan seemed to sink into the concrete a little bit and he was quiet for a while. They watched the sky fade to black, and when the stars came out he spoke up.

"I guess you're right. It's not all bad. I wouldn't mind bringing my wife here one day." Then he ran his hand through the air. "When all this is over."

Massey and Shaw looked at each other and then back at Hagan. He had a small smile on his lips and cradled his head with one hand, kept the other on top of his stomach, like he was watching a football game back home. Shaw looked at Massey. He was laughing quietly, doing his best to hold it in and not break Hagan's peace.

Shaw smiled. "You got a wife you're keeping from us, Hog?"

"Not yet," Hagan said. He kept his eyes to the sky, away from Shaw and Massey and the war below. "One day, though. Yeah."

Shaw nodded and smiled, and Massey clapped Hagan on the shoulder. Then they watched the stars and satellites trade places and dance around the sky until they got the 1.

They strapped on their kits just after 2300 hours and grabbed their weapons and helmets and walked outside. The heaters of the war room gave way to the hard, cold ground and the sky was clear. Their breaths fogged before them, rose like clouds. Fast-movers screeched above on their bomb runs and the wind bit at the skin exposed beneath Shaw's beard and above his top and kit. His beard was thick and he was glad for it.

"Closing the damn doors," Hagan yelled. "We're sure as shit closing the damn doors."

No one countered him, so they were all probably freezing. They sat in the Black Hawks while the birds spun up, then they clipped in and shut the doors and the birds carried them away. The Black Hawk was the taxicab of the American wars. Larger than a Little Bird but smaller than a Chinook, it was dependable and everywhere. It fought the strong crosswinds and the machinery groaned and whined as they flew on. The operators sat on the floor of the cabin with their legs cramped against the closed doors. They had to get creative to keep their boots out of one another's nuts, but eventually they settled in and waited for their legs and asses to go numb. They did soon enough. Hagan took out a pack of peanut M&M's and they passed them around and tried to find the ones they dropped in the dark. A low green glow from the gunners' NODs lit the cabin and a red light flashed every now and again and Shaw thought of the holidays he had growing up in Minnesota. They were flying high and opened the doors on the *Five mikes out* call. The cold air rushed in and hit hard. Hagan yelled out that he should've brought long underwear.

"Your nuts would freeze to your legs," Cooke yelled. "Stop being a pussy."

They all had a laugh and got some warmth, and hands got busy finding straps and snaps, checking weapons and seals on equipment. Shaw took off his helmet and put on a balaclava and then strapped up again. The other guys followed suit and let their legs dangle in the air. The wind blew Shaw's legs toward the tail of the bird and he could see small mounds of homes and scattered huts pass below them like moguls on a ski hill. Stag1's city was to the east, its lights scattered and twinkling soft on the horizon. It looked like a ski resort during Christmastime. Shaw could make out trees here and there without leaves, and they banked sharp to the north and then the pilots radioed in *Three mikes out*. Shaw put in a big chaw to get some nicotine and warmth flowing and gave one to Cooke. Then he cracked his neck and tried to loosen his shoulders. He looked past his boots and saw aviation fluid frozen to the underside of the bird, in front of the rotor. He thought of Stag1 and how he was probably sleeping in bed all warm next to his wife. Then he thought about how he was freezing and cold, and it made him feel old. He tried to scoot back and get his feet on the lip of the bird. Too much splatter and his bottoms would freeze.

The birds dropped them off three klicks northwest of the compound. They had a ridgeline of small hills leading to mountains at their backs and Stag1's compound to their front. There were open fields, dirt roads, and goat trails on either side of the walk and a stray compound or two in the distance and dark. They started their walk in staggered teams spanning the open fields. Shaw flexed and wiggled his fingers for a few minutes until his hands started to feel warm, then he stopped to keep from sweating. They painted the earth green and there was nothing but runoff from small pockets of snow blown into the air. The ground was mostly frozen over and it crunched under each step, the harvested blades of wheatgrass run down to icy stubs. It felt like walking on gravel or rocks.

Mines were all over fields like this. The teams avoided mounds of earth and stuck to lower elevations in the ground to bypass them. Shaw kept his eyes toward the location of the compound and tried not to think of getting his legs blown into his stomach or having his nuts torn off and splattered all over the frozen stubs and shrubs. Every hop they heard of a guy from another squadron or team who stepped on a mine and lost a leg or, if the mine was big enough, everything. They hadn't heard about any on the hop yet, so they might've been due. Shaw's footfalls felt clumsy and heavy.

"Mound to the left," Cooke said over the comms. He circled it with his laser and radioed back to the perimeter teams to watch it on their approach. It looked like a knee-high mound of animal shit.

The outline of the compound was starting to break through a staggered line of trees on the horizon that would eventually form the natural walls of the dirt path leading right up to the target house. Shaw had stopped thinking about his own nuts getting blown off and had moved on to wondering what kind of a life Hagan would live without his—he'd probably kill himself—when he saw the compound and started thinking of Stag1. He wondered if he was deep in the peaceful sleep of the innocent or wide-awake, moving from room to room throughout his house with his finger on the trigger. Searching for points of entry or ghosts from his past like Shaw imagined himself doing down the line. Intel had watched him for nearly a week and still couldn't get a full picture of the man. He fought in the region in the 1980s against the Soviets, and then he left it all to go into construction just to come back in another decade during another war. He seemed respected in the community and liked, not necessarily feared, but the two weren't far off. He didn't live in a mud hut hidden in the brush or a cave in the mountains but in a decent-sized stone compound set back from a dirt road and flanked by a half-assed perimeter. If he wanted to be in hiding, he didn't seem to know, or care, that he wasn't. None of it made any sense to Shaw.

Panther1 moving into position came over the comms, and then the other perimeter teams radioed in the same. Shaw and his team took a knee a couple hundred meters from the compound and let the perimeter elements settle in on their flanks. It was cold on the ground and the wind blew so hard he had to lean in to it. He painted the rooftop of the compound, ran his laser over its corners and blind spots, while the other guys did the same. The house, built of stone the color of sand, glowed green in the night. Panther1 radioed in that they were set and 2 and 3 followed suit.

Then the assault teams assembled their ladders and Shaw radioed in that they were approaching the wall. Mike's team split off to take the other side of the wall and their footfalls and the bangers and mags shifting on their kits seemed loud, but the wind picking up off the flat fields kept them quiet.

Dalonna put the ladder at the base of the wall, climbed it, and hopped over. Hagan, Cooke, and Massey followed him and then Shaw mounted the rungs last. The wall seemed ancient and was made of sunbaked bricks. It seemed odd and out of place, connected to the modern metal gate—a clash of cultures. Dust flaked and loosed from the foundation where the ladder was set against it, and Shaw rubbed the wall and came away with dust on the fingertips of his gloves. It was soft and grainy. He climbed and jumped into the courtyard and saw a tire swing hanging from the tree and rocking gently on the wind.

The perimeter teams lit up the windows and walls of the house and the assault teams approached the door. Shaw set up closest to the door on the left side and Mike mirrored his movements on the right, his team snaking behind him down the wall. Ohio was on his first mission back after getting shot, and he stood behind Mike, staring at the doorknob. He probably shouldn't have been out yet, but his fingers danced up and down the barrel of his rifle. He seemed eager.

Shaw ran his hands around the door frame, looking for wires and anything out of place. The wood door looked old and felt heavy and cold, but the lock mechanism was brass, shining and looking new. He didn't see or feel anything that made him think the door would blow and take them all out.

"Pick it," he whispered over the comms.

Hagan came to the door and took out his pick kit and got surgical on the lock. His big hands moved gracefully and light. Oddly enough, he was the best pick among them, bear paws and all. He let go of the lock and gave Shaw a thumbs-up. Then he put one hand on the knob and braced another on the door between the mechanism and the door frame. He whispered over the comms, "Breaching." Then he turned the knob and opened the door.

Nothing blew, so they flowed into the house, slow and smooth like honey out of a water glass. Moonlight came through the few windows in the landing and cast barred shadows of the window guards onto the carpets and tabletops. Mike and his team took the first floor and Shaw and his team toed their way up the stairs. A floorboard creaked when Shaw hit the first step and his boot sank a little into the carpeted stairs. He smelled nutmeg and warmth and a recently extinguished fire. He picked his way carefully up the stairs, sticking to the perimeter of the steps so they wouldn't groan. He saw thin cracks and streaks in the bare walls and then hit the landing. Four doorways split off from the hallway, two on either side. He broke off right, into the first doorway, with Hagan on his hip. The door was ajar. He nudged it open with his elbow and Stag1 was sitting on the edge of his bed, fully clothed, shoes on his feet. He had the window cracked and a cigarette in the corner of his mouth, and he watched Hagan and Shaw enter. Smoke trails snaked out the window. The room was small and drafty, and the tobacco smelled stale and harsh. Hagan walked slowly around the other side of the bed and lit up the man's wife and the rest of the room with his laser, checking under the bed and around the small dresser. Then he looked out the window and back at the wife.

Shaw turned on his tac light and lit up Stag1. He sat upright, rigid like a statue. He kept his eyes on Shaw, though away from the light. He was looking at Shaw's kneepads, and his shoulders rose and fell as if he was taking a relieved breath. No one said anything for a while and then he brought his hand up slowly to his mouth, a bracelet visible on his wrist. He grabbed the cigarette and brought it down to his knees. He blew the smoke at Shaw in a long stream and it hit Shaw's pants and rose up into his face. Then he shrugged, nodded, and patted his sleeping wife on the side. He tightened the covers around her and then opened his hands.

"I should stand, no?"

Shaw didn't say anything and neither did Hagan. They nodded. Stag1 stood and offered his wrists. Hagan cuffed his hands in front and then checked his arms and legs, the pockets of his pants.

"Cigarettes and a lighter," Stag1 said.

Hagan took a pack of Marlboros out of his pocket and a black lighter. They walked him out of the room and he didn't resist when Shaw put his hand on Stag1's shoulder to lead him down the stairs.

"My wife," Stag1 said, leaning toward Shaw. "She's a hard sleeper." Then he smiled. "I am not."

Shaw smelled the tobacco strong on his breath and figured he must've been smoking for hours, probably his whole life. They brought him to the landing and he looked past them, toward the children's rooms, then he nodded and walked down the stairs. Shaw expected the stairs to blow beneath them, but they stayed steady below their feet. They walked out of the house and all the teams trickled out of the home and into the fields and they started walking Stag1 to the exfil.

"Did you close my door?" Stag1 asked.

The words rolled out of him slow and proper, like he was reading a translation he didn't trust. Hagan told him they always closed them on their way out and Stag1 laughed and looked up at the sky.

"I've never been on a helicopter."

He raised his eyebrows and looked at Shaw. Then he looked

around at all the teams spread out along the fields walking to the exfil.

"So many of you."

Then it was quiet for a while and Shaw could hear only the ground crunching below their feet. He saw the birds approaching before he could hear them and they took a knee and waited for them to land so they could load up.

"There are mines in these fields," Stag1 said.

He jutted his chin out and looked around the land. His breath sent up a screen of white. The birds dipped their rotors and started to land, whipping up the frozen earth and sending hard pellets of ice and dirt into the air. He smiled at Shaw.

"Boom."

They handed Stag1 over to Intel once they touched down on the tarmac. Shaw was glad for it. Leaving an objective, most of their pickups were either in body bags or pissing on themselves, probably thinking they were going to get thrown out of the birds or shot in the back of the head. But Stag1 just sat cross-legged like royalty next to them. He didn't seem to mind rubbing shoulders with the men who had taken him, even fell asleep and leaned in to Hagan. Hagan nudged him back to the middle and Stag1 woke up and said, "Sorry," real loud. His warm breath flooded the cabin and his stale tobacco breath spread throughout. In the dark cabin he would smile every now and again and Shaw thought his teeth were brighter than the stars, brighter than any he'd ever seen.

Shaw walked back to the war room with Hagan.

"He was talkative," Hagan said.

"Yeah, he was. You think his wife was really asleep?"

Hagan shrugged. They spat on the tarmac and watched Intel walk Stag1 over to a set of huts sheltered by blast walls. "She didn't open her eyes. And her breathing seemed steady under the sheets."

Shaw nodded.

"Dude was waiting for us."

"Seemed like it," Shaw said. "Didn't particularly care for that."

"Me either. Gave me the creeps."

The tarmac died off and their boots hit the gravel.

"Did Dalonna and Cooke find the kids?"

"Yeah," Shaw said. "They were all asleep. The girl in her own bed and the two boys in one together."

"And the last room?"

"Empty. Some toys for the kids and a small bench with some shoes underneath, but that was it. They didn't find anything."

Hagan threw his chaw on the gravel and then took out his pouch and set a new one in his cheek. It looked like it might burst through the skin. "The house smelled good. The wife, too."

"Yeah to the house, and how do you know about the wife?"

Hagan shrugged. "Smelled like flowers. Lilac or some shit. You didn't smell it?"

Shaw shook his head and laughed. "Guess I don't have the nose for it. I didn't peg you for a botanist, Hog."

Hagan was quiet and they walked on awhile before he spoke up. "What the hell is a botanist?"

Shaw laughed again. "Someone who studies plants and flowers."

Hagan smiled. "No weaknesses. I love fucking flowers."

. . .

Intel handled Stag1 for a few days and the teams got briefed on the findings.

The first few nights he was very cooperative—smiling and talking a lot, looking the interrogators in the eye and speaking about his time during the jihad in the eighties and about the new life he made as a father and a construction contractor. He said the city was a peaceful one and that cells hadn't operated in or around it after they attracted drone strikes and bomb runs years before. Talking about his wife and kids lit him up. He was talking about all the good he was planning on doing once government contracts to rebuild the country started getting offered out. After the wars were over, of course.

After the second and third nights without sleep he started getting more reserved and less talkative. Irritable. The interrogators said they felt a façade shifting in him. Conversation steered toward how his family was carrying on in his absence. Intel told him they hadn't seen anyone visit, nor had his wife left the house, and he started getting frustrated, going on about how he hadn't done anything wrong and the jihad of the eighties was carried out in line with sharia law. The interrogators let him know they didn't give a shit about the jihad, even thanked him for helping them win the Cold War. Then they let him think about why he might have been in a dark wooden shack for the last few days if it wasn't about that. They let him get flustered for a while and honored his request to pray whenever he asked to. He decided not to speak to them for a day or two and they were okay with that. After he broke his silence they offered to take him home, but only if he told them why he hadn't been visiting the wife of his nephew after he'd died in the ambush.

"Then he broke," the CO told the teams assembled before him. He set images on a table in front of the men. "Stag1 admitted that while he's been waiting for the government contracts he's answered questions from cell leaders every now and again. He said they pay him for 'structural knowledge' and that he doesn't know what they do with the knowledge after speaking with him." He laid a picture of Scar1 and Scar3 on the table and photos of a few others the teams hadn't taken on yet.

"Specify 'structural knowledge,' sir?" Cooke asked.

The CO nodded.

"Points of weakness within compounds. Vulnerable points most likely to collapse an entire structure with concentrated explosives."

"A boom consultant," Dalonna said. "And he said he didn't know what they did with the information after that. Did they press him to take a guess?"

The CO smiled.

"I'm sure they had some colorful photos, probably with some children in them, to show him. We know of at least one or two bombings Scar1 orchestrated, so I'm sure they showed him pictures from those. Let Stag1 know what his expertise really bought."

He paused and then brought out another picture of a compound set among a small cluster of buildings following an arced ridgeline. It sat at the base of a hill that gave way to the same mountain range where they had killed the boy. The small group of buildings formed a ring around the compound and the compound sat like the pupil of the village eye.

"Stag1 said the last person he spoke to about 'structural knowledge' lived here," the CO said. He pointed to the large compound. "He said it was four to five weeks ago. We're going to monitor it for a couple days and see if we should pay a visit. We'll put up tape drills and be off the green until further notice in case we get reason for a 1."

Hagan spoke up.

"They letting Stag1 go, sir?"

"I think they might hold on to him for a little while longer."

They all nodded and the CO left. Shaw and Cooke gathered the images and went outside to set up the tape.

The next few days were so sunny they could hardly see the white tape laid out on the gravel outside the war room. They moved through the drills constantly, stepping lightly around the imaginary doorways, cabinets, and dressers they knew they would have to avoid. Shaw and Massey visited the CASH again and saw their bomb boy. He had recovered well. He smiled wide despite the missing teeth, and his black hair shined bright in the light. He clung to his mop tighter than the Snickers bar they had given him. It seemed to anchor him to the floor. They went into the children's bay and there was a whole new set of kids with new injuries that would leave behind new scars. Shaw and Massey didn't have a lot of candy to give out so mainly provided high fives and smiles. Shaw even hugged a little one just before they left.

"I'll have a bunch of Christmas cookies sent over," Massey said, when they were walking out. "Maybe Penelope can write the kids some letters or something."

"That's a good idea," Shaw said. He wondered if he knew anyone who could bake worth a shit, but he didn't.

The teams watched the pupil compound on the monitors in the TOC when they weren't shooting, working out, or running tape drills. Intel identified the target of the pupil compound as Iris1. He seemed to be the leader of the group occupying the dwellings, because he was followed the most and people always ran off after speaking with him. Intel thought Iris1 might be a Syrian transplant who hopped the border during the early years of the war after spending time in Africa and Southeast Asia, dodging international sanctions for his involvement in smaller bombings during the early 1990s. But they weren't entirely sure. He wore glasses under a large turban and had a mass of gangly hair spilling out of it like a ball cap set on top of a permed Afro. If he was the Syrian transplant, he didn't have any known children even though he had at least four known wives. His infertility was something rival cells and international watch groups liked to play up, so he countered by calling his followers his sons and targeting embassies and the children of other cell leaders. Intel got excited and wondered if he might be the leader of al-Ayeelaa, given the sensitivity of his infertility. A man who couldn't conceive might call his cell his family.

Intel monitored Stag1's house for the entire week he was being interrogated. They let the teams know that the home hadn't received any visitors, nor had the family left since they took him. They monitored the phone lines and didn't notice any irregular activity. The Iris1 compound, however, had been active constantly since they began monitoring it. Intel watched FAMs running hurriedly around the smaller structures and carrying things into the larger pupil. The pupil seemed to function as a life source for the revolving structures in its orbit. Men with rifles strapped to their backs brought supplies, cases, and munitions to and from the pupil to the surrounding structures, and everyone seemed to settle in the larger compound during the nights. Jeeps would be loaded up and roll over the hills and disappear into the mountains and plains behind the hill. Intel chalked up the activity and remote location to a likely cell training ground or supply center, so Shaw added tape layouts of the smaller structures around the pupil they already had on the gravel. It seemed more likely that they would make a move on the compound.

They were running out of gravel.

They got a 4 the day before Thanksgiving. They walked through the sunlight to the war room and their CO stood in front of images of Iris1 and the pupil compound at the base of the ridgeline.

"We're moving on this tonight. They're staging for something and we're not going to let them ambush some coalition convoy and blow them all to hell or set up cells across the border and infiltrate any more cities."

The teams talked about the hill that sat as a backdrop for the structures and how on the earlier op the Scar3 intelligence had directed them to the empty village with the nest of tunnels leading into the mountains. The CO nodded and answered eagerly.

"We'll put teams around likely exit points behind the hills and send breach and assault teams through any tunnels we find on the village side. We're not letting anyone slip away."

"Conventional-force add-ons?" Cooke asked.

"Yes. They'll set up blocking positions behind the hill and try to catch anything we flush into the mountains."

Hagan raised his hand. "Sir, why not just bomb the hell out of them?"

The CO sucked air between his teeth. "We could, but we don't know exactly who we're hitting yet. We need a positive ID on any bodies and if we send in drones there will be nothing but rags and blood on the rocks."

Hagan shrugged. "Lucky ducks."

The assault would be carried out with six teams from the two squadrons, thirty men. Shaw's and Mike's teams drew duties for clearing the pupil compound and the small shacks. They would move on and help the remaining teams breach any tunnel entry points they might find in the hillsides afterward. They agreed to hit the pupil and the smaller shacks simultaneously to maximize surprise.

While they were waiting to get spun up Intel told them they had released Stag1. Apparently he'd put on a good show during the days since he spoke about Iris1—crying and offering information readily—and they figured he was significantly scared shitless. They wanted to release him while he was still scared of them but before he started channeling his frustrations into anger that would lead to blowback. Revenge. They figured he'd be more willing to cooperate in the future if his fear hadn't had time to calcify into hate. They planned on watching him and keeping tabs on his movements.

The teams sat in the war room long after the sun set. They'd take the Black Hawks out to the ridgeline and start their infil a few clicks from the group of structures, then walk in to maximize surprise. Intel gave them briefings every hour. They reported a gathering of five to ten men in the pupil compound and mentioned smoke trailing from its roof for hours. For days, actually. The teams taped down their banger and frag pins and loaded mags, topped off water, and checked batteries and NODs. Then they sat in their kits as a group on the floor and waited.

"Big knockers or booty?" Dalonna asked after a while.

Hagan lit up.

"Both. Real men don't have to choose."

Everyone laughed.

"Bullet or bomb?" Dalonna asked.

They all answered *bullet* in unison.

"Catch a round in the nuts or lose both arms or legs?" Dalonna asked.

"Take my legs," Hagan said.

"Screw that," Cooke cut in. "Take my nuts. Intercourse is overrated."

Massey looked at Dalonna.

"If the beans are out, is the frank still good?"

"Sure," Dalonna said. "Why not?"

"Then take my nuts, too," Massey said. "I want my arms and legs."

"What have you guys got against your nuts?" Hagan said. He put a hand on his crotch like it had been burned.

Cooke shrugged and looked at the ceiling. "Guess we don't love nuts as much as you do, Hog."

Hagan flicked him off and threw a granola bar at him and they all laughed.

Dalonna leaned forward and raised his eyebrows. "Win the lottery or peace in the Middle East?"

They were all quiet and busy making colorful, confused faces. Hagan looked like he had lost something on the floor and Dalonna was smiling wide. He seemed to be getting off on his own private genius.

"What's the trade-off, Donna?" Shaw asked.

Dalonna waited. He laughed and turned up his palms. "Either way, we won't have to work."

Everyone smiled.

"Nice," Shaw said.

They all answered *Lottery* one by one.

Dalonna himself took the longest to answer. He looked at the picture of his kids on his locker after he did. "Hell, the lottery, I guess. What else would I do?"

The 1 beeped through around 2200 hours and they all got to their feet, relaxed and loose. Nobody's nuts got stomped or mashed in a flailing mass of limbs and no one had to pop diet pills to stay awake. They were ready. They racked their weapons and stretched to the floor and squatted in place. Shaw raised his knees to his chest and had Hagan crack his neck.

"Shaw, could you really go on without your nuts?"

Shaw told him he could.

"Crazy, man," Hagan said. "Y'all aren't right."

Shaw patted him on the back and they walked into the dark. The birds were all spun up and waiting for them on the tarmac when they got to the airfield. The operators grabbed their seats and waited to be carried away.

Flying to the objective, Shaw had his NODs down. A bright beam of green light split the clouds and dropped to the earth a few klicks out on the horizon. It looked like a green rope anchoring the sky to the earth. They flew on and after a minute or two a large white flash erupted where the green rope hit the ground. Whatever lay at the bottom end of the green rope had just been blown away. The empty plains below them swallowed the sound of the explosion and Shaw thought of the follow-on team, just like them, being sent in to survey the damage. He imagined them stepping over the skeleton of the compound and finding their target all blown to hell—an arm here and a leg and piece of torso there. Then he imagined them finding the target sitting peacefully in his bed with a smile on his face, small rivers of blood draining out of his nose, mouth, and ears—the runoff of his organs blown out inside him. Then he thought maybe the target wasn't even home, maybe his kids and wife were there instead. Maybe one of the kids had a buddy sleeping over. Then the green light shut off from the bird circling thousands of feet above and the sky was all black again. He tried to find the birds approaching the blast sight in the distance and the dark, looked for the team just like them flying through the night, not sure of what they'd find on the ground. He saw a flicker here and there and thought he had the strobe pinned down, but the stars were too thick to see anything else.

Five mikes out came over the comms, and Shaw gave up on trying to find the bird. He cracked his knuckles, then his neck, and rolled his shoulders back and then forward. He shook out one leg into the open air, and then the other. He breathed out and then opened his pouch and took out a big chaw. He wanted a real jaw buster for some reason, so he got a golf ball–sized wad and set it in his cheek. Hagan hit him on the arm and gave him a thumbs-up. Shaw handed him his pouch and Hagan grabbed a huge chaw and couldn't fit it in his mouth, so the flecks caught in the air and blew into the sky, disappearing in the dark.

"Did you see that hit?" Shaw yelled over the noise of the bird.

"What hit?" Hagan yelled back.

Shaw thought of the long green rope and the white flash.

"Some house just got blown away over there."

Shaw pointed toward the horizon.

Hagan shook his head. "I was sleeping."

Shaw nodded and Hagan started pressing his rifle in front of him and above his head.

"Getting the blood moving," Hagan yelled.

Shaw gave him a thumbs-up and then the birds dropped them into an opening a few klicks from the Iris1 compound. They took a knee and let the birds blow the snow into their faces, and then the birds lifted off and left them and it seemed like the whole world got put on mute.

The walk was nice. They had to look out for deep holes of snow, but only an inch or two covered most of the walk. The sloping earth gave way to mountains to the west and boulders as big as cars were strewn every few meters. The land made for poor farming so they got to walk between some trees. Shaw smelled pine and sap and the stars seemed to watch over them quietly. They could've been buddies on a hunting trip back home in Minnesota.

Shaw always remembered reading about Vietcong and Japanese snipers gathering food and ammunition and tying themselves into the nests of tall trees. It had stuck with him as a boy. Patrols would wade through the rice paddies and beachheads with their eyes and weapons to the front, only to get one between the eyes from the trees they walked under. Then flamethrowers would come in and burn everything down. As the teams made their way to the compound and the wind blew, Shaw would feel a cool breath on his neck and wonder if it was the first kiss of a bullet coming down from the trees. It made him shiver.

The smaller structures blended in well with the arced ridgeline covered in snow, but the smoke coming from the pupil compound in the middle of the structures did not. Whoever was in the building wasn't thinking about keeping their necks from getting slit but rather their nuts from freezing. The perimeter teams radioed in that they were breaking off and setting up around the flanks of the buildings. They would post up along the ridgeline and start looking for tunnels as soon as the teams started knocking down doors. They'd take care of anyone squirted out of the warmth.

When they were a couple hundred meters from the first few dwellings, Shaw radioed in that they were making their approach. The pupil compound sat above the others by at least a full story, but it was smaller than he thought it would be. Made of stone or dried mud, the second story sat above the small, wooden shedlike structures like a top hat. The sheds were even smaller—some entirely covered in snow. Mike's team got parallel to Shaw and they started their walk. The perimeter teams spread out around the compound and hugged the ridgeline, looking for tunnels. Shaw looked up and saw the strobe of a Spooky circling thousands of feet above. From the aircraft watching them on surveillance, the men must have looked like the expanding head of a firework just after it bursts.

A shed not tall enough for a grown man to stand upright in was the first structure on their movement. It didn't have a door, so Shaw just painted the inside, found it empty except for a shovel and a bucket, and they continued to the pupil. The ground between the structures was dirt beaten flat into hard-top by the weather and treads from the jeeps and pickups that disappeared over the hills. Snow was beaten down into the ground, and sparse patches of dead grass sprang out every couple feet like weeds through pavement. The air felt damp and everything smelled like wet wool and smoke.

They lined up to the left of the pupil's door and Shaw stepped into the doorway and ran his hands over the frame. There was a padlock the size of a man's hand on the door, holding a clasp lock shut. The door was flimsy and seemed out of place against the hard foundation.

"Hard charge," he whispered into the comms.

Mike came over the comms from one of the smaller structures to their right.

"We got three doors at head height," he said. "They're all padlocked. They look like a storage shed we could clear with a flashlight. Maybe we should breach the pupil all together and handle the sheds afterward. Advise."

That made sense. The pupil was far larger and Shaw could use Mike's team. Shaw looked at the clasp lock shut before him and thought about the shed he'd breached before. There wasn't a door on it, let alone a lock, and it was a genuine shed. Nothing but a shovel and a bucket inside. If the other sheds were that small it would be pointless to breach the pupil alone. But Mike said he had three head-height doors padlocked alongside one another. They sounded bigger than the shed Shaw had cleared.

"I'll come over and take a look," Shaw said.

Shaw stepped back from the door and looked at the height of the pupil. It seemed smaller now that he was standing in front of it. If it was smaller than they'd assumed from the satellite footage, then the sheds must be even smaller. If they were as small as the shed he had first breached, then they would all breach the pupil together and have the perimeter teams check the sheds. No matter how long they studied layouts, they always had to adapt to the situation on the ground. He looked toward the sheds surrounding the large structure and paused, almost told Mike to just come on over with his team and get on the other side of the wall. Instead he looked behind him and motioned to the door.

"Hog," he whispered. "We're blowing it. Get the charge set up and we'll blow it when I get back."

Hagan gave a thumbs-up and Shaw made his way over to Mike's team.

When the investigation into the bombing mentioned a pressure plate, Shaw knew that wasn't right. At least not if the plate functioned properly. He would've been blown apart before he even got a chance to finish checking the door frame for wires. It had to have been detonated by remote. The bomb was placed directly under the doorway like a welcome mat, only a few feet below the earth. The investigating teams insisted that a pressure plate could have been used, maybe Shaw had simply missed stepping on it, but once they reviewed the footage and saw him standing on top of the threshold they dismissed the possibility. They agreed that someone must have been waiting in the woods or on the ridgeline—maybe in one of the small sheds—and blown the thing by remote.

In the ambush sprung immediately after the blast from a few of the smaller shacks, the perimeter teams wiped out the nine fighters within seconds. Then a team found and entered a tunnel carved into the rock and killed Iris1 shortly after the other nine were killed. He was sitting on an ammo crate with a handheld radio, an AK-47, and two bodyguards. None of the bodies had a trigger device on them, but that didn't mean they didn't blow the device that killed Massey, Hagan, Cooke, and Dalonna. The teams might just not have found it. Or maybe they did and it was dialed from one of the eight phones the SSE teams picked up. Either way the bomb blew.

Shaw was told by those watching the monitors that he was blown into the shed with the three small padlocked doors along with Mike and Ohio, but he couldn't remember it. The rest of their team was blown behind the shed and across the fields, a few meters between each man, like leaves that had fallen from the same branch of a tree on a strong wind. The bomb completely destroyed six of the small shacks and nearly collapsed every other structure around the pupil. The pupil itself was sheared down the middle, the half housing the doorway leveled to a pile of stone and the other half knocked over completely and resting on its side. From above, it looked like someone had cut the building down the middle with a giant knife, smashing the doorway side into rubble and leaving the other half neatly resting on the ground relatively intact, as if the two sides might one day be reconnected in the middle.

There was nothing to find of Hagan. He was in front of the

door, directly on top of the bomb when it blew, and they couldn't tell if his body parts were any of the small bits of tissue, fatigues, and blood stuck in the rubble or blown into the walls of the surrounding structures. He was nothing but vapor and mist. Massey was last in line and they actually found the part of his torso with his dog tags zippered into the pockets, so they could identify him. He had the agate necklace in his cargo pocket and it was blown to dust. There was nothing left of it. There were pieces of arms and legs found under and between the rubble but nothing recognizable on sight. DNA matches were used to identify Dalonna and Cooke based off the small bits of flesh found somewhat intact—part of a hand or foot, a section of jaw with a couple teeth still in place—but that was it. Shaw never had the nerve to ask, but he heard of a hunk of wrist found with a pink yarn bracelet wrapped around the flesh. He never found out if it was true or not, and hoped not to.

6

Stag1's wife woke up the morning after her husband was taken and found the front door unlocked. They always locked their door. She could see faint lines of dirt or mud tracked in on the carpets as well, so she sat on the couch in the living room and told her children to play outside. She did not turn on the TV. She sat. After she'd fed her children their lunch she went to the backyard, put on plastic gloves, and thrust her hands into the compost pile. The compost covered a large section of ground, but they had dug a shallow hole in the middle of the pile and her hands found it. Then she found the phone wrapped in plastic and took it out of the compost pile. The battery and SIM card were separated and wrapped in plastic inside the larger plastic bundle. Intel did not have the phone from the compost pile traced. In fact, it was the first time it had been used. Stag1 bought the prepaid phone and the SIM card from different countries and buried them immediately. He'd never even turned it on himself, but now his wife took the phone, the battery, and the SIM card inside. Then she washed her hands and charged the phone for a few minutes. She put the SIM card in, turned on the phone, and called the wife of her husband's dead nephew as she'd been instructed. The wife she called had remarried the man the Americans referred to as both Pike1 and Iris1. The two code names were given to the same person. After the call, Stag1's wife hung up the phone, removed the battery and SIM card, and smashed the pieces with a hammer. Then she threw the broken plastic in the trash, packed bags for her family, and hoped her husband would return.

The call was too short to monitor the weak phone signal originating outside the home around lunchtime, and even if it could be monitored, the number couldn't be tracked. It had existed for only a moment. Iris1's wife told her new husband that Stag1 had been taken. He in turn immediately left for the mountains. His men had dug underground tunnels into the pupil years before. The tunnels led to the small shacks so the men could enter the pupil and move around the entire area underground without ever appearing to have left.

The bomb had been constructed inside the pupil and buried from inside by using a tunnel under the front door. No surveillance videos were able to detect it, but they did detect smoke. The smoke originated not from a fire to keep the inhabitants warm, as the operators supposed—the inhabitants had blankets for that—but rather from the cooking of the TATP used to detonate the device. Intel had been monitoring the very preparations for the deaths of Hagan, Dalonna, Massey, and Cooke all along.

After his release, Stag1 immediately gathered up his family and the silver piece-of-shit van picked them up and drove them into the city as they had planned. Drones followed the van during the whole ride, but as the bombing didn't happen for hours after his release, nothing seemed amiss. By the time the bomb blew, Stag1 and his family had picked up the wife of Iris1 and disappeared among the masses. Intel's been looking for Stag1, his family and the driver, and the piece-of-shit van ever since.

7

Shaw came to in the war room. He was surrounded by Slausen, Mike, and Ohio, and so many other guys he couldn't see the walls for all the camo in front of him. They gathered around him close to break the news and he fell into their arms. Later, Slausen had his hands on Shaw's face and was rubbing his cheeks. Shaw didn't know if Slausen was checking for broken bones or whether he had found something he was trying to put back in place. He couldn't feel Slausen's fingers until he took them off his skin, and only then because his face began to tingle. He never felt any of the sedatives or fluids Slausen had injected from the IVs into his veins. They kept him heavily medicated.

"Open your mouth," Slausen said.

Shaw did and Slausen put an opium lolli in his cheek, patted it gently with his hand. Shaw didn't remember anything after that, surfing the morphine swells as he was. He couldn't tell whether the hours on a clock were running forward or back until the CO and Slausen stood in front of him hours, maybe days later.

"Massey wants you to escort him home," Slausen said. "It's in his will."

Slausen's eyes were tiny black slits hiding in his red puffy eyelids. Shaw was sitting in a chair in the war room. He didn't say anything. It felt like milk was flooding his eyes, blinding him. Slausen and the CO were fading into Mike and Ohio sitting next to them, and they all just formed a big jumbled mass of beards and fatigues. Depression and pity. Anger. Slausen leaned toward him. Shaw felt a beard on his face, warm breath on his ear. He smelled Copenhagen and sweat. Slausen whispered soft. Slow.

"He wants you to take him home."

Slausen passed him a handful of pills before Shaw got on the bird with the caskets.

"Take all of them," Slausen said. "You'll piss hot, but everything will melt away. No pain. So no tests for two or three weeks."

Shaw nodded and popped them, ground them to powder, and swallowed. His mouth felt chalky and dry.

"Listen to me," Slausen said. "Get someone else's piss or tell them you need to see the shrink." He put his hands on Shaw's shoulders and brought his face close. Their noses nearly touched. "Do not piss for them. They'll kick you out."

Shaw ran his tongue around his mouth and swallowed some grains that'd lodged between his teeth. Slausen looked behind him, at the flags draped over the metal caskets holding what was left of their friends. He sniffed and shook his head.

"Don't kill yourself, all right? They already got four of us."

Slausen hugged him and then bit at his fingernails.

"Make sure you're sitting or lying down within a half hour. They hit hard."

Shaw nodded, didn't say a thing. He could already feel a tingling in the back of his head and spreading from his elbows. He kept licking his teeth.

Slausen looked him in the eyes.

"We'll see you in a week or two, okay? Come back."

They both nodded and Slausen turned away. The ramp started to close. From his seat, Shaw watched him walk away toward Mike and Ohio and the rest of the guys lining the airfield in the fading sunlight. Then Slausen stopped and turned toward the bird, his hand held up in a wave. Shaw watched his fingers close into a fist, then the ramp cut him off and the bird darkened.

Shaw never asked Slausen what he'd taken, but they worked. Everything fuzzed and melted away and he started feeling heavy and weightless at the same time. The person guarding the door of the cabin changed from a man to a woman and then disappeared entirely and he couldn't be sure there was anyone at all. He saw bodies and sad little girls and smiling friends who had been alive but were now lying dead in caskets at his feet. He didn't know if he clocked out at the half-hour mark like Slausen said he would, but the nearly daylong flight felt like only a few minutes. What he did remember of those few minutes seemed thick, cloudy, and invented like a dream.

Normally body parts of the fallen would be washed and prepared for burial after they were analyzed and the coroner's final reports made. Then the remains would be put in caskets and flown home to their families. Since the bomb turned the four of them to mist, Shaw wondered if he was sitting in front of four empty caskets. He thought maybe there was only the one chunk of Massey's chest and a couple jars of whatever they could find of Hagan,

Cooke, and Dalonna lying on the metal beds underneath their flag blankets. He almost got the nerve to look.

He vowed to quit, sitting in front of his friends. He finally admitted to himself that he couldn't do it anymore, that all the ghosts had finally caught up with him. He'd seen the young boy from the pass wave, not point at them, too many times, and the little girl's cries had turned into menacing laughter. The laughter was enlightened and harsh, like she was saying *You might have killed my parents, but you're the one who's fucked.* His grandma's face had come through the woman's chador after Hagan slit her throat in front of all those kids, and she had smiled at him. He thought if he quit maybe they'd all leave him alone, maybe he could get some peace. He thought maybe he'd be able to explain himself when they visited at night. He could tell the little girl her dad was an HVT, a known cell leader who massacred dozens of innocents, and that he was sorry about her mom and didn't mean to kill her. He could tell the boy in the pass that he should have hidden from them, kept himself alive, and that others like him had reported positions and gotten guys blown away. He could tell his grandma that they never killed the woman, he had only dreamed it, and that the children would put it behind them and study hard and make good lives for themselves.

And then Shaw remembered Stag1's smile, those white-as-shit teeth. He remembered the way he blew smoke at his knees and how it rose up into his face, and somewhere Shaw knew, even if Intel didn't yet, that Stag1 had screwed them. Shaw remembered Hagan's last words. They were *Getting the blood moving.* Shaw couldn't place last words to Dalonna, Cooke, and Massey, and that pissed him off, so he thought of Massey with those kids in the

CASH and Cooke cleaning his weapon as if it were a baby and Dalonna staring at the pictures of his family before leaving the war room to kill the fathers, brothers, and sons of others. He knew he could never escape the fate waiting for him at the end of some Hajji's det-cord or rifle barrel. If it wasn't one of theirs, it'd probably be one of his own.

Then he thought of Illinois. He knew he'd have to walk over the ice-chapped cornstalks of its southern border with Missouri and visit Massey's family, lay the box of what was left of him into the ground and never see the agate necklace around Penelope's neck. He thought of Chicago and how he'd have to visit Dalonna's wife and hug his daughters, maybe make them a bracelet with one of their dad's old bootlaces and how he'd have to see Dalonna's son grow up and turn into his father because there's no way he wouldn't. He thought of the dry West Texas plains and wondered if there was some drunk, hard father out there among the tumbleweeds who used to beat his kids and might give a shit to see one of them buried in the oil fields. He thought of Hagan, their Hog, and how he wasn't ever getting the wife he'd wanted to bring back to the land that killed him and show her how fucked up and beautiful it all was.

He thought about what Massey had asked him. About murder. He thought that even though that little girl probably just wanted her parents to braid her hair or read her stories before bedtime, her dad still needed to die. Her mom didn't need to, but the daughter she carried like a backpack looked a hell of a lot like the straps of a suicide vest and the operators died when they hesitated. He'd tell the boy they had no idea if he would rat them out or not and weren't willing to wait and find out. There were four of them and only the one of him and his weight was less than theirs. He'd tell his grandma that she was already dead and had left him alone long ago, that they left that woman and those kids alive to hate and love and become whoever they wanted to be after they left their town on fire.

If Massey were alive in that C-17, sitting next to him and not inside of a metal box, Shaw would finally be honest with himself and say yes. Yes, he did feel like a murderer sometimes, and before everything had happened he would've hoped that that realization alone would've made him stop. But sitting next to the caskets, he knew then that it wouldn't. He'd like to tell that little girl in the poppy fields he was sorry about her mother but not her father. So where does that leave him? He's killed far more than he murdered and there's no way of knowing how many attacks they prevented, or how many they caused. The squadrons will keep going back long after the conventional units and all the news cameras have pulled out. They'll outlast all the foreign aid. Not until long after the officeholders stop uttering the country's name in anything but political-poison whispers and schoolchildren no longer recognize the significance of its syllables in their classrooms will the squadrons leave. And then they'll just go to new places, different lands. Shaw knows there will always be Stag1s to chase until they killed them all, and they never will. Never could. So he can go on chasing them forever and they him until his ghosts have all left him. And they never will.

He'd rather charge among them than flee only to be overrun in the end.

GLOSSARY

.50-CALIBER: A large round, roughly the size of a thumb from the last joint to the tip of the fingernail. The round is devastating and utilized by sniper rifles, GMVs, and multiple aircraft.

5.56: The most popular round used by Western militaries. It is smaller and lighter than the 7.62-millimeter but more accurate, thus favored by units specializing in close-quarters combat and in need of precision firing. About the size of a sharpened pencil tip.

7.62: Large-caliber round fired by the AK-47 assault rifles and other large assault weapons. About the length of a fingernail.

AAR: After-action review. A debrief, or meeting, that discusses and analyzes the events that transpired during an operation or raid.

AH-64 APACHE: Attack helicopter with tandem cockpit for a two-man crew.

AK-47: The assault rifle most widely used throughout the world. Known for its durability and firepower. Fires the 7.62-millimeter round.

BANGERS: Flashbangs. Stun grenades. Typically nonlethal cylinders, with holes drilled into the housing, that emit loud noises and flashes.

BARAH: Arabic pronunciation for “Get out.”

CASH: Combat support hospital.

CH-47 CHINOOK HELICOPTER: Heavy-lift helicopter with wide loading ramp in the rear of the fuselage. Roughly ninety feet in length and used to transport heavy machinery and climb high elevations. Capacity of up to fifty men and a max speed of 170 knots.

CHADOR: A traditional full-length female garment with a face opening, worn in certain Middle Eastern cultures.

CLP: Cleaner, lubricant, and preservative for weapons. Gun oil.

CO: Commanding officer.

COMMS: Radio communications.

CSAR: Command search and rescue.

D-RING: Carabineer.

DASTHAA BALAA: Dari pronunciation for “Hands in the air.”

DET-CORD: Detonating cord. A thin, plastic tube of explosives that detonates a large explosive device. Det-cords explode instead of burn, enabling faster and more precise detonations.

EKIA: Enemy killed in action.

ERFA YADAYK: Arabic pronunciation for "Hands up."

ETA: Estimated time of arrival.

FAM: Fighting-age male.

FAST-MOVERS: Fighter jets.

FLEX-CUFFS: Plastic ties used to restrain individuals (similar to handcuffs).

FOB: Forward operating base. A secure military base of varying size used to support tactical operations in foreign lands. Some FOBs are vast, containing large airfields and hundreds of buildings, while others are smaller and more primitive, consisting mainly of strands of barbed wire and concrete bunkers.

FRAGS: Fragmentation grenades.

GMV: Gun-mounted vehicle. Typically a Humvee or a Stryker.

HOP: Deployment.

HOUSE CALL: A raid targeting a residence.

HVT: High-value target.

IED: Improvised explosive device. An IED is usually a rudimentary bomb of varying size and power. Some are rather primitive, consisting of hastily combined wires and explosives, while others are quite advanced. An IED is a lethal weapon, so long as it is operational, no matter what its appearance. Can be small enough to fit in a backpack or larger than a standard bathtub.

INSHALLAH: Arabic pronunciation for "God willing."

JDAM: Joint direct attack munition. A guidance kit attached to munitions that acts as a GPS device for the weapon system. The "smart" element of a smart bomb.

JIHAD: A contentious issue among Muslims. Jihad, once declared by a religious leader, is an Islamic duty among Muslims, often interpreted as a "holy war" against nonbelievers. Jihad can have many meanings and be interpreted in numerous ways.

KAFIR: An unbeliever; one who denies the truth of Islam and its teachings. A Muslim accused of being a *kafir* would likely take great offense.

KIT: Configuration of body armor, pouches, et cetera.

KLICK: Kilometer.

MADRASSA: Arabic word for an educational institution, often assumed to be of a religious nature when used in Western cultures.

MAG: Magazine. A detachable metal device in which bullets are loaded into and fired from.

MH-6 LITTLE BIRD HELICOPTER: Light helicopter with a capacity of six men. Max speed 150 knots

MIKES: Minutes.

MINIGUN: A mounted eighty-five-pound machine gun that shoots 7.62-millimeter rounds at two thousand to six thousand rounds per minute. Commonly mounted on helicopters.

MOTAR SAKHA RAA WUDZAI: Pashto pronunciation for "Get out of the car."

MP: Military police.

MRE: Meal ready to eat.

MUEZZIN: An individual who leads and recites the call to prayer in a mosque, often through speaker systems that reach large areas of a town or countryside.

NIGHT- AND DAY-ZERO: Process by which gun sights/lasers are modified to ensure accuracy at night and during the day. Process in which operators ensure that their rounds will strike where their weapon sights/lasers intend them to.

NODS: Night optical device. Night-vision goggles.

NWFP: Northwest Frontier Province; a former province in Pakistan.

ORP: Objective rally point. Preestablished place of meeting during or after a mission/movement.

PELTORS: Ear-protection and communication device. Advanced headphones used by military and SWAT teams.

POPPING HOT: Technological process by which a target is pinpointed and its location confirmed.

RPG: Rocket-propelled grenade.

SALAT: The practice of formal worship in Islam—the proscribed set of rituals of prayer in Islam.

SALAT AL-'ASR: Afternoon prayer of the five prescribed prayer periods in Islam.

SALWAR KAMEEZ: Traditional dress of Middle Eastern cultures. The salwar are loose trousers and the kameez is a long shirt.

SAS: British Special Air Service. Special Operations unit.

SHARIA: Moral code and religious law of Islam.

SHIITE (SHIA) ISLAM: Second-largest sect of Islam, behind the Sunni sect.

SKEDCO: Plastic portable emergency sled that rolls into a tight cylinder and expands into a litter longer than an average man.

SPOOKY: AC 130 Spectre Gunship. A nearly hundred-foot-long airplane bristling with numerous cannons and rocket systems. Often used for close-air support in combat situations.

SQUIRTERS: Individuals who escape from a secured objective or perimeter.

SSE: Sensitive site exploitation. Process in which the rooms of a compound are physically searched to find and gather sensitive or valuable information.

SUNNI ISLAM: The largest sect of Islam.

TAKFIR: The practice of one Muslim declaring another Muslim an unbeliever. A bold, combative declaration.

TAQIYAH (TAQ): A short, round skullcap often worn by Muslim men.

TATP: A white powder high explosive that smells like bleach. Often used as a primary explosive for large IEDs.

TOC: Tactical operations center. Mission control, where a command team can monitor numerous operations at one time.

UH-60 BLACK HAWK HELICOPTER: Medium-lift helicopter with a capacity of up to eleven men. Max speed 193 knots.

ACKNOWLEDGMENTS

When I think of wars I don't think of parades or conquests, victories or defeats. I think of scared young boys in foxholes, firing lines, and foreign mounds of earth. I think of sad mothers and fathers, brothers and sisters, and sweethearts. I think of the children left behind and those who were never born. I hope wars end. I think human beings aren't born with the claws of a bear or teeth of a shark for a reason. I think we were given advanced brain function with the burden of using it. So here's to peace and to all the sons and daughters who never made it back home. And here's to David, for giving this thing a shot. Here's to Aileen, Phoebe, Linda, Kylie, Amy, and the rest of Blue Rider and Penguin for all the tireless work on this. A special thanks to William for giving me a chance and for all the advice and hard work. Thanks to my teachers and family and friends—both old and new—for all the lessons and smiles and beers and love. Thanks to everyone who never gave up and never will. Thank you.

ABOUT THE AUTHOR

Ross Ritchell is a former member of the 75th Ranger Regiment, a United States Special Operations Command direct-action team. He conducted classified operations in the Middle East, and upon his discharge, he enrolled at Northwestern University, where he earned an MFA. He lives with his family and dogs in the Midwest.